JUST
MAYBE

HOME IN YOU SERIES
BOOK THREE

Crystal Walton

Impact Editions, LLC
Chesapeake, VA

Impact Editions, LLC
www.crystal-walton.com

This is a work of fiction. Names, characters, places, and incidents are a product of the author's imagination. Locales and public names are sometimes used for atmospheric purposes. Any resemblance to actual people, living or dead, or to businesses, companies, events, institutions, or locales is completely coincidental.

Book Layout ©2013 BookDesignTemplates.com

Cover Design ©2021 Blue Water Books

Author Photo by Charity Mack

Name: Walton, Crystal, 1980-
Title: Just Maybe / Crystal Walton.
Identifiers: LCCN 2017914545 (pbk) | ISBN 978-0-9862882-9-6 (pbk)
BISAC: 1. FICTION / Clean & Wholesome Romance 2. FICTION / Contemporary Inspirational Romance

Library of Congress Control Number: 2017914545

Escape

It wasn't supposed to be like this. The speed, the distance—it should've been enough, should've let him outrace the regret.

Like an echo, Cooper Anderson's legs throbbed each time a distant red light flashed from somewhere above him. Thunder raged through the ringing in his ears, but he couldn't silence the words he'd lost his chance to say.

Fragmented memories from only hours ago pulsed in and out of focus: a canopy of black umbrellas failing to shield them from tears, his five-year-old niece needing arms of comfort he couldn't offer her. Not today.

Cooper squeezed his eyes tighter and strained to breathe against the weight crushing his sternum as fiercely as it had at the funeral. He'd stood beside the open earth like a glued-together statue. Cold, unfeeling. So shattered, one breath of wind would've crumbled him into the grave that'd stolen his father from him too soon.

It all closed in. The faces, the voices. "*From ashes to ashes.*"

No. He jerked his head to the side. Wet, ragged gravel pressed into his cheek, but his limbs wouldn't move. Without ceasing, memories stormed over a body trapped by the car wreckage pinning it to the grainy pavement.

Another flicker. Another scene. At the edge of the cemetery, his brother had grasped Cooper's shoulder before letting him get into his Audi. *"Be safe."*

Safe. The word had burrowed inside him and rebounded off his need to soar across uncaring pavement. To screech around curves and lose all connection with the loss haunting him.

Clipped memories struck him again. An oncoming car, a jerk of the wheel, sounds exploding from every direction. Aches had racked his body. One blink, one breath, and the windshield had shattered to pieces the way his world already had.

Time slowed until another roar of thunder brought him from the brink of unconsciousness.

Sirens broke through the fog blocking his ears while fast, heavy footsteps pounded the pavement. Lights flashed. Voices rang. Someone's knees hit the ground beside him, a second pair close behind.

A battle of relief and anger warred inside as he watched the escape he'd chased outrun him one more time. Helpless to stop it, all Cooper could do was lay on that stretch of dark highway and promise nothing would leave him this undone again.

CHAPTER ONE

Chase

Six Years Later

Thirty seconds. That's all it took for Cooper Anderson to reach his date across the gala floor. He cupped her arm. "Is everything all right?"

Tanya set her empty glass on a waiter's tray. "You should've heard what that man just asked me about us."

Cooper caught a glimpse of the guy's wet face and dress shirt before he skirted into the men's room. If it was bad enough for her to toss her glass of wine in his face, Cooper wasn't inclined to let it slide.

Grabbing his sleeve, she stopped him mid-stride. "I already handled it."

When his gaze jumped back to Tanya's, his irritation gave way to a grin. "Remind me not to get on your bad side."

"Luckily for you, you always know the right thing to say." She looped her arm around his, and remorse doused him in a splash of its own.

He knew that look in her eyes. Had seen it more times than any single guy should. She wanted this to go somewhere it wasn't—past a second date to a relationship he couldn't offer her.

Holding a smile in place for her sake, Cooper nodded to the door. "How about we get out of here. I think I've had enough hobnobbing for one evening." After two hours of making the rounds with business contacts and potential clients, he was more than ready for a secluded night alone back at his lake house.

She tilted her head, lips to the side. "You read my mind."

If only he knew how to change it so he wouldn't hurt her.

At the door, Mitch from Schroeder Financials intercepted them before they could pass. "Well, if it isn't the man of the hour."

Cooper tugged his ear. "Considering it's your fundraiser, I'd hardly say that."

"Considering you're the one up for Top Entrepreneur this year, I'd say you're rather modest."

Tanya pressed closer to him as if enamored by the title, and Cooper cringed at the whole scenario.

"I'd reckon more conversations revolved around you and your ... *ambitious* international plans than around any of the auction pieces tonight." Mitch slipped a stem glass off a waiter's tray and motioned for Cooper to take his own.

He held up a palm. "We're actually on our way out."

The guy who'd offended Tanya earlier stepped out of the bathroom, still dabbing his wet shirt with a paper towel. He scanned the room until he locked gazes with Cooper. Visibly on a mission, he started toward them.

"Always in a hurry," Mitch droned on. "No one should be surprised it took you a mere year to reach the financial status many of us have spent a lifetime building."

Heat waves from outside poured into the air-conditioned room as someone passed through the door, and Cooper adjusted his tux collar. "I guess hard work still pays off these days. That and a little luck." He prodded Tanya forward. "Listen, we really should be—"

"Mm." Mitch swallowed a sip of champagne. "I'll agree with the first part. The second?" He shook his head. "I only believe in things I can put my hands on." His gaze flitted to Tanya for the briefest moment before retracting to Cooper. "Which is why I'd love to get my hands on a partnership with you. Between the two of us, imagine what we could turn Schroeder Financials into."

And there it was. The same pitch half the men in the room had tried to slip his way tonight.

He sent a glance toward the restrooms. Though the guy still had his focus trained on them, he'd gotten held up by another fast-talking businessman.

Cooper redirected his attention to Mitch and worked his stiff jaw. "I appreciate the offer, but my investment overseas is already a done deal. Plane ticket's bought, house is up for sale, the shop's grand opening is already set and publicized." He reached for the drink he'd declined a minute ago and raised it in a toast. "Three more weeks, and I'll be on the shores of Indonesia."

"Until you change your mind."

"Excuse me?"

Lowering his near-empty glass to his side, Mitch brandished a look of superiority. "A start-up business in a foreign country? We're talking about more than just tying up your resources, Cooper. The demands will consume every part of your life and leave no room for ..." His eyes drifted to Tanya again. "Other interests."

The insinuation and assumptions about his lifestyle sank into Cooper's stomach and soured. He returned his untouched drink to the tray. "I think I'm more than prepared for that." He stayed unattached from relationships for a reason. "Now, if you'll excuse us."

"If you change your mind ..." Mitch called behind them.

Doubtful.

Outside, the fresh air he needed coated him in a thick layer of humidity instead.

Tanya flittered in front of him. "It's not a bad idea, you know."

Cooper's shoulders slumped at the meaning embedded in her words. "Actually, all of this is. Tanya, listen—"

"Mr. Anderson?" The guy who'd been trying to get to them flung a voice recorder in his face while weaseling Tanya out of his way.

She backed into the brick edging behind her, snagged her heel, and fell to the concrete.

The guy blocked Cooper's path to her. "Can you give us a statement about your decision to move out of the country so quickly? Does this have anything to do with the recent allegations against Shore Corporation?"

A reporter. He should've known. Ever since this Top Entrepreneur of the Year nomination put him on the radar, the media had been prying into his personal life and hounding him for interviews he wasn't about to start giving now.

The thought of whatever intrusive questions he'd asked Tanya earlier burned in his chest. He grabbed the reporter's shirt. "If you ever knock a woman to the ground again, I'll have your credentials stripped from you before you can so much as turn your recorder on." He released his shirt with a shove. "You want a statement? Stay away from me and the people in my life."

Cooper got Tanya in his Audi and gunned away from the curb before he did more than merely push the guy out of the way.

A good five miles passed before he'd calmed enough to look across the console. "I'm sorry."

She smiled it away. "The price of fame, right?"

A price he wasn't willing to put anyone else through. As soon as he got her home, he'd make sure she understood this was their last date.

A flash from beside him brought a black Impala into view with a telephoto lens pointed at him from the passenger seat. "You've got to be kidding me."

"What?" Tanya leaned around him. "Wow, that creep doesn't know when to quit."

"Different guys." Cooper changed gears and soared up the road. He shouldn't be surprised the media would be prowling nearby after catching wind he'd be attending tonight's function.

The Impala edged closer, driving Tanya's side of the car dangerously close to the guardrail. She braced a hand against her door panel and scooted in his direction. "Cooper."

"I see it." After a quick glance to make sure her seat belt was fastened, he slammed on the brake, fell back, and switched positions with the Impala.

The other driver didn't lose speed. Side by side, both cars flew down the pavement, straight toward a divider.

Tanya darted her other hand to the dashboard. "Tell me you see that, too, right?"

"Hang on." Cooper jerked the emergency brake up at the same time he circled the wheel, fanning the car to one side to force the Impala off the exit.

Sideways, his Audi skidded to a stop in the middle of a cloud of burnt rubber and smoke. "Are you all right?"

Tanya transferred her death grip to her seat belt and nodded. "Where'd you learn to drive like that?"

"I've had practice." Not wasting any leverage, Cooper released the brake, let up on the clutch, and spun in the opposite direction.

"I thought we were going back to my place."

This close, it'd be too easy for someone to follow them. "Change of plans." He'd take the long route to his lake house, ensure no one tailed them, and call her a cab from there instead.

"Amy was right," Tanya said once they were almost to his home.

"About?"

"You being an adrenaline lover." She shifted in her seat. "That's part of why you never go on more than two dates with the same girl, isn't it?"

Exhaling, he slowed the car as he turned onto his street. "Tanya, you're a sweet girl, but—"

"I get it."

After tonight, she should understand it didn't have as much to do with adrenaline as she might've once thought.

She reached for the door handle when he pulled into the driveway.

"Wait." Cooper stretched across her seat and tugged the door shut. "Stay put for a minute." In his rearview mirror, the sight of an old Camry parked along the curb caused his pulse to rise. The media might be able to catch him at a publicized business function, but they shouldn't know where he lived. He'd worked hard to keep it that way.

Shoulders drawn back, he got out of his car the same time a middle-aged man and woman exited the Camry.

"Mr. Cooper Anderson?" he asked.

"Can I help you?"

"You're one tough man to track down." He flashed some kind of identification at him. "Dillan Miller. My coworker, Julie. We're from Social Services. Did you know a woman by the name of Megan Neilson?"

Megan? His heart rate doubled without explanation. He hadn't seen or heard from her in almost two years. "Briefly. What's this about? Is she all right?"

At the look of sympathy on Dillan's face, the word "did" finally registered. His stomach twisted. "She's …?"

"Car accident." He lowered his gaze to the driveway. "I'm sorry."

Cooper clenched his jaw and raked both sets of fingers through his hair. "When?"

"Just earlier this week."

The familiar sting of regret seared into him. He should've fought harder when she cut ties with him after that summer they'd shared together. Should've tried to change her mind about them, or at least about staying in touch. Something.

The sound of a car door opening joined a series of cries that turned Cooper back around. Julie stood beside the car, bobbing a baby in her arms.

Dillan cleared his throat while opening a manila folder. "Miss Neilson left you as the sole guardian of…" He slid on a pair of reading glasses and shuffled through the file. "Brayden Ryan Neilson. We'll have to take care of some paperwork, of course, but—"

"I'm sorry." Cooper blinked, swallowed. The trees in the background slanted, the air too thick to breathe. He looked from the boy back to Dillan and strained to make sense of what he'd just said. "Are you trying to say he's—?"

"Your son."

CHAPTER TWO

Elusive

Why here? A self-made billionaire could have a villa on the coast, a secluded beach house anywhere in the Outer Banks. Shoot, a guy like Cooper Anderson could own a private bungalow on an island if he wanted. Instead, he'd holed up in Littleton, NC. Population: 625.

And he wanted people to believe there wasn't a story under all this? Please. Maybe one that most journalists didn't have the skills to shake out, but Quinn Thompson wasn't about to be lumped in with the others who'd walked away empty-handed. She had too much riding on this feature.

A flicker of dread passed through her at the sight of the quaint lake homes streaming by the window. Squelching it, Quinn tilted the A/C vent toward her face.

So what if this lead meant going back to her hometown after four years? It was just a quick interview. In and out. She'd be back in Cape Hatteras by tomorrow afternoon. Sunday at the latest, if Cooper wanted to be extra difficult. It'd be fine. *She'd* be fine.

Yeah, if fine meant being as nervous as a long-tailed cat in a room full of rocking chairs.

Quinn almost flinched at the phrase springing to mind out of nowhere—in Mama's country drawl, no less. She cringed. She hadn't even turned her car off yet, and her roots were already trying to strangle her. As if the blazing July heat weren't doing a good enough job as it was.

She leaned forward in her seat to air out the back of her blouse. A lot of good it did. A drip of sweat careened down her spine straight into her underwear. She sighed. *Welcome home.*

Alongside the curb, a layer of acorns crunched under her Altima's wheels like a giant sheet of bubble wrap. She shifted into park, looked from the sticky note on the center of the steering wheel to the house matching the address, and breathed in.

One lead story. That was all she needed. Just one solid push to show her boss she had the journalistic instincts to hack it as executive editor. Then she'd at least have access to Cruella's ear every day. Could maybe even convince her to stop being a tyrant micromanager before she drove their magazine into the ground. She was running out of time.

Echoing the thought, Mama's unanswered voice mail from days ago weighed Quinn's cell in her pocket like a lead sinker.

She withdrew her keys from the ignition, straightened her back, and pushed every apprehension aside. The chance of getting this promotion was worth any cost, even enduring a torturous hour with some rich stockbroker playboy.

A dog barked somewhere nearby. Without thinking, Quinn slid down her seat faster than a hot knife through butter.

A hot knife through butter? Really? Where were these random phrases coming from?

Quinn peeked over the rim toward a woman walking her collie. Wow. That fluorescent visor she was sporting might've shielded her eyes from the sun, but nothing was blocking the glare coming off those bright pink flamingos on her apron.

At least she didn't recognize the lady. With no one else in sight, Quinn inched all the way up. If this interview didn't kill her, returning to Lake Gaston clearly wanted a stab.

She draped her arms around the wheel and tapped her forehead against them. "This lead's right up your alley, Thompson," she mimicked in her boss's raspy voice. She'd like to show her an alley, all right.

The Cruella De Vil song blared into the car and sent her juggling her phone. Jeez, it was like the woman had her Altima wired or something. While trying not to curl a lip at the image of her boss on the screen, Quinn composed herself and answered. "Hi, Chri—"

"Give me the scoop. What do you have?"

A splitting headache? "I just pulled up."

"Time is money, Thompson. You left four and a half hours ago."

"Well, I thought about bringing empty bottles so I wouldn't have to stop to use a restroom but decided against it." Quinn grasped at the runaway words spewing from her mouth, but they were gone before her fingertips ever grazed them. Chewing her nail instead, she slumped in the seat and waited for impact.

One tick. Two. The seconds hung on her boss's delayed response.

"Considering you're showing up unannounced to land an interview with a guy who's skilled at turning them down, you better have spent your trip thinking of something other than your bladder."

Even 230 miles away, Cruella could still make her feel as small as a minnow in a fishing pond.

Her jaw clenched before she even finished the thought. So help her, if one more suppressed country saying slipped through her subconscious, she'd—

"I expect to see an update in my email within the hour. Are we clear?"

Another sigh. "Crystal."

"Good. And, Thompson? Don't even think about asking him if you can use his restroom."

Her knuckles whitened around the steering wheel. The minute her boss hung up, Quinn chucked her cell into the cup holder, peeled her damp shirt away from the leather seat again, and craned her head back.

Buying a car with black interior definitely fit on the ever-growing list of "shouldn't haves" she'd racked up in life. But nailing this piece? No way. She had to make it work.

Her best friend's ringtone rang like a warning bell. They'd worked together long enough to know what was coming.

"Cruella isn't roaming the halls on one of her rampages already, is she?"

Ava snorted. "Are you seriously asking? I'm pretty sure another Dalmatian just lost its life somewhere. Let me guess, you didn't have anything to give her yet?"

Quinn tore into a half melted dark chocolate bar she'd stashed in her bag of road trip snacks. "I just got here. I don't know what she expects."

"Of course you do, and you're the crazy girl who assured her you'd deliver."

"I'm not crazy," she mumbled through a mouthful of sticky chocolate getting everywhere. She eyed her messy fingers. "Okay, maybe I am. Ugh. I swear, that woman has it out for me."

"She has it out for everyone. No one can live up to her expectations."

"Yeah, but she didn't send everyone out on a career suicide mission. She wants me to fail at this. And I just had to say yes anyway, didn't I? What in the world is wrong with me?"

"Oh, there are so many adjectives I want to insert right now."

"Very funny." Quinn balled up the empty candy wrapper in hopes her nerves would crumble with it. Crazy expectations or not, she couldn't afford to prove her boss right. "You know what? Forget my rambling and just keep running interference for me, will ya?"

"Instead of trudging through this endless trough of stock photos? I'll see if I can tear myself away, but I'm taking my chair with me. I swear, Cruella's gonna start putting them on eBay just to boost our bottom line this quarter."

"Our bottom line's fine, and it's a good thing you're paid to have a flair for the dramatic, you know that?"

"Says the girl about to interview our competition's pick for the hottest guy in business this year."

"Top Entrepreneur."

"Whatever. Oh, speaking of which, what are you wearing right now?"

"Ava."

"I'm just saying. If you want an in with a guy like Cooper Anderson, you gotta play the part."

"Or I could just be myself. You know, that really skilled journalist who can get an in without any tricks." The very sophisticated one with chocolate all over her. Right. She grabbed a hand wipe from her purse.

"You mean the really geeky *editor* who pretends she's satisfied with book boyfriends instead of a real relationship. Give it up, girl. You're gonna fall all over yourself the minute Mr. Elusive opens the front door. Ooh, now *there's* a story worth pitching. I can meet you there this afternoon. You know, for an unbiased viewpoint."

Quinn rolled her eyes. "I'm hanging up now."

"Don't forget to take pictures!"

"Bye, Ava." Shaking her head, she tucked her phone in her purse and extracted the pencil holding her hair up in a twist. As it spilled down her shoulders, she refocused on the house and the task before her. She wasn't pretending anything. She was making things happen. Same as she'd done the last four years.

She yanked the sticky note off the horn and opened her car door. Cruella wanted the impossible? That made two of them.

Outside, a lake-scented breeze swam across her face and hedged all reservations inside the car where they needed to stay. This small town didn't leave room for second guesses.

A *For Sale* sign in the yard drew her to a stop along the driveway. He was moving? Sunlight crested the roof and intensified the heat already claiming her cheeks. A good journalist would've known this already. She kicked herself the rest of the way to the front door. What made her think she could do this?

Stop it, already. She could handle this. She just had to get Cruella out of her head.

On the porch, she straightened her navy-blue wrap midi skirt. With another calming breath, she rang the bell and tapped her pencil to her thigh until she caught a glimpse of her reflection in the glass panels. A double take sent her scrambling to smooth out the humidity-induced frizz time-warping her back to the eighties.

The sound of a baby crying stopped her halfway into reaching for her brush. She scanned all around before leaning an ear closer to the door. Okay, something was off. She checked the house number on the siding against her sticky note one more time. Her source better not have gotten the address wrong.

A sinking feeling seized her stomach. What if it *was* someone else's house? Someone she knew?

She latched onto the doorknob for balance and adjusted the strap to her slingback. Stupid. What was she thinking? She shouldn't be here. If she ran into—

The door whisked open, gravity took over, and she stumbled right into Cooper Anderson's solid bare chest.

Good thing she'd just sucked in that giant gasp of air, because her lungs were about to prove Ava right.

"I'm so sorry." Embarrassment trumped the summer heat infusing every inch of her skin. Skin. Gah. She flung her hands off his brawny arms like they were hot coals. Once back on the porch, she shoved her long hair out of her face with her forearm and resituated her purse and heels. "I, um … Sorry, I just lost my …" Dignity? Professionalism?

In nothing but plaid pajama pants, Cooper stood in the doorway, a slow grin sloping toward his sandy blond hair.

Sanity. That's what the heck she'd lost. All grasp on sanity. She knew better than to take Ava's call. It had her all messed up. Now, she'd have to backpedal without looking completely neurotic, if that were even possible.

A high-pitched wail from inside erased the fleeting amusement from Cooper's face. With a cell in one hand, he waved her in with the other. "Thanks for responding to my ad."

Ad?

"Sorry about the mess." He scooted an open moving box out of the entryway and tossed a pen over a folded-up newspaper on top of it. "It's been a little" —he raked a hand through his messy hair— "crazy here lately."

A man's voice sounded from the phone at Cooper's side, and he offered Quinn a weary smile. "Excuse me for a minute." He brought his cell to his ear. "Yeah, Jim, I'm here ... I don't care what her lawyer said, I ... Yes, I knew about her dad. But what about her mom, her brother?"

Another set of airy cries drew Quinn's attention from one distressed male in the room to the other. Seated in a high chair, a brown-haired, red-cheeked baby boy—probably a year old—smeared what looked like sweet potatoes across his face while rubbing his eyes.

Wait, Cooper Anderson had a kid? She knew there had to be missing pieces to his story, but this? No. Uh-uh. Couldn't be. Maybe he was a nephew. A girlfriend's son?

Whomever he belonged to, one thing was clear. He obviously missed them.

Instinct kicked in, and Quinn forged a path through a mountain of toys surrounding the high chair. "Hey, little guy, you're ready for a nap, aren't you?"

Though, truth be told, the coffee fumes bouncing off the lofty ceilings were strong enough to give the kid a secondhand buzz. It was only nine a.m., yet it smelled like Cooper had brewed a good four pots already.

She cleaned off the baby's fingers with another hand wipe from her purse and set her keys in the one clear spot on the tray in front of him. He picked them up, cries morphing into babbles of curiosity. The transition uncovered a sweet little boy, and the center of Quinn's chest constricted at the sight of him.

Cooper paced in the hallway. "There's got to be someone. You have three weeks to resolve this. Three. I'm running out of time and ..." He stopped mid-stride, turned in Quinn's direction, and almost dropped his phone. "Jim, let me call you back."

Though he stayed in place, a dozen questions raced past his eyes. "How'd you do that?"

"Do what?"

He waved a hand at the baby like he was hunting for words. "That. Silence. You got him to stop crying."

Quinn bit her lip to keep from grinning. So, even the elusive Cooper Anderson could be caught outside his element. Interesting. "Keys. They work every time."

"Keys." He looked across the plethora of toys he'd piled in front of the kid as if he were a buyer at a toy fair. Still without blinking, he started toward her.

Frazzled, sleep deprived—whatever might've been going on with the rest of him, it obviously didn't affect his eyes. They locked on to hers with the kind of charisma he was known for. So much so, Quinn backed into a box behind her as he neared.

"You're hired."

"Excuse me?"

"The nanny position. It's yours."

"Nanny pos ... ?" The ad. He thought she was here because of an ad to come work for him? "Oh, um, no, sorry. I think there's been a—"

"Name your price." He edged a step closer, hazel eyes confiscating her voice. "It'll only be for three weeks, but I'll pay you six months' worth, if that's what it'll take." Another inch toward her. A nod. "Please."

Five blinks finally untied her vocal cords. Not that it mattered. They obviously had a mind of their own. "Wh... when do I start?"

He looked at the ceiling, exhaled. "Now." When he faced her again, visible relief awakened a smile even more dangerous than those enigmatic eyes of his. He extended a hand. "Cooper Anderson."

Willing her response to remain schooled, she slipped a hand into his. "Quinn Thompson. Pleasure's mine."

"I think I may have you beat on that one." A soft, almost vulnerable laugh curled around her as he let go and kneaded the base of his neck. "You've been a lifesaver already."

Seeing him in this context had her fighting a bashful smile. "I haven't done anything."

A mystified look took her in. "You have no idea."

And he had no idea the effect he was having on her. Or maybe he did. The thought alone jolted her out of a trance she'd never live down if Ava could see her right now. She shifted her focus to the high chair. "What's his name?"

"Brayden." A waver caught between affection and regret shook his voice. He cleared his throat. "You can have the guest room beside his. You should find everything you need, but let me know if not." His phone rang. "We can finalize the rest of the arrangements this evening."

"Okay, but I should tell you—"

"Six o'clock." Unfair dimples deepened as he backed up. "A lifesaver, Quinn Thompson." Cooper brought his cell to his ear and turned toward a room she presumed to be an office. "Ray Williams. Tell me you found a new buyer."

As the conversation drifted out of reach, the possibilities before her slowly sank in. She could process her normal workload from here for a few weeks while warming him up to the idea of an official interview. Admittedly, an in-home nanny wasn't exactly the in she had planned, but she'd be crazy to pass up an opportunity handed to her like this. It was perfect. More than perfect, it was an exclusive, inside look into Cooper's life—the one no one else got to see.

Grinning, Quinn shot off a text to Ava.

Tell Cruella this feature's in the bag.

Cooper Anderson was about to meet his match.

CHAPTER THREE

Trouble

With Quinn there through the night, Cooper had slept for the first time in a couple of days. Not that it had made much difference.

Fifty feet from his house, he cut his WaveRunner's engine and gripped his thighs. Being on the lake wasn't the same as surfing the ocean. But after the week he'd been having, he needed the water this morning. Needed the rush of flying against the wind, the freedom of cutting ties from the shore.

Sunlight clung to his back and dried each streak of water running down his hot skin. Other than an occasional striped bass popping up or an osprey whistling in the distance, stillness surrounded him. His WaveRunner rocked in the breeze, his thoughts rippling. He sat back, forked his fingers through his wet hair, and scrubbed a hand down his face.

A son? How could Megan keep this from him? Maybe that summer in Ocracoke was just a fling to her—a temporary escape from everyday life. He got that. He'd encountered the same mentality every summer since he was born. But to walk away with something more and never tell him? She could've tracked him down, could've—

His neighbor's lab barked from their dock where Mike and his seven-year-old son were pulling up a crab pot together. Excitement from bonding with his dad ran across the kid's face as it did most mornings.

The tighter Cooper grasped the handle bars, the more the image gripped him with the answer to his own questions. He couldn't blame Megan for protecting her son. She knew better than to seek out a father who didn't know how to be one.

His heart winced. Would taking Brayden with him prove her wrong? He closed his eyes under the sun and shook his head. Yeah, and offer him what? A capricious life overseas that would keep Cooper away from home half the time? A reckless dad making every mistake known to man, trying to raise him on his own? Nights of nearly being run off the road by reporters?

He may not like Mitch's insinuations about his *interests*, but the man was right about the demands and risks in his life. With or without a start-up business overseas, that wouldn't change. Brayden deserved more than a single parent tossing money to a caregiver to make up for the time and parenting he couldn't give him.

The ache of regrets coiled into his side—the mistakes he'd made, the life he'd been living. He released a hard exhale and the naiveté of thinking things could be different.

Fragments from the night Dad died blurred into flashes from his latest run-in with the media and solidified his decision. He'd never be able to provide a son with the kind of upbringing his father had given him, but finding Brayden a good family was the closest he could come to the sacrificial love Dad had lived every day.

Drowning his doubts, he turned the ignition and jetted the rest of the way to his dock. Megan did the right thing for her son, and now it was his turn to do the same.

The sun-heated planks warmed the soles of his feet as he toweled off. He slipped on his flip-flops and snagged his cell from the bench as it rang.

Barry Jedson. Just what he needed to deal with right now—damage control with an overly reactive client.

Cooper whipped the towel over his bare shoulder. "Barry, my man, how we doing this morning?"

"How *we* doing? One of us is staring at my stock dash-board, trying not to lose his breakfast. Why don't you tell me what the other of us is doing? And please tell me it involves recouping the money I just lost."

Cooper craned his head to the sky while trekking up the yard to his back deck. "Forecasts are always going to fall after a major recall announcement. You have to expect a hit to the market, but now's not the time to pull out." He slid open the screen door. "Trust me on this. I'm watching your portfolio. Your investments are going to be fine."

"But what about—?"

"Have I ever steered you wrong?" He stood over the threshold and pinched his forehead. Coffee. He needed a cup. Or twenty.

A scent he couldn't place wafted from inside—something almost honey-like. He peered around, listened. Instead of baby cries, a soft hum blended into the sounds of someone stirring in the kitchen.

Barry must've rambled off at least a page worth of sentences, but Cooper didn't hear a one. "Have a drink with your wife today, Barry. Everything's going to work out."

"Are you sure?"

"Positive. I'll be in touch." Cooper ended the call before another unwarranted question could sneak through. A few tentative steps brought him to the center of the living room. The aroma grew stronger, the humming transitioning to lyrics. It almost sounded like ... Yep, she was definitely singing Boyz II Men.

He might've been able to hold in a laugh if the view around the open doorway left him half a chance. Waving an oven mitt in one hand and a muffin tray in the other, Quinn swayed to the music coming through her earbuds.

His gaze bounced from her to the baby monitor on the counter and on to a series of pink sticky notes attached to every drawer and cabinet in his kitchen. Wow. He'd seen a lot of clashing images in his time, but this one might've topped them all.

Midway through the song, she spun around and gasped. The pan hit the floor, muffins rolling across the tiles. "Jeez." She yanked her earbuds out and curled a wayward strand of brown hair around her ear. "Sorry, I was just, um ..."

"Having a dance party in the middle of my kitchen?"

A rosy hue set off the flour smudges on her cheeks. The girl was cute. He'd give her that.

She ran her white Converse along her calf beneath her capris' cuff. "Thinking," she offered instead. "I mean, baking. Well, both, actually. One usually helps the other. The music was just kind of a break." She shut her eyes and mumbled, "Like the one I should be giving my mouth right now."

Cooper leaned an arm into the jamb and bit back a grin. Definitely cute.

The second she caught him smiling, she looked away and dropped to her knees to gather the runaway muffins.

"I didn't mean to startle you." He joined her on the tiles. "If it makes you feel better, you were dancing pretty good."

"Well."

"I'm sorry?"

"It's dancing *well*, not good." She put the muffin he handed her back into the tray without looking up from the floor. "And don't worry about the muffins. There should be plenty. I made two dozen earlier."

While adding another dozen reasons Cooper could barely hide his amusement. Did she really just correct his grammar?

When she still didn't so much as blink in his direction, Cooper tilted his head under hers. "Something wrong?"

"No." She rose to her feet, cradled the pan to her chest, and sent her gaze flitting across every corner of the kitchen as though scouring for an exit. "You have something against shirts?"

That was what had her all flustered? He glanced at his bare chest as he rose. "I was out on the water. *Thinking*." His lips quirked. "Guess you could say one usually helps the other."

Quinn met him head-on. With a glint in her amber eyes that he'd probably just provoked, she set the pan down and crossed her slender arms. "I don't blame you. It's hard to think in here with everything disorganized. You're kind of a mess."

Cute, geeky, *and* brazen. He ran his tongue along the corner of his mouth. "Getting ready to move has a way of doing that." She didn't need to know the place would be a wreck regardless. "Guess it doesn't matter since I see you've remedied that for me."

"Just trying to get my bearings. Hope you don't mind."

For three weeks? He'd deal. "Don't mind at all."

She tossed the muffins in the trash and ran the tray under the faucet. "So, where are you guys moving to?"

"You guys?"

"You and Brayden." Loose strands of hair fell from a messy bun as she peered up from the sink.

"Uh, yeah, it's just me." He backed against the counter and retied the strings on his board shorts. "I'm heading on a cross-country trip July Fourth weekend. Once I make it to LA, I'm catching a one-way ticket to Indonesia."

The pan clattered into the sink. She spun around, hands covered in suds. "Indonesia?"

"It has some of the best waves on the planet."

Shock dissolved behind a telling look that said she had him all figured out. "You're moving across the world to surf?"

"To open a boat shop. It's something I need to do." Why was he telling her this? He let go of the strings, grabbed one of the good muffins from a platter, and slanted a brow. "And the view's not half bad." He expected her to get the implication. If she was so sure she already had him pegged, he'd play the part.

Hopefully, she did a better job at baking than she did attempting to keep a blank face.

"Seems like the view here suits you just fine." She dried off her hands and motioned to the only two sticky notes without capital letters labeling a compartment.

He peeled them off the counter to find phone messages from two girls he'd gone on dates with last week. Nothing like playing right into her hand.

"I'm not trying to be your personal assistant or anything. I just didn't want the phone to wake up Brayden."

Cooper set the notes aside and looked from the baby monitor back to Quinn's fiery, flour-coated cheeks. "Sorry about that. I don't give out my cell number to women." He'd barely finished his sentence before his cell rang like a gavel she probably assumed was proving him a liar. Perfect. He turned and answered. "Anderson. Talk to me."

"Cooper, it's Ray. We have a new potential buyer interested in the house. A well-established couple—highly motivated, already pre-approved. I have a good feeling about this one."

About time. It had taken months after the first contract had fallen through to find another qualified buyer. This couldn't end in anything but a quick sale. They were cutting it too close to his move-out date. "When do we settle?"

With his usual patronizing laugh, Ray fit right in with half the businessmen Cooper had worked with through the years. "Easy, cowboy. Let's not get ahead of ourselves. There are negotiations to be made."

Of course there were. Cooper clenched the muffin. "Such as?"

"The couple's asking for a new pier."

"What's wrong with the one that's here?"

Even the guy's pauses could be patronizing. "You know how these things go. They look at other houses in the area. Comparisons are made. You can't blame people for wanting the best. Am I right?"

When Cooper didn't bite, Ray switched gears. "We're not talking major reconstruction here. Just a little upgrade. Maybe, say, switching those worn pine boards for red cedar. That's all."

Sure that was all. "And what about *my* negotiations?"

"It's a buyer's market, kid. You want a quick sale? You agree to terms."

Cooper glanced at Quinn, busying herself with the rest of the dishes. He set the muffin down. "You know what? Fine. Done. I'll repair the deck."

Dollar signs from Ray's expected commission hung on the tail of an audible smile. "I'll make the call."

After pocketing his phone, Cooper gripped the edge of the counter with both hands and leaned into it. Money wasn't a problem, but he'd rather do the work himself. At this point, he could use the distraction. It might even be therapeutic.

Right beside him, Quinn gently touched his hand. "I'm fairly certain it's not the countertop's fault."

White skin on his knuckles beamed up at him. He let go. "Sorry, it's—"

"Not my business."

True. None of it was. Why was he trying to defend himself anyway? He opened a cabinet labeled *MUGS* and withdrew his favorite Tar Heels one. That coffee was way too many phone calls overdue.

Still beside him, Quinn peeled a liner off a muffin, one side at a time. "I know I just finished saying it's none of my business, but I *am* kind of curious why you have to leave in three weeks. I realize your plans are already set, and believe me, I know how that goes. But it seems like staying longer might take some stress off."

He hung his head, sighed. "It's not an option." He couldn't let Dad down again. Not this time. As hard as it would be, he had to secure a stable home for Brayden before the Fourth.

"Okay," she dragged out the word. "Business deal gone bad?"

He faced her. "What makes you say that?"

"It's kind of hard to live in Hatteras without hearing about the fallout with Shore Corp Investments."

He cocked a brow. "You're from Hatteras?" Why hadn't she said anything about it yesterday?

She diverted her attention to the muffin she was dismantling piece by tiny piece. "I've lived there for four years."

And was clearly hiding something about it. He tipped his head to read her eyes. "What brought you to Lake Gaston?"

Cornered, she backed up. A frazzled look scrunched her forehead but only for a moment. Replacing it, a seemingly satisfied grin made a slow climb to the left. "The view."

Oh, this one was trouble, all right. He liked her already.

Her cell buzzed on the counter. She snatched it, shoved it into her pocket like contraband, and dodged his gaze again. "Coffee," she blurted out. "You wanted some coffee, right?"

Not as bad as she obviously wanted a diversion. He would play along. For now.

"There's a canister in the cabinet above the microwave. But you probably already know that, given you've dissected my entire kitchen."

"Actually, it's over here now." She motioned to a cabinet two over from the sink. "It makes more sense to keep it here. You'll thank me later, and sorry, but that's not coffee."

She had to be kidding. He retrieved the canister, opened it, and inhaled. A rich, nutty aroma met him like a therapist. "Italian roast. This stuff is amazing. My sister-in-law got me hooked on it last summer." He smiled at Ti's new designation. Drew was a lucky guy.

Quinn sent a skeptical appraisal over the clear canister.

"Let me guess." Cooper closed the lid. "You're looking for some venti whip frou-frou thing."

She didn't deny it.

A city girl out of her element. He could have fun with this one. "I'll tell you what. There's a café up the road. If I nail your order, you have to answer my earlier question."

"What are we? Ten?"

"You don't strike me as the type to back down."

"I'm not." Shoulders squared, mouth tight—he had her now.

Her cell buzzed in her pocket again. She strained to pretend she didn't notice.

"You gonna answer that?"

"Nope." She pulled a pencil out of her dark hair and grabbed her purse from the table.

"Going to replenish your sticky note supply?"

The stiff smile she sent him wrinkled the freckles on her nose. "We're going to get coffee. And I'm buying."

Of course she was. He could certainly add stubborn to her list of endearing traits.

He cocked his chin. "We can take my bike."

A simpering laugh shifted her demeanor. "Might be kind of hard to strap a car seat to a motorcycle."

Brayden. How could he forget he was here so easily? Sure, Social Services had dropped the boy off at his house only two days ago, but still. A pang quaked through him. What had Megan been thinking, leaving Brayden to him? Even a stranger could see he wasn't cut out to be his dad.

Quinn seemed to be trying to interpret his thoughts.

He crammed them aside before she saw things she shouldn't and hooked a thumb behind him. "We can take the Audi instead. I'll just go …" He fought a grin. "Grab a shirt."

"Make sure it's big enough to fit over your inflated head," she said once she probably thought he was out of earshot.

He wouldn't have been surprised if she'd launched one of those muffins at him next.

He laughed on his way to his room. Apparently, he wasn't the only one who liked a challenge. From the sounds of it, he wasn't alone in keeping secrets either.

CHAPTER FOUR

Roots

Quinn huffed to herself on her way down the hall toward Brayden's room. A shirt, indeed.

A replay of her fumbling those muffins stopped her in the doorway. Ugh. She bumped her forehead against the trim. *You have something against shirts?* She just had to let that come out of her mouth, didn't she? Now, he knew she noticed *and* admired. Double ugh.

She could hear Ava's write-up already: Mr. Elusive turns Miss Uptight into a puddle on the kitchen floor with nothing but a crooked smile. Quinn shook her head. Stupid water droplets clinging to his perfectly messy hair. Like his commanding presence wasn't attractive enough.

Straightening, she gave herself an internal Gibbs-smack. So, the guy had charisma. Big deal. So did half the men she rubbed elbows with every day. Just because most women couldn't stop themselves from stumbling under his charm like it was a spell didn't mean she had to fuel his fire. She worked for *News First*, not *Seventeen Magazine*.

If her own pep talk wouldn't work, her boss's nagging voice surely would. Quinn withdrew her cell and opened the messages she'd ignored in the kitchen. First, a text from Ava:

Cruella just let Brad in Advertising go. If I'm next, I'm taking my desk chair with me.

Despite her best friend's teasing, Quinn's stomach dropped. That was the third termination this month. If she didn't do something about their boss's firing spree soon, she'd be letting down all her coworkers counting on her to take *News First Magazine* in a new direction.

Her thumb hovered over the voice mail icon. Maybe she'd better listen to it later when she actually had something to report other than rolling muffins and hypnotizing eyes.

Admittedly, she had learned a few new things about Cooper's future plans, but his past was what she needed to break. Cruella didn't care that he was up for Top Entrepreneur of the Year. She wanted to know how he'd gotten there in such a short time. She wanted the gritty secrets, the scandals, the reason he'd been hiding out in Lake Gaston for a year.

But what if it wasn't that simple?

A singing toy went off across the room. Quinn tiptoed over. Brayden lay awake in his crib, seemingly content to play with his jungle blanket. He lowered the corner from his mouth when Quinn leaned over the railing. Sunlight coming through the window lit up an innocent smile, and everything else faded with the shadows.

"Hey, little guy. Have a good nap? Wish I could take one. But time is money," she said in Cruella's annoying voice.

Wiggling a finger to his belly, she tamped down the pang his cuteness stirred and kept her tone light. "Luckily, you have a while before you have to worry about that. How about we settle for taking a ride?"

Squealing, he flapped his arms and legs in the air as if she'd spoken a secret password into his world.

"Ah, you know that word, huh?"

He clung to her two index fingers to pull himself to his feet and batted Cooper's same crippling hazel eyes at her. He *had* to be his son. But then how could he leave him behind to go all the way to Indonesia, of all places?

Maybe he was a loner—along with a host of *other* nouns Quinn could add—but something didn't add up with this. She just had to find out what. Well, and then actually get him to agree to let her print it.

She brushed a thumb over Brayden's soft hand. Was she going about this all wrong? She used to swear she could do whatever it took to be a solid journalist, even go undercover if a lead required it. But being underhanded wasn't her style. Despite how perfect the nanny cover had sounded yesterday, this whole idea turned her stomach into a maze of nerves now.

At least she had some time to figure it all out. Amazingly, Cruella agreed to let her stay the three weeks. Almost a little too easily. Man, she must really want to see Quinn screw this up. Then again, Quinn could do her job from almost anywhere, so being away from the office for a few weeks wouldn't cause her to fall behind on her regular responsibilities.

Getting Cooper to open up in that time frame, on the other hand ... The knot in her gut expanded. Maybe she could talk him into an exchange—her help as a nanny for his cooperation on the feature. She rolled her eyes. Lame. He'd toss her out the second she dropped the big "media" word on him. There had to be another way.

Completely unaware of the thoughts running laps in her mind, Brayden let out another soft squeal that lifted his adorable chubby cheeks.

"Oh, you think you're cute, too, don't you? Uh-huh. I see you flashing those dimples no girl could turn down."

"Cah. Go." Brayden spouted off a string of gibberish with only a decipherable word here and there.

"See, it's not that hard to get guys talking. You just gotta mention cars. Add in a little flattery. What do you think? I can be smooth, right?"

Without his smile even twitching, he passed gas.

Quinn cracked a laugh. "Well, I guess that answers that." After changing his diaper, she shimmied a fresh T-shirt over Brayden's head and lifted him onto her hip. "Come on, Dimplestiltskin, let's go show Daddy how it's done."

By the front door, Cooper stood in leather flip-flops, low-hanging jeans, and an O'Neill T-shirt, stark white against his tanned skin. Figures he'd look even better with one on. Though, she had to admit, his laid-back style wasn't the look she'd imagined for a guy with his drive and reputation. Iron Man's chest plate, on the other hand—

"What?"

She peered up from the hardwoods. "Hmm?"

"Something has you smiling. What are you thinking about?"

She bit her lip as if that would curb the answer. "Nothing." With Brayden clinging to one shoulder and his diaper bag on the other, Quinn looked around the modest home.

He studied her. "Something wrong with the house?"

"It's gorgeous, just not what I anticipated. Honestly, I half expected you to have one of those fancy bidets in the bathroom. Or at least a knockoff of Tony Stark's secret chamber downstairs."

His mouth pulled sideways. "Does that make you Pepper?"

She brushed past him to the door. "You wish."

A trail of deep laughter followed her outside into the already-fuming day.

Quinn finished buckling Brayden into his car seat, twirled her hair into a bun, and threaded a pencil through it. Cooper met her gaze over the hood of his SUV, taking her in with an expression she couldn't interpret.

Her arms slid to her sides. "What?"

"Nothing," he said in the same nonchalant tone she'd dished out a minute ago.

In the car, he cranked the A/C while the hint of a grin brought out his dimples.

Quinn pulled a pen out from under her backside and added it to a random collection in the cup holder. "Just say it already."

He laughed. "You're quick on your feet."

"Is that a bad thing?"

Cooper cocked his scruffy jaw while shifting into reverse. "Just not what I anticipated."

She crammed her seat belt buckle in. "You find that amusing, don't you?"

"If you only knew."

Arms crossed, she faced forward and tried to pretend his luxurious leather seats weren't remotely comfortable lest she boost his ego any more. Cruella seriously better give her more than a promotion after surviving three weeks with this guy.

As they drove, glimpses of the lake filtered through the sideline of trees. Families were already out on the water, creating summer memories.

Quinn blinked away from the window and noted the direction he was headed. Just perfect. "Since when did Littleton get a coffee shop?" How much else had changed since she'd been home?

Cooper glanced across the console. "You're familiar with the area?"

Way to go, Quinn. "I've been here once or twice." Or a thousand.

At least the chances of her family trekking to a café were next to zero. And the odds of catching her ex away from work this time of day were probably no more than ten percent, maybe less. Heck, for all she knew, Brian had moved away years ago.

Okay, fat chance. The man's roots were embedded in this town's soil deeper than an oak tree's. Inhaling slowly, she fished her oversized sunglasses from her purse and clung to the comfort of Cooper's tinted windows.

"What's with the Hollywood disguise?"

"Sorry?"

Cooper gestured to her sunglasses. "You look like you're hiding from the paparazzi in those things."

They'd probably be easier to fend off. She straightened the glasses on the bridge of her nose. "You shouldn't underestimate the effects of UV rays."

"UV rays," he said with far too much lilt in his tone. "I see."

Yeah, more than he should.

"Okay, look." She twisted in her seat. "There might happen to be some people here who I'd rather not run into. That's all."

"It's not that small of a town."

Quinn snorted. "You don't know it like I do." She flung a hand over her big fat mouth. What was the deal with this guy pulling secrets out of her before she even realized it? It was supposed to be the other way around.

Surprisingly, Cooper didn't run with it. He jerked the wheel to the right, and Quinn bumped into her door panel. She flung a glance at him. "Should I be driving?"

"Sorry." He steered his gaze from the car passing them on the left back to the road and exhaled. "Thought I saw something. It's nothing."

Clearly, she wasn't the only paranoid one. She might've pressed it if they had pulled up to a café like she was expecting. Instead, he parked in front of a Piggly Wiggly.

She stared at the grocery store. "Need to go shopping?"

His dimples flexed. "Just for some coffee."

If she had a steaming cup to dump in his lap right now, she'd be oh so tempted. Leaving a scathing glare for a response, she hopped out of the SUV and backed against the hot door panel while heat waves rose from the asphalt. She should've known he was messing with her.

The driver's door closed, the car still running. "Oh, c'mon. You know as well as I do there's no Starbucks around here," Cooper said on his way around the bumper. "I just came here to give you a hard time."

"And now we're both without our morning coffee. Congratulations."

"Only because you're too stubborn to take my word on the good stuff. And relax, I have an alternative."

Her arms came uncrossed. "Stubborn?"

"Don't worry, QT. It's not a bad thing. Tenacity will take you places."

The next time tenacity led her to Timbuktu, she'd remind herself to pass. She took off her sunglasses and glared at him. "Wait a second. Did you just call me, cutie?"

"QT." He splayed his hands out at the obvious connection. "Quinn Thompson."

She rolled her eyes. "Don't call me that."

"Why, does it unnerve you?" He sauntered closer.

More like those ridiculously captivating eyes did. Forget writing a breakout article. If she patented a way to keep from drowning in those beauties, she'd be rich. Downplaying her reaction, she kept her shoulders as relaxed as his. "I bet you think that's original."

He rubbed the whiskers along his jaw while edging another step in. "It's not?"

"Hate to break it to you, but you might want to brush up on your flirting skills."

Right in front of her now, Cooper held her gaze while tucking a strand of hair blowing across her forehead behind her ear. "Guess I'll need to practice a little more."

Breath. Where was her doggone breath?

"You ... I ..." Apparently, her lungs were withholding words too.

Cooper finally released her eyes, withdrew his hand, and squeezed the crook of his neck instead. He looked up from the pavement and nodded to his SUV. "C'mon. We might not have lattes here, but I know something just as good."

They both got back in the car. But even before their doors shut, an overpowering stench vanquished her appetite for coffee. Or for anything else.

Cooper covered his mouth and nose, his face a scrunched look of repulsion. "What *is* that?"

Quinn's pinched lips barely contained her laugh. "Never had to change a dirty diaper before?"

He whipped around to Brayden's rear-facing car seat. "*You* did that? Not cool, hoss."

Brayden kicked the seat, the mirror showing an expression caught between a laugh and a cry.

Cooper rolled down the windows. The second he uncovered his nose, he dry heaved. "Aw, man, I think I'm gonna..."

Quinn buried her face in her elbow but laughed so hard, she snorted. "Let's just hope nothing squished out of the diaper."

A look of horror seized Cooper's face. Priceless.

His chest convulsed, gag reflexes in full swing. Quinn took one look at the sweat starting to bead across the top of his forehead, and she couldn't help it. She tossed her head back and cracked up.

He nudged her in the arm. "I'm glad you're enjoying this."

"If you only knew," she mimicked in his same lilt from earlier.

His eyes roamed over her, and for a minute, she wondered what he was seeing. His usual grin re-emerged. "Congrats on the uptake, QT." He flung his hand in the air like he was waving a white flag. "Now, can we do something about little Atomic Bomb, here?"

Laughing all over again, Quinn got out and handed Brayden to Cooper so she could spread a changing mat on the floorboard. She turned to find him dangling smack in front of her. Cooper extended Brayden an arm's length away like he wasn't sure how to hold him.

Quinn rolled her eyes, laid Brayden down, and slid a clean diaper under his backside. The minute she unfastened the tabs on the dirty diaper, Cooper dashed backward like she'd pulled the pin from a hand grenade.

She shook her head and wiggled a baby wipe over Brayden's nose. "Men are such wusses, aren't they? Yes, they are," she said to his giggling smile as she finished changing him.

"You're not married."

Quinn jumped at the sound of Cooper's voice behind her again. "Excuse me?" Where had that come from?

He nodded to her left hand. "No wedding ring."

"Your point?" She shoved the balled-up dirty diaper into his stomach.

He raised a brow, once again pushing her buttons to reveal things she didn't want him to see. "You're good with kids." He shrugged. "Just an observation."

She got Brayden situated in his car seat while dodging the now-glaring spot on her finger where an engagement ring once sat. "I have a ton of cousins. Being the oldest meant I learned a lot." She turned and almost bumped right into him.

His arms might not have closed around her, but his gaze seemed to. "Why do I get the feeling it's more than that?"

She darted her glance away from him and drew on her years of experience rehearsing a lighthearted tone. "'Cause you're caffeine deprived and going crazy?"

Though the depth in the way he studied her didn't let her off the hook, he dipped his head anyway. "Then I guess we better get to where I really wanted to take you."

Adding a stop at a winery would be nice while they were at it.

On the drive, she glanced behind her seat. "He doesn't say much, does he?" Maybe she should be taking lessons.

"He doesn't walk yet either. Do you think that's weird for his age?" The slightest tenor of concern rang in his voice.

"He's about a year, right? He might be a little behind the curve, but every kid is different. Not to mention lots of outside factors come into play."

Cooper whipped into the next lane, a clipped huff following. "Yeah, like losing his mom and being dropped off at some stranger's house." He'd said it so softly, Quinn might've missed the underlying turmoil in his words if she didn't see it tearing down his face.

Before she could come up with something to say in return, Cooper jabbed on the radio, obviously as quick to curb his feelings as she was.

At least he had the advantage of being somewhere other than in his hometown. A wave of nostalgia broadsided her the moment he pulled up to Wakeboard Willie's Ice Cream Parlor.

Cooper draped an arm on the wheel and faced her, his playful side back in gear. "You may think my Italian roast isn't good enough, but I'd like to see you turn down Willie's coffee ice cream."

One look at the goofy expression baiting her to the challenge, and all she could do was shake her head. "Fine. But if I eat more than you, *I* get to ask *you* a question you can't evade."

He scuffed the back of his hand under his chin while sizing her up. "Deal."

Coffee flavor wasn't bad, but the taste of sweet victory always blew everything else away.

"I'll get the orders. You get Dimplestiltskin into his stroller."

Cooper raised both brows. "Dimplestiltskin?"

She opened her door. "Careful, or I might start calling you that too."

His dimples caved into his cheeks as if soaking up a compliment. Of course.

"And please tell me how you've managed never having to change his diaper before?" She lugged her purse from the floorboard. "What, do you have doting neighbors at your beck and call or something?"

Cooper's crooked grin stiffened.

"Oh my word, you do." Why'd she even ask? She climbed out of his SUV and ducked back in. "If you tell me you take him to grocery stores to pick up chicks, you're gonna have to add vomit to the list of stenches in your car today."

The slightest flicker of something unreadable creased his face before his practiced smile drove it away. "Now, QT, you gotta give me a little more credit. The beach is much less cliché than grocery stores."

Rolling her eyes, she shut her door and mumbled, "Men."

Too bad she couldn't write a piece about Cooper Anderson, the ladies' man. It would probably sell better. Even if there was some big scandal, did anyone really care about why he left Shore Corp two years ago and how he got rich so fast? They had probably stopped wondering a long time ago.

Halfway up to the line leading to the blue building, her feet froze. People around these parts would never stop wondering what made someone leave. She knew that better than anyone.

Her throat tightened as she looked around the front patio full of tables. She'd been too caught up in Cooper's games to think about being in her old stomping grounds. Maybe she should've swallowed her pride and let Cooper pay this time.

With a quick check at the time on her cell, Quinn exhaled. Only the vacation crowd would be getting ice cream at 11:00 a.m. Just in case, she crammed her sunglasses on her face once she reached the back of the line and fixed her attention on another text from Ava.

Cruella's already pushing me for a cover shot. Make sure to get me something I can work with.

Trying to coerce Cooper into opening up was hard enough. Now she had to talk him into a photo shoot? Piece of cake. Sure.

She seriously needed to up her skills. She peered back at his Audi, where some oiled-up girl in a skimpy tank over her bathing suit was eagerly helping Cooper with the baby stroller. Quinn let out a sardonic laugh. If *those* were the kind of skills she needed, she was in big trouble.

"Quinn?" someone called from in front of her.

The knot in her gut tanked like lead. She inched around, breath lost.

"Well, I'll be. Quinn Thompson finally made it home."

Blood thudded in her ears as she stared at the couple waiting for her paralysis to heal. Her gaze slanted from a girl's pregnant belly to the man beside her.

"Brian."

CHAPTER FIVE

Sucker Punch

Surely, she wasn't seeing this. Quinn raised her sunglasses to the top of her head and squinted harder at the girl's perfectly round stomach. Nope, still pregnant. She looked back at Brian.

When the girl's gentle cough didn't disconnect Quinn and Brian's gazes, the petite thing curled a ring-clad hand around a bicep that still looked just as defined as it was tender. "Sweetie, it's rude not to make introductions."

Brian blinked toward her then. "Of course. Forgive me. I'm just a little stunned is all."

That was one word for it. Sucker punched was another.

The girl extended a dainty hand in the air. "I'm Cindy Mae."

Perfect. Her ex-fiancé married Cinder-freaking-ella. Could the knife dig a little deeper?

Quinn fumbled for any kind of response halfway resembling southern hospitality. But if birds showed up with strings of beads hanging out of their mouths next, Cooper wouldn't be the only one fighting a gag reflex.

A breeze slapped a whiff of sickeningly sweet ice cream across Quinn's face.

"You'll have to excuse my husband. Men just get all out of sorts when they're off work, don't they?" In a hat with a red sash matching her polka dotted sundress, Cindy Mae leaned into Brian. "But I'd be lost without him this week, trying to get things ready for little Miss, here," she said while patting her stomach. "Me and him spent half the morning adding the final touches to the nursery, didn't we?"

Quinn tried not to twitch at the grammatical error. "He and I," she mumbled under her breath.

"What's that?"

"... E-I." She froze, realizing she'd just blurted that out like she had Tourette's or something. "Um, I was just saying, E-I-E-I-O. You know, like the song." She slid her sunglasses off and folded the arms into the frames, back and forth. "Could be a fun theme for a nursery."

Cindy Mae's blank stare followed Brian's.

Someone rescue me.

Brian tugged on his ear the way he always did when uncomfortable. "So, uh, what brings you home to Littleton after all this time?" His eyes widened. "Your dad ... he isn't ...?"

All at once, everything she'd left behind wrenched around her like ivy choking the life out of a tree trunk. Summer heat drilled into her skin as the look of concern on Brian's face burrowed into places she couldn't give him access to.

The sight of him with Cindy Mae took another blow: the perfect southern wife, a precious daughter on the way, a legacy in Littleton—all the things Quinn couldn't have offered him.

She stared Cinderella down, wanting to resent her. But the truth was, she was adorable and sweet and everything Brian deserved.

"Are you all right?" He set a hand to Quinn's forearm with a familiar touch—once comforting, now laden with regret.

Wind blew her hair along her sticky neck. Her pulse raced. She needed to get out of there. "I ... um ..."

"Wanted it to be a surprise." An arm curled around her back. Cooper. He tucked her shoulder under his as if he'd done it a hundred times. With his confident eyes fixed on Brian, he held out an equally self-assured hand. "Cooper Anderson, Quinn's boyfriend."

She dropped her sunglasses. He did not just say ...

Cooper squatted at the same time she did and handed her the glasses along with a go-with-it expression. When they both stood up and he roped an arm around her again, the only thing she wanted to go with was the fastest track out of there. Especially when a convoluted mix of emotions spread across Brian's face as he leaned his head toward Brayden's stroller.

He pulled his focus back to Cooper. "I'm Brian Meadows, Quinn's ..." His focus gravitated to her. "An old friend," he revised. His warm smile melted over her. "I'm really happy for you, Quinn."

And he was, genuinely. Because that's the kind of guy he was. The sting of that truth sawed through her layers of insulation as if they weren't even there.

"You're a lucky guy, Cooper. Quinn's one of a kind."

"She sure is."

At Cooper's obnoxious tone, Quinn elbowed him. But when another trace of unanswered questions shadowed Brian's eyes, she had to lean into Cooper for balance.

He tightened his grasp around her waist and gently rested the side of his chin to her temple as if he understood somehow. "Only a crazy guy would let a girl like her go."

If Cindy Mae caught the insinuation in Cooper's jab, she didn't show it. Brian, on the other hand, adjusted his collar.

Yet instead of unleashing the arsenal of questions he'd had years to accumulate, a hint of unresolved pain was all his expression offered. "Then you better hold on to her tight," he said without releasing her gaze. Brian dipped his head at both of them like a cowboy tipping his hat. "Give your father my regards."

Even after he and Cindy Mae had made it into the parlor, Quinn stayed tucked under Cooper's arm. He stood like a firm pillar beside her—one she shouldn't have leaned on but couldn't bring herself to pull away from.

"Are you okay?"

Not even remotely. "Fine." At least it was over and out of the way.

Panic climbed her neck in a rebuttal. She hung her head in her hand. "If my mom hears about this—"

"Quinn Mary Beth Thompson."

No. It wasn't fair. Her muscles constricted, willing the sound of Mama's voice back to some hidden part of her psyche. *Please be dreaming.*

"Mary Beth?" Cooper mouthed with too much amusement.

Quinn would've popped him if she could move.

Mama and Aunt Loraine scurried over to them like two chickens just let loose from a henhouse. Cooper seemed to take the cue to let her go and squatted to Brayden's stroller instead. Wise man.

"As I live and breathe, that *is* you." In a short-sleeved white button-up plagued in a pattern of oversized cherries, Mama raised a hand to her mouth, to her heart, and then to Quinn's arm. "My baby girl." A watery gaze swam over her. "Just look at you. A sight for sore eyes, isn't she, Loraine?"

"You sure are, darlin'."

A quizzical look tipped Mama's head to the side. "Now, sugar, I think your hair dresser must've been standing on a slant when she cut your bangs."

And so it began.

"They're supposed to be slanted, Mama."

"Is that right?" She swept a glance to Aunt Loraine and back. "Well, isn't that precious." She reached up. "Maybe if we just—"

"No one teases their bangs anymore," Quinn said, ducking away.

"Don't be silly. Everyone knows, the higher your hair—"

"The closer you are to God," Quinn finished with her.

Yeah, a lot of good that did any of them. She lifted on her toes to scope out the line to the door. She needed something to occupy her mouth before she said something she shouldn't.

Mama squeezed her hand. "Why didn't you tell me you were home, sweetie?"

"It was a surprise." Cooper rose to his feet, making things ten times worse without even knowing it. Or maybe he did. "Pleasure to meet you, ma'am. I'm Cooper, Quinn's boyfriend."

Quinn darted him a tight-lipped smile as he curled her into his side again, clearly enjoying this whole shenanigan far more than he should.

Two doe-eyed gazes soaked in the full-length of everything that made up Cooper Anderson. Mama fluttered a hand in Aunt Loraine's direction in search of something steady to grasp. "Baby, you could've warned me you were bringing such a handsome young man home. I would've gotten my hair done."

"You look lovely, Mrs. Thompson." Cooper leaned down to kiss the back of her hand.

Mama waved her free one over her flushed cheeks. "Oh, my."

Oh, brother.

He moved on to Aunt Loraine. "Is it Mrs. Thompson as well?"

"*Ms.* Thompson." Still swooning, she ran her fingers along an oversized necklace. "But you can call me whatever you like."

As long as someone called Quinn a cab. She had to get out of there. The odds of running into them at this time of day were supposed to be next to nothing.

Fine, so she'd dropped statistics in college. That didn't mean it had to take a vengeance on her now.

Another zing of panic barreled into her. What came out of her own mouth shouldn't worry her. The things Mama might spill in front of Cooper could ruin everything.

Mama fluffed out her short, layered hair, recovering. "I don't understand why you wouldn't tell us you were here."

"That's my fault. I've kept her to myself." Cooper squeezed her close. "Though, we still have *so* much to talk about, don't we, QT?"

This was some sort of retribution for going along with the nanny thing, wasn't it? She probably deserved it.

"Pet names," Mama practically hummed. "Well, aren't you two just as sweet as summertime peaches. We certainly have a lot to catch up on ourselves." She exaggerated a wink to Quinn like everyone in a three-block radius couldn't see her failing miserably at trying to be subtle.

The wrinkles jutting out from the corners of her eyes deepened in a visible question. "Now, honey, I'm just a little confused. I thought you were dating someone named Gil."

Cooper raised an amused brow, and Quinn clasped her sunglasses so hard, she almost broke them. Was there no end to the humiliation?

"Oh, um, Gil, yeah. We had a bit of a time-distance problem we couldn't overcome." As in, he lived in the imagination of a century-old author. "But we stay in touch." Every time she picked up *Anne of Green Gables*. Really, it was the perfect relationship.

The clank of one of Brayden's toys hitting the ground ignited a round of cries. Aunt Loraine knelt beside the stroller and held her ice cream cone out to him. "Doesn't that look good? Now, you just come on over to Aunt Loraine, darlin'. I'll make it all better." She finagled him out of the straps, hung him on her hip, and held the cone for him.

With one of his carefree smiles, Brayden swung his hands together in excitement—straight into either side of the scoop of ice cream. Dollops of chocolate splattered across Aunt Loraine's face.

Looking stunned, she blinked the melted chocolate off her lashes while Brayden kept clapping his goopy hands together, making it all the worse.

Cooper buried his chin in his shoulder, his chest shaking with silent laughter. Quinn bit her lip to keep from joining him.

"Stop it," she whispered through her teeth.

Aunt Loraine stilled Brayden's hands. "Well, aren't you just a little booger?"

Once Cooper regained his composure, he reached for him. "I can take him."

"No point in you getting dirty, too, darlin'. We'll be right back."

As they flitted toward the parlor to use the bathroom, Mama took both Quinn's hands in hers and sighed. "I still can't believe it. My Motel 6 baby, finally home."

Cooper pointed a look at Quinn. "Motel 6 baby?"

Shoot me now. "We really should be going."

"I'm sure we have time for a few stories." His lopsided grin nearly toppled his whole head sideways.

Quinn's eyes narrowed, but the moment Cooper extended his arm, Mama took him hostage for a stroll down memory lane. "After Quinn's daddy and I got married, we got this silly notion in our heads that we'd go all the way up to see the Statue of Liberty."

She patted his bicep, chuckling. "We didn't even make it past the North Carolina border before turning right back around. But it was so late, we stopped at this Motel 6 off Highway 87." A rosy blush of nostalgia swelled across her sun-spotted cheeks. "And well, our little Quinn came nine months—"

"Okay, Mama. We really have to leave. Brayden needs some lunch." And she needed an exit route. Now.

"Bring him on back to the house. I have plenty of mac and cheese from last night. It'll just take a—"

"No," Quinn almost shouted.

"Heavens, child. What's the matter with you?"

Quinn stole a minute to iron out her shirt and her voice. "Sorry. I'm just here for a few weeks and trying to work on a routine with Brayden. Plus, we still need to get some shopping done. Lots to do today." Like drilling a hole in her head.

"Fine, but you make sure you pick up a bushel of peaches while you're out." Mama leaned toward Cooper. "She makes the best peach cobblers. And her vanilla custard?" She fanned her lashes. "To die for. Our Quinn is exceptional in the kitchen. Always has been. Did you know she ran her own food blog for a while?"

She listed off Quinn's cooking skills like she was posting an ad: Single woman desperate to be a southern wife. If Quinn had a peach, she'd surely be gagging on it right now.

Mama bobbed her brows at Cooper. "Be sure to save at least one cobbler for the cookout at our house Sunday after church. You do go to church, don't you, honey?"

Quinn's throat turned to sandpaper. Forget ice cream. She needed something to drink. Water, whisky—whatever.

Cool and smooth as usual, Cooper flashed his mind-stopping grin at her. "We'd love to come by on Sunday. Thank you for inviting us, Mrs. Thompson."

"Please, you call me Paula, you hear?"

Quinn speared a glare at him. This wasn't happening. "But you have to work on your deck, remember, *honey?*"

His eyes teemed with inward enjoyment. "It'll get done. I'll work fast, dreaming of your vanilla custard."

He wasn't the only one dreaming about it. She had already envisioned ramming it into his face ten times since this conversation started.

Aunt Loraine meandered back over and set Brayden in the stroller. "As good as new." When she straightened, an unexpected look of pity touched her face. "I saw Brian and Cindy Mae inside. It was big of you to speak with them, sweetie. I'm sure it was hard, seeing her like that and all."

Quinn tried not to twitch. "I'm fine."

"Well, of course you are." Mama looked between her and Cooper. "You have a new beau now. Everything's going to work out."

Seriously? Ugh. "Bye, Mama." She turned to leave, but Aunt Loraine's frantic plea to wait stopped her.

"You're coming to the cookout, right? We'll be brainstorming Ginny's sweet sixteen party and could really use your help. And just wait till your daddy sees you." A nonstop beam of hope glowed at her.

Chin down, Quinn dragged the tip of her Converse in circles in the dirt. "How's he doing?" she all but whispered.

Mama's delayed response drew her gaze from the ground toward a notorious southern smile Quinn could see through. "Oh, he's just fine, sugar. Has his good days and bad days." She gave Quinn's arm a gentle pat. "We just keep praying for more of the good ones."

What was the point? It wasn't like prayers ever got answered anyway. A river of buried brokenness forged through her walls. If a single tear escaped in front of them, she'd—

"It was so good to run into you ladies." Cooper pressed a comforting hand to her lower back, once again sensing more than she ever intended him to. "But we really do need to get going." He prodded her toward his SUV while pushing Brayden's stroller.

"Don't forget to bring your desserts, sweetheart," Mama called behind them. "Just wait till you taste them, Cooper. One bite, and you won't want to let go of our Quinn."

Quinn whipped an exasperated stare around toward another animated wink proving her life was a walking Jane Austen novel. If Cooper wanted to go to her parents' house Sunday, he'd better polish up his Mr. Knightly impersonation. Or they'd both be in trouble.

CHAPTER SIX

Intervention

Cooper tried to keep up with Quinn's beeline to his Audi. He lifted Brayden into his car seat while Quinn paced back and forth a few feet away on a silent rampage. "Take it from me, hoss," he whispered to Brayden. "It's better not to ask."

After two minutes of messing with the stupid straps, he leaned back and wiped his brow across his arm. If he could analyze financial markets all day long, he should be able to figure out a stinking car seat.

His incompetence must've been some sort of Quinn-magnet. She shimmied her way into the space and managed to fasten the buckles in two point five seconds.

She backed out of the car and held out her hand. "Keys. I'm driving."

Red flag. Uh-uh. Back up. "I'm sorry, do you think that's a good idea?"

"Keys!"

He yanked them free from his pocket but held on. "You know the speed limit's thirty-five, right? As in, throughout the entire town."

Her amber eyes answered for her as she snatched the keys and whirled toward the driver's side.

Cooper looked at Brayden in the mirror. "Just be glad you have a harness."

With his own seat belt fastened, he waited for a mile to pass before peering her way to gauge the level of heat waves still steaming off her. "Do you want to—?"

"No."

"But don't you think we should talk abou—?"

"No." She snapped on the blinker and whipped onto a side street.

Okay then. No talking it was.

"Seriously, what was that back there?" she rambled off faster than she was driving.

Apparently, talking was back on the docket.

"What was what?"

Quinn flicked a glance at him. "Pretending to be my boyfriend. 'It was a surprise,'" she mimicked in a sappy voice that sounded nothing like his.

He leaned into the door panel and stared at her. "It's called an intervention," he ribbed right back in that same ridiculous voice. "Those were the people you were hoping not to run into while here, I take it?"

Mouth tight, she careened into the Piggly Wiggly parking lot, of all places, without responding.

"You had a problem that needed a solution. Simple as that."

"Simple?" She sped into a parking spot and jerked the gearshift into park. "And who said I had a problem?"

"Your trembling shoulders, for one." He couldn't just stand there, watching her hurt like she was. He had to do something. Didn't she see he was trying to help?

Her demeanor shifted, and a glimpse of a frail girl hiding something unspoken broke through the mayhem.

He tugged his ear. "I'm sorry if I went too far. I was trying to make things a little easier on you."

"This isn't simple or easy." She looked away and massaged her temples. "It's a disaster."

"I'm sure it's not that bad."

"Did you just meet my mom and aunt? Or did I imagine that? Because I'm pretty sure if you were actually there, you'd at least halfway understand."

He strained to hold in his amusement at her frazzled expression. Recounting the little run-in with her family wasn't helping.

She flung her hand in the air. "See?"

His laugh tumbled out. "Okay, fine. So, you have some country roots. Big deal."

"Big deal?" With another exasperated shake of her head, she opened her door. "Stay here. I need to shop."

Didn't have to tell him twice. He hadn't come anywhere close to cracking girl-code, but he'd wager 'need to shop' translated into 'don't come near me unless you want your head bitten off.' *Copy that.*

"Women," he muttered into the quiet car and then twisted around to face the mirror in front of Brayden's car seat. "You have a lot to learn, hoss. Starting with the fact that women are 100 percent complicated. Don't try to figure them out. You can't. Trust me."

He glanced toward Quinn as she strode into the grocery store. "Save yourself some headaches and just accept that they're beautiful, mysterious creatures capable of driving you insane and leaving you undone at the same time."

Brayden twisted a crinkly book, elated at the simple noise it made.

Cooper laughed at the clear disparity. "That's right. Keep it uncomplicated. It's how we men roll."

"Roll!" Brayden waved the book against the seat at the same time a text from Ray Williams popped up on Cooper's cell.

Call me. The buyers just informed me of a house sale contingency. This could delay our original schedule.

Not again. He stared at yet another pressing reminder of why he shouldn't get involved in Quinn's problems right now. But as his gaze drifted to the empty driver's seat, his focus strayed into a replay of what had just gone down at the ice cream parlor. She'd obviously lied to him about being from here. Was she that embarrassed about her family?

Though, to be fair, he couldn't exactly fault her for wanting anonymity when he wanted the same. But something about it all felt a little off. If she wanted nothing to do with this place, why come back for a temporary nanny job?

And how was it that she was mad at him for helping her save face in front of her ex-boyfriend, or whoever that Brian guy was? "You were there," he said to Brayden. "It was perfect, right?"

A plastic keyring set nailed him dead in the face, followed by an all-too-amused coo.

"Oh, you think that's funny?" He stretched around the seat and reached to tickle Brayden's leg, igniting a round of baby laughter. It filled the SUV with a sound Cooper wasn't used to having in his life.

A mirror reflection of his own eyes smiled back at him and caught him low in the gut. His chest tightened at the tender look on Brayden's face. He'd been so consumed by the shock of finding out Megan had kept their son from him, he hadn't allowed himself to feel any other response. He had immediately jumped into troubleshooting mode and defaulted to keeping Brayden an arm's length away like everyone else.

But Brayden wasn't just anyone else.

The implications of that truth tore him down the middle, pulling one side from the other. He swallowed hard at the impact of mixed emotions and toyed with the jumbo keys in his lap. Some problem solver he was. Not only had his irresponsibility with Megan ultimately put Brayden in this situation to begin with, he couldn't see a way to ever make it right. No matter what Cooper did, he'd fail him in some way.

Megan must've known it too. If she thought he was suited to be in Brayden's life, she wouldn't have kept him out of it until she had no choice.

A car door slammed beside him. Tensing, he reached for his seat belt buckle while turning around. Just a kid getting out of a back seat to follow his mom.

Cooper shook his head. Things with the media might've died down the last few days, but that didn't mean they'd stay that way. How long before they caught wind that he had a son he hadn't even known about until this week? It would take them all of three seconds to twist it into some slanderous story to smear across the papers to validate what people already thought about him.

He hung his head. Tanya was right. His profile came with a price. Which was exactly why he needed to shield Brayden from it—and anyone else he might end up caring about.

Another glance toward the store ended in a hard exhale. How many more blatant reasons did he need to convince himself he had enough complications overtaking his world without adding Quinn Thompson to the mix?

Except, he already had.

The sorrow in her eyes broke into his thoughts with the same ache that had driven him to rescue her from it back at the parlor. As preoccupied as he was with everything else, he couldn't ignore she stirred something in him. Maybe he didn't get her sticky note fetish, coffee snobbery, or grammar fascination, but pain he understood.

He craned his neck and let out a moan. *Three more weeks.* "Either I'm about to crack girl-code or get a good crack to the skull. You ready to weigh the odds?"

A puzzled look peered back at him from the mirror. He could joke about Quinn being crazy, but he was the one out here having a man-to-man talk with a one-year-old.

He smiled on his way out the door, leaving the sudden on-slaught of emotions in the SUV.

With Brayden in one arm, he stood at the trunk, trying to shake open the stroller. He probably should've gotten it out first, *then* put Brayden in it. *Real smart, Anderson.*

His cell rang from his pocket. Hands full, he shook the annoying stroller even harder. "Hang on a sec," he said as if the person calling could hear him. But by the time his hands were finally free, his voice mail was already dinging with a message from his realtor.

Cooper raked his damp hair back while peering against the hot sun toward the store. He would return Ray's call when they got home. Right now, he had bigger problems to deal with.

"C'mon, hoss." He pushed the stroller forward. "It's time to learn how to be the southern gentleman your mom would want you to be."

A rush of A/C and beeping registers greeted them inside the grocery store. Cooper stopped short on his way to start weaving through the aisles when the sight of Quinn's yellow shirt up near the checkout lines caught his eye. Huh. Faster than he thought.

"Looks like we might've lucked out." He maneuvered through the line to reach her, took one look at the cram-packed cart, and leaned down to Brayden. "Then again, maybe not. Reinforcement time."

He jumped right in unloading the shopping cart onto the conveyor belt. Chocolate ice cream, dark chocolate bars, chocolate sauce. Yeah, definitely not out of danger territory yet.

He'd never seen someone binge shop before, but from the looks of the tower of butter, sugar, and spices, he was pretty sure that's what just happened. If the etched lines still creasing Quinn's face were any indication, a binge eating session was probably about to follow.

At least she didn't argue about him coming in after her. He set a three pack of mac and cheese on the belt. "I know you're worried about going to your parents', but it's gonna be fine."

When she didn't tear her focus off her arsenal of coping supplies, Cooper leaned an arm into hers. "If you want to use Brayden as a diversion to keep the conversation off you, I won't judge. I mean, it *is* almost as bad as using him as a chick magnet, but I'll let it slide."

The faintest smile graced her lips, but whatever tangle of thoughts were keeping her shoulders looking that tense clearly hadn't released her yet.

As the pepper-haired woman behind the register ran each item past the scanner, Quinn stared at the magazine rack like she was silently rewriting the headlines on each cover.

Cooper glanced at Brayden, who'd already passed out. *Way to have my back.*

He wheeled the stroller around Quinn. "Listen," he half whispered. "There's no reason to be embarrassed about your roots. And you never know, things might've changed since you were last here."

He ran his hand up and down the back of his hair when she still didn't respond. Okay, complicated was obviously just the start of it. If she had the same caffeine headache he did right now, it would be hard to blame her.

He withdrew his wallet when the cashier finished up checking them out. "How you doing, ma'am?"

"I'll be more better as soon as my shift ends, honey."

A twitch pulsed above Quinn's eye. "I'm sorry, did you just say more—?"

"I bet it's hard standing on your feet all day." Cooper scooted Quinn to the side before her grammar twitch turned into convulsions.

"It was them beans and rice I ate at lunch." The woman shifted on her feet and circled a hand around her stomach. "Ooh-wee, they sure enough went straight to my backside. Yes, they did." She made a strained face the way Brayden did when he was about to pass gas.

Cooper paused with his Visa pulled halfway out of his wallet, mouth slack. Without moving a muscle, he cut a glance at Quinn.

Her blank expression transitioned from stunned to delirious. An airy laugh shook her shoulders, almost folding her in half the louder it grew. She swung a finger between the woman and him. "Things might've changed," she squeaked out like he'd made the punch line of the year. She strode away with Brayden's stroller, mumbling something about living in a walking cliché.

Cooper offered the cashier an apologetic smile and his credit card. "Long morning."

"Don't I know it, honey."

All paid up, he pushed the cart full of Quinn's nervous breakdown remedy over to the front of the store where the wall was holding her up.

She picked at the rubber coating on the stroller's handles. A rueful expression tinged with sadness looked up at him when he approached. "She's having his baby."

He made a face. "The kid probably won't even be cute, and it wasn't like she was glowing or anything. Did you see how swollen her ankles were?"

Quinn gave in to a smile. "She did have cankles, didn't she?"

"Hideous."

She cracked up then, and the sound lit something off inside him.

Wiping her cheeks, she met his gaze again. "You're kind of sweet, Cooper Anderson. A terrible liar, but sweet." She dragged her fingers back and forth along the top of the stroller. "I'm sorry I didn't warn you about all this."

He raised a shoulder. "It's none of my business."

"I still should've told you."

"I understand."

She curled her bottom lip in, looking torn about whether to say more.

Cooper jutted his chin toward the exit. "Let's get out of here. I'll make you some coffee."

"Does that come with a tall glass of wine?"

"I don't know." The corner of his mouth sloped sideways as they walked. "I wouldn't want to interfere with all those peach cobblers you're gonna make me."

Wide-eyed and adorably appalled, Quinn gave him a solid shove across the lane. "You just wait. You have no idea what you're walking into."

Finally, something they could actually agree on.

CHAPTER SEVEN

Predicament

D ays passing only intensified the dread building in Quinn's stomach.

She snapped her laptop shut on the patio table and switched her cell phone to her opposite ear. "Chase, you can't let me walk into an ambush at the cookout today. You know how Mama and Aunt Loraine are. You *have* to be there as a buffer for me."

"I can't just hop on a plane. I'm in the middle of a job. And from what I hear, you're not going alone."

Perfect. The news had already traveled across three states. Why was she not surprised? "Kill the singsong tone. It's not what you think."

"Littleton's prodigal child coming home with an eligible beau at her side? Oh yeah, it's exactly what I think—Mom's dream come true."

Cringing, Quinn dragged her cool orange juice glass along her forehead. "At least help me come up with an excuse to get out of going."

Her brother's obnoxious laugh cut right through her flimsy plea. They both knew good and well there was no getting out of this. "It won't be that bad. I'm sure Gramps will limit his inappropriate commentary to only half the day." A string of laughter rolled through the line.

"I hate you right now, you know that?" She set her glass aside, hoisted her leg up in the patio chair, and dropped her head onto her knee. "Why am I even talking to you about this?"

"I've been asking myself that same question since you woke me up first thing this morning."

"You're impossible."

"And you're overreacting." His tone shifted with the breeze fanning Quinn's bangs across her lashes. "Relax. Mom's just glad you're home. It's been too long, Quinn."

He was right. Months had turned into years, just like the space she'd needed had turned into an excuse to hide. "I know." But that didn't make it any easier.

"Then live it up at the cookout for me, will ya? Never know, you might actually end up having fun."

Or a coronary. "I'm hanging up now." Man, he was almost as bad as Ava. Though, at least he'd answered his phone this morning. Quinn checked her cell for any missed messages. Still no returned call. Knowing Ava, she was still asleep after a *lively* evening last night. Like another someone she knew.

She glanced at the closed blinds on Cooper's room. He'd gotten home long after she'd gone to bed, probably out on a real date—unlike the fake one she was dragging him on today.

Wait, this whole predicament was his fault. Well, sort of. Okay, fine, so she'd spun her own mess, but he didn't have to go pouring gasoline on it by romping around as her pretend boyfriend.

Quinn reopened her laptop, stared at the single paragraph it had taken almost an hour to write, and slumped in the chair. Who was she kidding? She was just as much of a fake.

Cruella wanted a briefing every day, but even after being here a week, Quinn still didn't have anything substantial. She could only write so much fluff before her boss nailed her for not being able to cut it as a journalist. How was she supposed to prove she was equipped for the executive editor position if she couldn't even master the tasks of the people she'd be over-seeing?

She should probably stick to basic editing. She'd obviously lost her writing skills. Maybe she never even had any.

A skinny black cat jumped into her lap out of nowhere. Quinn froze with her arms hovering above her keyboard. If the cat sensed surprise, she didn't let on. The little thing pawed around Quinn's legs, rubbing her head up under her arms as she circled.

"Um, hi there. Where'd you come from?" Cooper owned a cat? She ran a cautious stroke along its back. But when the little purr box walked her two front paws up Quinn's stomach and went to nuzzle her adorable wet nose under her chin, Quinn melted.

"Aren't you just the cutest thing ever." Bright green eyes, tuxedo markings, the tip of her right ear missing—she liked this cat already. "Scrappy, too, huh?"

Still purring, the cat made bread against Quinn's stomach, which tightened without warning. If she was honest, she could use a friend here.

Not that Cooper was hard to live with. He was surprisingly kind of sweet, and his coffee wasn't exactly terrible after all. Maybe this pretend relationship thing was a blessing in disguise.

"Couples talk, right?" she said aloud. "They share secrets and stuff." Rubbing the cat's head, she reclined against the chair back. "What do you think? Should we give it a shot?"

The cat launched off her lap onto the deck and scampered through the railing slats.

"Too much talking?" Quinn called after her. That was probably a bad sign. Stupid. It would never work. What made her think she could do this?

Ava's ringtone lit up her cell on the table. Quinn bumped into her laptop, stretching for it. "Finally," Quinn said, skipping hellos. "I've been trying to reach you all morning."

"Really? I had no idea. Your fifteen texts didn't clue me in."

"Yeah, well, this is an emergency. Cooper and I ran into my mom yesterday."

Ava took a sip of something. Probably a caramel macchiato—the same cup of deliciousness *she* would be drinking right now if she weren't in the sticks.

"Just tell her he's Gil. She gets to put a face to your imaginary boyfriend. You get to keep her off your back for a little while longer. Problem solved."

"No, you don't understand. She's having us over today. *My mom*, Ava. As in, the woman who's at home right now, already planning our wedding. How am I supposed to keep Cooper from finding out I work for *News First* when she's going to pounce on him with my entire life story the minute we walk through the door?"

"Here's a thought. Why don't you tell him the truth. Just lead with an Anderson Cooper joke. It'll be awesome."

A joke. Right. Her coffee obviously hadn't kicked in yet. "I'm sorry, you do know our boss, right? The woman itching for an excuse to fire me? I can't ruin this."

Ava's lack of response from the other end of the line pulsed with something she wasn't saying.

"What now?"

"Don't worry about it."

"Ava."

"Fine." Her best friend sighed. "Remember Chad? That guy from Corporate I went on a few dates with? You're not going to believe what he told me last night." In classic Ava style, she stretched the dramatic pause.

Quinn's grasp tightened around the phone. "If you don't just spit it out, I'm gonna—"

"Cruella's job is on the line this quarter!"

"What?"

"It's about time, isn't it? The woman can only strut around on her power trip for so long before someone puts her in her place."

Quinn swirled her orange juice in the glass, a jumble of thoughts circling into each other. "You think she knows?"

"Doubt it. If she did, she might be thinking twice about letting people go just 'cause they have a single hair out of place." Voice sobering, Ava sounded like she was tapping a fingernail to a desk. "This could be good for you, Quinn. Her plan in sending you out there could totally backfire on her."

"What are you talking about?"

"The feature on Cooper. You don't think Corporate's going to take notice of you after this? And if Cruella's position ends up being open …"

Editor-in-chief? She'd be lying if she didn't admit she'd had her eye on that job since day one. The creative changes she could make, the chance to lead and honor the whole team—it was what she'd always hoped for.

Pressure expanded in her gut. What if she wasn't ready for Corporate to look at her? What if failing to come through on this piece only proved that Cruella should stay and Quinn should be demoted, fired even? How could she face her family if that happened?

Her eyelids caved shut. She had to make this work. "I need more time." She draped an arm over the top of her laptop. "Maybe if I tell Cooper—"

"Tell me what?" he asked while opening the sliding screen door.

Quinn swung her laptop shut so fast, two birds on the rail tore into the trees as if a gunshot had gone off. "Gotta go," she whispered into the phone before hanging up. Deep breath. She could handle the pressure. Just had to play it cool.

Carrying a plate of the breakfast she'd left in the kitchen, Cooper pushed Brayden's umbrella stroller on his way across the deck in his pajama pants. Thankfully, he had a T-shirt on this time.

He parked the stroller beside the monitor Quinn had brought out with her and dropped into the opposite seat.

"You found the breakfast I left you," she said.

"I saw the sticky note." The corner of his mouth lifted in obvious amusement. But the minute he took a bite of his omelet, his warm smile sprawled across her with the morning's sunshine. "You keep cooking like this, and I might not let you go."

She looked from his playful eyes toward Brayden instead. "Going for a walk this morning?"

When a question arched his brow, she pointed to the stroller.

"Oh, nah. I just figured it'd be easier to bring him out here in that. Plus, he seems content in his car seat or stroller most of the time, so I thought it might keep him happy."

Quinn scanned over Cooper's messy bedhead, bulky arms, and aggravatingly cute dimples that dipped the slightest bit each time he chewed. Player turned father. Who would've pictured it? "Looks like you're getting this parenting thing down pretty well."

He paused with his fork halfway to his mouth, eyes dimming. "It takes more than a random observation to make a good parent."

Setting his fork to his plate, Cooper seemed to ward off whatever was bothering him. "What is it you need to tell me?"

So much for sidetracking him. She pulled her leg up again and tucked her ankle under her thigh, but Ava's nudge to tell him the truth kept weaseling in. "Uh, yeah, so, funny story.

I'm actually kind of a writer." There, she'd gotten it out. That was good enough, right?

Cooper looked at her like she'd just confessed something already written in blinking billboard lights. "Uh-huh."

"You already knew?"

"Normal people don't go around correcting people's grammar."

She stifled a laugh. "Writers aren't normal?"

"They're ..." He looked from the acorns covering the deck to the moss-covered tree branches above them as though hoping the right adjective would drop into his lap. "Creative," he finally said.

"Sounds like you've known a few."

"Creatives? Wait till you meet my sister-in-law." He linked his hands together over his head and stretched from side to side.

Quinn darted a glance from his flexed muscles back to Brayden, already drifting off to sleep, and took a sip of her orange juice.

"So, you're writing a story about me?"

Juice sprayed down her chin. In a scramble to wipe it off without looking like a lunatic, she tapped her chest and coughed. "Sorry, I think a gnat got in my drink or something."

"If I didn't know any better, QT, I'd think you were blushing." He crossed an ankle over his knee.

Darn slanted grin. She downed the rest of her OJ. "I've always been a little uncomfortable talking about my writing, that's all." True enough.

"What do you write about?"

Clearly, he missed the uncomfortable part. Or maybe he didn't. *Punk.* She shrugged. "Oh, you know. Stories, news." Things far more interesting than her own life. She ran a fingertip along the perimeter of her laptop. "I don't want to bore you."

Eyes not leaving hers, his gaze somehow deepened. "There's nothing boring about you, Quinn Mary Beth Thompson."

What good was chugging OJ when her mouth went completely dry two seconds later? She shielded her face with her hair. They needed a subject change.

Of course, she wouldn't be that lucky.

"In all fairness, it was more than just your grammar skills that tipped me off. Your mom mentioned you used to write a blog."

Right. Why couldn't he have missed that part?

"That was forever ago, and it was stupid."

"I doubt that." He took another bite of his breakfast, still looking at her as if what she had to say couldn't be anything less than fascinating.

Little did he know how easily she could prove him wrong. "Oh, no, I assure you it was. It was called Biscuits and Gravy and All Things Crazy."

When he struggled to swallow through a laugh, she jutted her glass at him. "See! I told you. Trust me, you can't even classify it as real writing. It was just a silly blog about family stories and recipes. No one read it." Thankfully. Just the thought of it still lurking around the internet mortified her.

Not that her writing had improved since then. If it had, she would have more than a single paragraph written for this feature by now.

"You know," he said, his tone shifting. "About yesterday... I gotta admit, I thought your mom wanting to marry you off was kinda cute, but I really wasn't trying to make things worse for you. I was trying to help."

"I know." She dropped her gaze to the puddle of condensation her glass had left on the table. "I'm sorry for how crazy they were acting. I honestly don't have an excuse for my mom, but my aunt's been through a lot. She's the youngest of my mom's siblings and ended up with some health problems."

Biting her lip, Quinn fingered a string of moss that'd fallen onto the table. "She and Uncle Carter tried for years to have kids, but eventually he gave up and left her."

"What?" The disgust in the single word echoed the feelings Quinn kept to herself.

"The ironic thing was, he left the same month she found out about Ginny. On one hand, it was a miracle. She'd finally conceived." She flicked the moss onto the deck. "On the other, her marriage was already ruined."

Looking back, Quinn shouldn't have been surprised to see prayers get only partway answered. Like a tease, the hope they spurred never left a shadow of disappointment too far behind.

Her chair screeched against the grains of wood beneath it when she moved too quickly. "Anyway, I don't mean to unload a bunch of family baggage on you. Just wanted you to know why she might come off a little man hungry."

Her laugh fell flat, especially when Cooper's tender eyes burned a hole of compassion into her chest like he could read the hidden meaning no one else could see.

"I know there's a lot I don't know or understand about your past." He lowered his foot from his knee and dipped his head to catch her gaze again. "But I didn't miss the way your ex looked at you yesterday."

She almost snorted. "Like he was trying to figure out why in the world he was ever with me?"

"More like why he'd ever let you go." Cooper's sincerity gripped her. "Some guys don't realize what they have until they lose it." His brow furrowed with the kind of regret gained from experience, and the stereotype she'd boxed him into crumbled a little more.

A pair of jet skis soared by the end of his property, rousing Brayden awake. He squirmed in his stroller and rubbed tiny fists into his eyes.

Grateful for the distraction, Quinn brought the monitor to her lap and checked the volume. "I didn't hear him crying earlier."

"He wasn't. When I checked in on him, he was just laying there, awake in his crib."

Lying there. Quinn tamped down the urge to correct his grammar and smiled while wiggling Brayden's toes. "Was he sucking on his blanket?"

"He did not get that from me."

"So, he *is* your son." The words spouted out on their own like water from a hose. She stiffened, not wanting to meet whatever reactive expression might be on Cooper's face.

"So I'm told."

Her head shot up. "You didn't know?"

He peeled the lining off one of her banana wheat muffins and balled it into a tight wad.

It all registered then. "His mom?"

Cooper left the muffin on his plate and peered down toward the lake. "Car wreck," he said faintly.

Her heart sank. "I'm so sorry."

"Not as sorry as I am." He cleared his throat and turned toward her again, his confident aura back in place. "But we'll make it."

"I thought you said Brayden wasn't going with you."

He tore a piece of muffin off. "He's not."

Quinn's gaze bounced from him to Brayden's precious cheeks and back. "I don't understand. How could his not going with you be right? He just lost his mom. He needs his dad."

Cooper shoved his chair away from the table and bolted to his feet. "He needs a family who can raise him."

"What makes you think you can't?"

His usual charming smile turned piercing. "Based on all your assumptions about me, I'm sure you can answer that." He strode to the rail facing the lake and clutched the wooden edge.

Brayden started to fuss, and Quinn moved into Cooper's abandoned seat to try to soothe him.

Cooper threaded both sets of fingers through his hair and then let his arms drift to his sides. "I'm sorry," he said before turning around.

"No, you're right. It's not my place to say anything."

He wandered back over to the table with his head down in an image of vulnerability she guessed most people rarely ever saw. "I guess we both have things we'd rather not talk about."

A quick glance at her laptop sent her stomach churning. Her cell went off with an impersonalized ringtone. She grabbed the phone, silenced the call without looking at the screen, and rose beside Cooper. Whoever it was could wait. She rested a hand to his arm. "For what it's worth, Cooper, I think you might surprise us both."

His hazel eyes found hers, and her grip around his arm tightened more than she meant it to. Mama used to say windows were the eyes to the soul. Quinn'd had hers boarded up for so long, a guy she hardly knew shouldn't be able to peer inside without a single word.

Her pulse overpowered the growing chirping from nearby grasshoppers.

Neither of them moved until his cell broke the silence. Clearing his throat again, Cooper backed up a step and withdrew his phone from his pajama bottoms' pocket. "My lawyer."

She nodded, still searching for her voice.

"I have some business to take care of this morning, but I'll be ready in time for the cookout."

"Sure you don't want to do something else today? Maybe go drown ourselves in the lake?" Reread the entire *Lord of the Rings* boxed set? Anything?

Cooper laughed while backing up toward the sliding door, phone still ringing. "You just have those cobblers ready, QT.

I'll take care of the rest." He raised his cell to his ear and stepped inside. "Jim, what's the word today?"

As he wandered out of sight, Quinn turned toward Brayden, blanket in his mouth. She cracked up. "You learned that from your daddy, didn't you? I know."

His face scrunched, on the verge of a restless cry.

She unbuckled him, hoisted him onto her hip, and walked along the deck's warm boards under her bare feet. When he still seemed fussy, she dug around his stroller for the plastic keys Cooper had promptly bought him the first day she was here.

Instead of the keys, Brayden's attention stayed glued to the glass door Cooper had just closed behind him.

Quinn's stomach pinched. Of course there was more to his story. There always was. But what if it wasn't what she thought?

Another glance at her laptop sank the blow even deeper. Trying to dislodge it, she kept bouncing Brayden as she walked. "How about we see who called Ms. Quinn, huh?"

She held her cell in place with her shoulder while waiting for the voice message to play.

"Quinn, hi, it's Brian."

Her feet stumbled to a stop.

"I'm sorry for how awkward things were at Wakeboard Willie's yesterday. You caught me a little off guard." One of his self-conscious laughs trickled over her and blended into the same steady voice she'd curled into so many times. "I was hoping we could get together and talk. Just you and me. This is my new number, so, give me a call when you can. Please. It … it'd mean a lot."

Her pulse ticked in his pause.

"It was good to see you, Quinn. I hope you'll call."

Her arm slid to her side, a clear view to the lake grabbing hold of her.

Brayden's keys clattered onto the deck and elicited a round of cries, but she simply stood there. Staring. Remembering. A flag whipped in the wind along the edge of the dock as written-off emotions blew through her.

Brayden rubbed his face back and forth against her shoulder.

She blinked toward him then. "Shh. It's okay," she whispered, maybe more to herself than to him. "Everything's going to be okay."

Swaying, she fell into a natural rhythm she'd long given up on feeling. When he cuddled his head under her chin, she gripped the railing and breathed in.

Cooper stood in his office, wielding his commanding presence on the phone. One glance from him to Brayden, and Quinn's insides constricted. Could she really keep doing this?

She smoothed Brayden's hair across his forehead and forced herself to turn back to the lake she'd left four years ago. Heaven knew she needed a breaking story more than anything. But what happened if coming home broke her first?

CHAPTER EIGHT

Intrigued

Quinn dropped her elbow from the car's door panel and fidgeted with her seat belt. Other than swinging by the kitchen for some lunch and a peek at her cobblers, Cooper had stayed busy with work all day. She should've been grateful for the distance and chance to gain her wits about her. Still, rehearsing her last conversation with Cruella wasn't getting the job done.

Spit it out already. She unwrapped her fingers from the seat belt and tapped her thighs. "It's really peaceful here, isn't it? In that off-the-beaten-path kind of way."

Cooper checked his rearview mirror before making a right-hand turn. "By peaceful, you mean boring?"

Man, she stunk at this. "No, really. I mean, it's not for everyone, but there's a certain appeal in avoiding crowded cities, traffic...the stress of corporate life," she slipped in quickly. "Is that why you moved out to the middle of nowhere?" Holding her breath, she looked across the console.

He didn't let an iota of a reaction pass his face. "Guess you could say that."

Okay, this wasn't working. Quinn twisted in her seat toward him. "Seriously, Cooper? C'mon, you gotta give me something. No one just up and leaves a business like Shore Corp for no reason. Especially to move *here*. Were they not paying you enough? You found out someone was cooking the books? Had a blowout with the boss?"

Circling the wheel, he sent a smile her way. The kind that said, "Don't you wish you knew."

Two could play this game. "It must be some big secret for you to be all closed-mouthed about it." She pinned two satisfied arms over her chest and cocked her chin the way he usually did. "Cooper Anderson has a few skeletons in his closet, doesn't he?" How was that for bait?

One amused dimple chased the other. "How else can a guy keep a girl intrigued?"

Crazy. The man was driving her plum crazy. She pulled her Converse up to the edge of the seat and retied her shoelace, feigning disinterest. "Don't flatter yourself."

His warm laugh filled the car and dismantled her attempt at not returning it. Why'd she ever bother? Stinking charm.

Quinn let her foot drift back to the floorboard. "Well, you can't blame people for wondering about you. Shore Corp undergoes a major investigation right after you quit. Then you reappear on the radar out of nowhere as a self-made billionaire up for Top Entrepreneur of the Year. People are going to talk. You have to admit. It does sound a little susp—"

The car braked out of nowhere. Her head pitched forward and then hit the headrest while a family of geese took their sweet time crossing the road like they owned it.

The distinct furrow pinching Cooper's brow softened at the sight of them.

"Just be glad they aren't cows," Quinn said, only half joking. A second later, her stomach lurched. She'd been so preoccupied with cracking Cooper's secrets, she'd sidetracked herself from worrying about the cookout. Or maybe she'd just flat-out repressed the idea of going home at all. Four years of practice was bound to catch up eventually.

She rubbed the skin between her eyes. "Uh, Cooper? Speaking of cows ... If my mom comes running out with a herd like some sort of dowry, feel free to bolt in the opposite direction. I'll make sure they don't chase you. My mom included."

Another laugh soothed and prodded in its usual unfair way. "I'm sure it won't be that bad. It's just lunch with family, right?"

"Right." She dished a you've-been-warned expression at him. "Just a little family time. I mean, you might be walking into an episode of Duck Dynasty, but" —she raised her shoulders and batted her lashes— "How else is a girl to keep a guy intrigued?"

With eyes that seemed far more intrigued by her than they should be, Cooper set one hand on the wheel, the other on the gearshift, and smiled with enough fuel to rocket them the rest of the way to the house. "If that's a challenge, QT, you're on."

A challenge against a guy with breath-stopping eyes. Yeah, that was a grand idea.

"The road's clear," she managed to eke out. Because, obviously, that was the only logical response to make. *Smooth, Quinn. Real smooth.*

He started forward again while she contemplated diving into a ditch on the side of the road. But when her childhood home came into view, another unbidden rush of nostalgia rolled in with the scent of overgrown grass waving in the neighboring fields.

Cooper eased his SUV along the bumpy dirt driveway and parked behind Mama's old caravan. "Ready?"

Did hyperventilating count? "Yep." Quinn sucked in a breath like she was about to plummet to the bottom of the lake and got out of the car. She went to unbuckle Brayden from his car seat, but Cooper was already on it.

She raised an impressed brow. "You're getting good at that."

"Don't sound so shocked."

Before she could tame his gloating expression, Aunt Loraine came swishing down the driveway on an automatic path straight for the baby. "There he is. Just look at those cheeks. Did you miss me?"

Cooper strolled up beside Quinn. "How you doing, Ms. Thompson?"

"Just fine now that I've got my hands on these adorable munchkin legs." She swung Brayden up and planted a raspberry on his chubby thigh. Brayden's giggle must've sufficed as a reward. Aunt Loraine's face lit up, and so did Quinn's heart.

The screen door opened on the porch, followed by Mama zipping down the stairs toward them. "Well, aren't you three just adorable together."

Oh boy, here we go. Quinn glanced behind her mom. No cows. That was a good sign.

Mama gave Aunt Loraine a pointed look. "Don't think you'll be hogging that sugar all night, now."

"He remembers who gave him ice cream." She wiggled a finger over his belly button. "Don't you? And guess what Aunt Loraine has for you today? Watermelon."

Brayden's wide eyes mimicked her excitement.

Cooper leaned over to Quinn and whispered, "I'm a little scandalized. You, using a baby for distraction like this. Very cliché."

"Funny," she mumbled through the smile she'd managed to keep plastered on so far.

Aunt Loraine turned for the backyard.

"Wait." Quinn handed her his diaper bag. "Be sure to put sunscreen on him."

"Oh, and here." Cooper reached back in the SUV, swung around with a miniature version of his Tar Heels hat, and fit it onto Brayden's head. "There ya go, hoss. Now you're rocking."

He thought to get Brayden a matching hat?

"What?" He eyed her surprised expression.

She pinched her lips together. "Nothing."

Aunt Loraine brandished a telling grin, then moseyed toward the backyard with Brayden, leaving Quinn and Cooper standing in front of Mama like two deer point blank in shooting range.

She slid an unabashed smile down Cooper's tall profile. "It's a good thing my daughter met you before I did."

"Oh, Mama, really? Can you at least let him make it inside before you completely gross him out?"

Cooper rested his hands on Quinn's shoulders from behind, his lips to her ear. "Luckily, I'm already taken."

More like he was lucky his touch incapacitated her. Quinn maneuvered out of danger territory and started for the house—away from ridiculous attractions that would end up going nowhere. Aside from being unprofessional, letting misguided feelings take root would only result in hurts she knew to avoid.

"There's nothing wrong with letting a man know he's attractive, sugar."

Quinn didn't turn to witness the wink she was sure Mama had just flaunted at him.

"I'm only teasing, dear." She scooted past Quinn on the porch and opened the front door. "You know how foolish I am about your daddy." A glint of mixed emotions trickled from her eyes to a smile that seemed to struggle to stay in place. She blinked away. "You all come on in and make yourselves at home. Food's almost ready."

Cooper held the door open for Quinn. Even from this angle, she couldn't miss the enjoyment playing with his features.

"Your mom thinks I'm hot," he whispered on their way in.

Quinn rolled her eyes. "Yeah, well, she also thinks William Shatner's hot, so take it for what it's worth."

His laughter rang into the sound of his cell ringing. He took one look at the screen and offered them both a nod of apology. "Excuse me for just a minute."

Once he returned outside, Mama handed a small gift bag to Quinn along with a questionable bob of her brows. This couldn't be good.

One glimpse of lace inside explained why. She crammed the tissue paper back in. "A push-up bra? Really?"

"Now, sweetie, don't go flying off the handle. A little help goes a long way."

Tell me we're not actually having this conversation. "Thanks, but I'm good." She shoved the unsolicited gift back at her.

Bypassing the bag, Mama reached for the bra Quinn currently had on. "Are you sure? Let me see."

"Oh my word." She skirted out of her reach. "Yes, Mama, positive. Everything's ... perky."

"Okay. No need to pitch a hissy fit." She gave a mollifying shrug and turned. "But don't say I didn't try to help."

Yeah, help her into a wedding chapel and right out of a job. Which reminded her ...

"Mama?" Quinn called before she made it to the kitchen. She folded the hem of her T-shirt back and forth while taking in the dated pictures lining the living room walls. "Listen, I have something I want to tell Dad ... about work, but I need to wait a couple more weeks. So, can we not bring up anything about the magazine tonight? I'd rather keep the whole topic off limits for now." That would work, wouldn't it? Besides, it was all true.

Mama tied her apron on, her stare silently dissecting Quinn's request. "Sure, darlin'. But don't think you're getting out of filling us in on Mr. Wonderful and that precious baby of his."

"Wouldn't dream of it."

"Uh-huh." With a stern mother-hen look, she waved her toward the hall. "Go on now and wash up so you can help me in the kitchen. We can't be sitting around like a bump on a log."

"Yes, ma'am." At the door to the bathroom, Quinn paused and then kept trekking toward her old bedroom. Considering she'd only packed for a weekend, she wasn't beneath raiding her closet for some extra outfits.

A single glance inside almost changed her mind. She pulled out a plastic hanger with a ribbed tube top pinned to it—two sizes too small. She laughed. "That'd be one way to prove I don't need a push-up bra." She hung it back up and kept sifting.

Thankfully, Mama had kept a small section of clothes Quinn had worn the year before she moved away. They'd do. Well, minus the overalls. And the Peace Frog shirt. Okay, so, there were only a couple of salvageable things, but it was better than nothing.

She separated out the less atrocious clothes to grab when they left tonight and turned back for the bathroom. A sight across the room brought her up short—a tie hanging on her bedpost. She'd almost forgotten about it. Or maybe it was another part of her past she'd suppressed. Not ready to unearth it, she turned yet again, but her old vanity practically grabbed hold of her next.

Memories rushed in as Quinn glided a finger along the edge of the furniture an inch at a time—things her parents had taught her in this room, beliefs she wanted to be true for their sake. In the mirror, she studied a reflection that knew better. But how could she tell both her parents they were wrong about her?

She never should've come back, and she definitely shouldn't have let Cooper run with this fake boyfriend façade. Now she would doubly disappoint her family when they learned it was just a ruse. Hardly a full day with him, and they were already starting to fall for the idea of them as a couple. Far worse, she might've been too.

For everyone's sake, she needed to get the truth out in the open—the feature, the pretend relationship, all of it—before things spiraled even further.

"Quinn, dear?"

"Coming." She ran her hands across her cheeks, faced the mirror again, and drew her shoulders back. *Start with making it through lunch.*

Cooper wrenched the bill of his hat up and wiped his forehead, regretting taking Jim's call right now. "What do you mean they said no?"

Were Megan's mom and brother trying to spite him? Some kind of payback for resentment they held? This wasn't the time for petty family drama. This was Brayden's future they were talking about here.

"Just moving into an assisted living facility rules Megan's mom out as an adoptive parent. Her brother's in no state to raise a child. After alcoholism ended his marriage this past year, the only thing he needs right now is rehab." Jim cleared his throat away from the phone. "You could ask your brother—"

"No." Cooper yanked his hat back down and slumped against the tree trunk. He wasn't heaping another mess on Drew to clean up. He probably shouldn't have even told Drew and his family back in Ocracoke about this whole dilemma to begin with.

A stagnant pause stretched through the line. "Then we look into private adoption."

The suggestion weaved a knot in his chest. "Would that be best?"

"Best?" Another weighty pause. "It's an option, Cooper. Right now, that's all we have to work with. I'll touch base when I have an update."

Had he known about Megan's family's situations, he wouldn't have bothered asking Jim to look into it. Truthfully, he'd acted too fast. If he'd thought about it first, he'd have realized Megan's mom and brother weren't the best options for Brayden. He needed two parents who were ready and equipped to welcome him into a healthy family. Cooper just had to find them. They were running out of time.

The phone and all the unanswered questions hanging on to the end of their conversation dragged his arm to his side.

He lifted his face toward the splinters of sunlight filtering through the oak leaves.

Memories with Dad flickered images of the life Brayden should have the chance to live too. A grounded home without moving around, a stable father without a wild reputation or the media banging at his doorstep—things Cooper couldn't provide him.

Please, let me give him that life. That's all I'm asking.

Brayden's innocent smile swelled to mind and compressed around his heart. He looked to Cooper as if he could make things right, but he didn't know him yet. Didn't know how he always ended up disappointing those he loved.

A dragonfly zigzagged past him on a hay-scented breeze. Right behind it, barbeque aromas trailed with reminders of why he was here.

He pushed off the tree and tucked the effects of his phone call away for now. He didn't have all the answers, and he might not know what awaited him at this cookout, but whatever was in store the rest of the day, surely, it would keep his mind off the things he couldn't control.

He hoped.

CHAPTER NINE

Fragile

In the kitchen, Quinn's mom looked up at Cooper from the open oven and brushed back wisps of dyed hair curling above her forehead. "There you are. I hope you came hungry. Lunch will be ready quicker than two shakes of a lamb's tail."

She angled her head at him when she must've caught the expression he'd meant to leave outside. "Everything all right, honey?"

Cooper set the cobblers Quinn had made on the table. "Just fine." At least, they would be. Wouldn't they? He straightened a place mat under one of the dishes and stared at the tinfoil to keep from meeting Mrs. Thompson's intuitive stare.

"Well, okay, then. You just make yourself at home. Quinn should be along in a minute." With oven mitts up both arms, she carried some type of casserole dish to the back door.

Cooper opened it for her, and she replied with an appreciative nod.

"You know," she said. "If everything weren't okay, this meal would be sure to remedy that."

He returned her warm smile. "I'm sure it would."

A man Cooper assumed to be Quinn's grandpa passed her mom as she made her way down some rickety back steps. He stopped right in front of Cooper in the doorway, a grin of missing teeth less than a very uncomfortable inch away from him.

Cooper looked in every direction but right at him. "Hi. I'm Cooper Anderson, Quinn's date."

"I know who you are, son." He set a hand on his shoulder and kept his face right in front of Cooper's till he had no choice but to look him in the eye. No words, Grandpa simply stared, all while continuing to showcase a moonshine-ridden smile.

Cooper tried not to breathe directly in his face. Darting his gaze to the floor might've helped if it didn't intersect with Grandpa's unzipped fly. He shot a glance up to the ceiling instead and scratched his cheek. "Does it feel kind of drafty in here to you? Or is it just me?"

A glazed-over look kept beaming his way.

The screen door whined open again, freeing them from the more-than-awkward pose they were stuck in. Another guy—probably a year or two behind Cooper—wedged between them and clapped the old man on the shoulder. "Your fly's down, Gramps." He flicked his chin at Cooper while continuing his trek into the kitchen.

At the fridge, he ducked inside, withdrew two brews, and offered one to Cooper. A cold one had never looked better. He clanked his bottle with Cooper's. "You look like you could wet your whistle."

"Um, thanks. And you are …?"

"Chase?" Quinn said from behind him.

They both turned toward her, standing at the edge of the kitchen and the hallway. A sunray streamed through the window onto an expression bright enough to light up the whole room.

She raced over and flung her arms around Chase's neck. "What are you doing here? I thought you said you couldn't make it."

"When your crazy sister screams SOS, what's a guy to do?"

Quinn jabbed him in the chest as she lowered her feet back to the floor. "Doofus."

"Just looking out for you, Drama Queen."

When Cooper cocked his head, Chase clapped him on the back and flaunted a grin that made it clear he enjoyed baiting Quinn as much as Cooper did. "You'll learn soon enough."

On his heels, Quinn practically kicked him through the door.

Cooper was about to follow when her grandpa wheezed a laugh from the other side of the kitchen. He pointed a finger in the air at him. "Drafty." He slapped his thigh and let out another raspy laugh.

Cooper tipped his brew at him. Better late than never.

Outside, he walked right into an argument between Loraine and a teenage girl in the corner of the yard.

"If you're making me be here, at least you can let me invite Clay over."

Loraine transferred Brayden to her opposite hip. "Sweetie, I doubt your boyfriend wants to help plan your sweet sixteen party. Besides, this is family time."

The girl texted on her cell. "Whatever," she huffed.

Loraine shook her head at the sky and prodded the girl toward the rest of the group.

One glance up from her phone, and the girl's already rigid expression turned lethal. "What's *she* doing here?"

Quinn's hopeful smile shattered.

Loraine shifted almost as uncomfortably as Quinn did. "Ginny, baby, your cousin Quinn's home for a visit. Just in time to help plan your party. Isn't that nice? It'll be like old times."

Ginny snorted. "Super. Then she can turn around and leave without telling anyone." She shot a glare at Quinn. "Like old times, right?"

"Virginia Anne!" Loraine's face turned a shade darker than the checkered tablecloth.

Ginny scoffed while stalking toward the picnic table, tapping away on her cell again.

Frustration blended into the embarrassment flooding Loraine's eyes. "I swear that girl could start an argument in an empty house if she had a mind to." She handed Brayden off to Quinn's mom. "Excuse me."

Silence added to the tension already clinging to the thick humidity.

Time to intervene. Cooper curved an arm around Quinn's back. "You were right about your daughter's cobblers," he said to Mrs. Thompson. "Quinn's an amazing baker."

Her mom ran with the diversion. "Just wait till you taste her custard. Quinn, sugar, have you made any meringue for him yet?"

Though Quinn narrowed her eyes at him, the way she'd leaned into his side a moment ago let him know she was as grateful for the distraction as her mom seemed to be.

While everyone headed to the picnic table, a salt-and-pepper-haired man came out of a barn in the back corner of the property, wiping his hands on a rust-colored rag.

Mrs. Thompson settled Brayden in an old wooden high chair, pulled her apron off, and set it on the table before starting for him. "George, honey, look who's here." At his side, she looped an arm around his and steered him toward Quinn. "Our baby girl came home."

Quinn's expression warmed the way it had when she saw Chase. She curled her arms around his broad back. "Hi, Daddy."

"It's Quinn, dear." The noticeable waver in Mrs. Thompson's voice reached her eyes when her husband's only response was a vacant stare. "Our little girl's home for a visit. You remember—"

"It's okay, Mama." Quinn stepped out of an unreturned hug. Sorrow tore down her face, tugging Cooper's heart with it.

The back door squeaked open again, and Quinn's grandpa stumbled out with whipped cream layered in his wiry mustache. "Those darn raccoons got into the dessert again."

Everyone failed to hold in their laughter, thankful for levity.

Another woman, who Mrs. Thompson introduced as Nurse Murphy, joined them a few minutes later, carrying a handful of dishes of her own to add to the spread.

Chase brought over the rest of the meat from the grill while everyone else took their seats on the picnic benches. Like most southern meals, the food was rich, filling, and perfect.

Despite the few times Quinn whispered that she was about to crawl under the table to hide, she carried most of the conversation about Ginny's party like a hired event planner. She already had the baking part down. Somehow, Cooper wasn't the least bit surprised she'd be a pro at managing the rest of the details while dodging the ice spears Ginny kept shooting across the table with her eyes.

Quinn had skills *and* chops. No doubt about that. But she had holes in her armor like everyone else.

Cooper lowered his glass of sweet tea. "Ginny, why don't you come over to the lake house this week. We'll take you out on the water."

Quinn kicked his shin under the table.

"Really?" A spread of braces shined in the sunlight.

"Sure. It'll be fun. While you're there, you and Quinn can talk about which band you want to have play at the party."

Slower at downplaying her excitement than she probably wanted, Ginny strained to school her expression. "Yeah, okay. I guess I can fit it in sometime."

"Great." He flaunted a celebratory bite of pecan pie in Quinn's direction.

She shook her head and took her own bite but couldn't stifle a grin.

"Does anyone want seconds?" Quinn's dad said with an open and somewhat distant gaze traveling around the table.

Everyone shook their heads.

"I'm full as a tick." Loraine sat back and patted her stomach. "But I bet this munchkin wouldn't mind a little something as sweet as he is." She wiped up a drip of watermelon juice running down Brayden's chin. "Isn't this precious baby just a gift from God? Handing you a family like this, it's amazing, Quinn."

Whipped cream from the pie practically sprayed from Quinn's mouth. She swiped a napkin and coughed so hard her face turned red.

Loraine set her fork of watermelon down. "My, child, are you all right?"

Chase stretched across the table. "Aunt Loraine, did I show you my pictures from a recent trip to Oklahoma? They had hail the size of baseballs." As he redirected Loraine's focus to the images on his phone, he cast a subtle wink at Quinn.

"Thank you," she mouthed.

"Would anyone like seconds?" her dad asked again.

Everyone's gazes bounced around the table in an awkward dance of not knowing what to say.

Chase tapped a hand over his dad's. "You just asked us that, Dad. Everyone's all set."

A squint of confusion sputtered across his face.

Mrs. Thompson glanced from her husband to Quinn, a fractured look stealing the usual glint in her eyes again. She sprang up from the bench. "Good gracious, I almost forgot the ice cream."

Cooper rose. "Let me help you with that."

Inside, Mrs. Thompson busied herself with pulling out bowls from the cabinets. "There's vanilla and rocky road in the freezer, dear."

He withdrew the tubs of ice cream and set them beside her working space on the counter. Above the sink, the window brought a clear view of Quinn playing with Brayden outside. Someone must've turned on a sprinkler. As soon as the water touched Brayden's skin, his smile almost outshined hers. Few people had the kind of smile that could change a person.

"She's a special girl," her mom said.

Cooper blinked away from the glare outside. Heat climbed his ears at knowing she'd caught him admiring Quinn from a distance.

"She's as determined as they come, that one." Her eyes dimmed. "And more fragile than she lets on."

With the scoop over one of the bowls, she shook off a glob of ice cream along with whatever it was she wasn't saying.

Cooper's phone rang from his pocket. Drew. He ignored the call, not ready to deal with trying to hide things from his brother right now.

Mrs. Thompson tapped the scoop over another bowl. "Something you and Quinn have in common."

"What's that?"

"Business." She motioned to his phone. "Our girl's always been so driven. Once she was fixin' to do something, we knew to clear the way. And ooh-wee, that girl got madder than a wet hen when things didn't go according to plan." Her hand stalled, her chuckle tapering. "I suppose that kind of drive will take you places."

He peered out the window again. "Why'd she be interested in nannying, then?" The question slipped out before he could stop it. It was one thing to have questions. It was another to meddle. He didn't want to interfere with her family's shot at reconnecting with her today.

"Nannying?" Mrs. Thompson fumbled with a handful of spoons. In a quick recovery, she resumed her task. "Well, she's always loved children. They seem to take to her more than other people."

Cooper glanced at Quinn and Brayden again. "So I've noticed."

She flipped the lid over each tub and peered through the window as well. "I reckon it fills a void for her. Makes her happy." With a sad smile, she patted Cooper's hand. "Be a doll and bring this tray out to the gang, won't you?"

The screen door opened behind him.

"Better watch out," Quinn said. "Mama can talk your ear off if you're not careful." From the look on her face, she was worried about what that talk consisted of.

Mrs. Thompson waved a dishrag at her. "Phooey. We were having a lovely chat. Weren't we, honey?"

"Yes, ma'am."

Her mom strolled toward Quinn. "Don't worry, sugar, I'm not stealing him from you." She winked. "Yet."

"Mama."

"Oh, lighten up. My sight may not be what it used to, but I can still see when a man's heart is already taken. A little teasing isn't gonna change that."

Quinn swatted her mom's hand away when she reached for what looked like an inappropriate part of Quinn's shirt. Cooper wasn't about to ask.

"Cut those lights off when you come back out," her mom called.

The door closed behind Mrs. Thompson, and Quinn's gaze automatically found a stain on the floor to fixate on. "Sorry about that. All of it, really. I plan to set them straight about us today, so don't worry. You won't have to deal with this much longer."

He stopped in front of her with the tray of ice cream between them. "Take your time. I'm doing just fine."

Still avoiding eye contact, she pulled in her bottom lip and played with a strand of her hair.

At least, he was doing fine a moment ago. She killed him when she looked that cute without even realizing it.

He cleared his throat. "This ice cream, on the other hand, isn't gonna make it much longer."

Quinn looked at the fast-approaching soupy ice cream and opened the door. "Right. Sorry."

Mrs. Thompson flagged them over. "Sugar, we were just talking about that old dance you and Dad used to do at all the cookouts each summer. 'Member?"

Quinn dipped a napkin in her water, took Brayden from Loraine, and wiped his red-stained mouth. "That was eons ago."

"But wouldn't it be so fun to do it again?" She squeezed her husband's shoulders from behind him.

Quinn's napkin dropped to the ground and started to blow away. She caught it with her foot, her voice apparently not as fast on catching up. "No one wants to see that dance, Mama."

"I don't know," Cooper said. "I'm *intrigued*."

She cut him an I-hate-you glare. "We don't have the tape anymore."

"You mean, this song?" Ginny held up her phone, a country tune bellowing from the speaker.

Mrs. Thompson practically cheered. "I'll go get the boots and hat."

"What?" Quinn whirled around to her mom already hurrying to the back steps. "Mama, no—" But the door had already swung behind her.

Cooper had no idea what this dance was all about, but one thing was for sure. If it involved Quinn wearing a cowgirl hat, he was dying to find out.

CHAPTER TEN

Dance

"Great." Quinn held Brayden out to Cooper. "I hope you know you're in for it later."

"Can't wait."

She dipped her fingertips in her water and flicked drops at his face.

When her mom came out brandishing a dusty off-white cowgirl hat and a pair of equally faded leather boots, his chuckle morphed into outright laughter.

"You're lucky you're holding Brayden right now." Quinn made a face at him while begrudgingly taking the gear Mrs. Thompson presented her like a prized family heirloom.

Chase flicked the tip of her hat. "Don't act like you don't love being the center of attention."

"You know these boots have spurs, right?"

Cooper joined in her brother's amusement until Mrs. Thompson struggled to help her husband up from his chair. Nurse Murphy intervened and led him to the front of the table where Quinn stood looking more helpless than nervous.

Something in him flinched. He'd wanted to prove her wrong about coming here today. To show her family was family, and if she gave it half a chance, she might even have a little fun. But now that he'd seen glimpses into why she'd left to begin with, he felt more like a heel than a hero.

"It's your dance, George. Remember?" Mrs. Thompson looked to Nurse Murphy, who gave him a gentle nod of assurance.

He took Quinn's hand as the music began, but he might as well have been sleepwalking, each movement slow and unfamiliar. The pain on Quinn's face deepened the longer the song dragged on until Cooper couldn't bear it any longer. He held Brayden out to Chase, about to rescue her, when something shifted in her dad's countenance.

He grasped her hand tighter, the motions more fluid, more certain. A step at a time, life seemed to surge back to his vacant eyes, and Quinn was no longer leading. He was.

As the song waned, he stopped shuffling in the grass and cupped both her cheeks as though seeing her for the first time. "My baby girl." A sheen coated his eyes. "You're home."

"Yeah, Daddy." Her chin trembled. "I'm home."

He curled her into the kind of hug Cooper missed from his own dad. The ones that let you know everything was going to be okay.

All-out tears overtook her mom's cheeks, while Loraine covered her chest.

Brayden dragged a plastic spoon over the table and threw it on the ground, fussing. Thankful for the opportune interruption, Cooper rose and walked Brayden along the opposite end of the yard. Sometimes the pain of missing Dad caught him in the gut without warning.

He turned and almost smacked right into Quinn's father. He set her hand in his. "It's only fair you get a dance too, young man."

Cooper looked from the awkward tension in Quinn's eyes back to her dad. "Oh, sir, I appreciate that." He lifted Brayden up. "But I'm on baby duty."

"Nonsense." Mrs. Thompson came over, arms outstretched. "I've been itching all night for dibs on this cutie. Come to Nanna," she said to Brayden before waving them off. "You two go on. Have some fun."

Ginny must've turned up the music on her phone. Even the fireflies seemed to be urging them to join their dance floor.

"Scared I might out dance you, partner?" The playfulness in Quinn's tone lured Cooper's gaze to an even more impish grin. She was in for it now.

He stole her hat and swept her into his arms. "Ask me again when we're done."

Head back, hair flowing in the wind, she laughed with a melody that topped any song. His stomach tightened. It was a good thing he wasn't sticking around Lake Gaston. 'Cause if he wasn't careful, he could fall for a girl like Quinn Thompson.

"How'd you know Ginny would want to come over to the lake?"

Where'd that come from? He leaned back slightly to read her expression, then shrugged. "The chance for a suntan before her party? Especially with a boy to get dolled up for? Made sense."

Her feet stalled. "Should I be scared or impressed that you think like a girl?"

He chuckled. "I have a niece."

"Mm-hmm."

"I lived with my brother for a while last year. Took Maddie paddle boarding a lot. We got close."

"So, you—"

"Look at you two." Her dad approached again with a glint of awareness still in his eyes. He patted Cooper's back. "I've been waiting a long time to see my Quinn in love."

She dropped Cooper's hand, her face falling with it. "Daddy."

"What? There's nothing wrong with a father wanting to see his little girl happy and taken care of."

A silent fury Cooper didn't fully understand ransacked Quinn's embarrassed expression, all while her dad's continued to brim with affection anyone would be blind to miss.

He nodded at Cooper. "Forgive an old man's sentiment. I won't interrupt you two again." After a pat to each of their shoulders, he turned back toward the picnic table.

Cooper drew Quinn into a dancing hold again to give her a chance to calm down, if nothing else.

Behind them, her dad sat Brayden on the grass in front of Loraine and led her mom up from a wicker chair into their own dance. Cheek to cheek, they swayed in a world that, for the moment, clearly belonged only to them.

His stomach tensed. "You can't tell them, Quinn."

"What?" She leaned back.

"Your parents. This—us—it obviously means a lot to them. What's it going to hurt to play along?"

Her features hardened. "They can't let their happiness ride on whether or not I get married. I have … *other* things that make me a success on my own." She glued her focus to her Converse sneakers as if they held the answers to life's great mysteries. "Once I get past one more hurdle, it'll finally put me in a position he can be proud of me for."

Did she not see the way her dad looked at her? Cooper lifted her chin. "I think he already is."

A tear as stubborn as she was hung to her bottom lashes, refusing to escape.

He brushed her bangs over to her ear. "I'm not saying you shouldn't tell them. Just not today."

Quinn glanced behind her and back without answering, a dozen emotions still churning in her brown eyes. She needed to get her mind off things. To be honest, he did too.

He twirled her around, drew her in, and dipped her like a professional dancer.

Angled downward, she raised a brow at him. "Going for a trophy?"

"If our fan club over there has anything to say about it, I think I just won it." He lifted her upright and motioned to the faces following their every move from the opposite end of the yard.

Sass returned to her eyes as she stepped out of his hold. "Don't be so sure. They're a tougher crowd than you think."

"Then I guess I better find another way to impress them." He took her hat off, nestled it onto her head, and curved her hair around her ear. "They want to know you're with someone charming, gentlemanly."

"Mm." She nodded, evidently placating him. "Well, you *are* a good actor."

"Who said I'm acting?" He countered her raised brow with a steady gaze. "In fact, I think they'd be pretty disappointed if I didn't kiss you right now."

"Is that right?" She stood her ground, but the slightest flutter on her neck told him the distraction was working.

"Mm," he mimicked, edging closer. "Question is, would *you* be?"

She set a hand to his chest. "Ask me again when we're done."

Despite the tease in her voice at using his own lines on him, his heart rate picked up. A breeze blew through her hair, tangling him in an aroma of flowers and summer and things able to bring him to his knees.

Her fingertips reached for his collar, her eyes never leaving his. Her alluring expression nearly consumed him until a laugh breached the tiny space between them. "Sorry, that was totally lame, wasn't it?" She tugged her hat down. "I don't know how to play the smooth card like you do. I'm too much of a dork."

"No, uh…" Cooper ran a knuckle along his jawbone. "That was, um, really good, actually."

"Yeah?"

Recovering, he slid his fingers in her hair, his grin to the side. "Yeah." With his lips to her ear, he whispered, "But you should probably keep practicing."

Her breath fluttered when he grazed a kiss to her cheek.

He leaned back, winked, and started toward her family, who were still watching them like they were about to bust out popcorn. Halfway there, an acorn nailed him dead in the back of the head. He swung around toward an overly satisfied grin.

"Good thing my arm doesn't need any more practice."

He lit up in laughter. Yep, he could definitely fall for Quinn Thompson if he wasn't careful.

At the table, Quinn picked Brayden up from the grass.

A yelp drew all their glances toward her dad almost falling off the back steps, her mom and Nurse Murphy on either side of him. Cooper and Chase reached them in a second.

"I'm all right." Mr. Thompson waved them all away.

"It's that faulty step there." Quinn's mom pointed to a splintered section of the wood. "Been meaning to fix it for ages."

Cooper squatted to examine it. The old stairs had rotted in several places. It was a wonder they hadn't fallen through yet. "I'll be happy to come mend that this week. Won't take long."

"Well, that's mighty sweet of you, dear. A man who knows how to work with his hands is definitely a keeper." Beaming, she sent two more conspicuous winks at Quinn.

She massaged her forehead. "We should really get going. Thanks for lunch, Mama."

"Glad you could come, sugar." She kissed Quinn's cheek. "Drive safe, now."

"Safe*ly*," she muttered under her breath as she turned.

Though her mom probably missed it, Cooper couldn't help chuckling at the involuntary shuddering Quinn failed to hide.

After saying the rest of their goodbyes and ensuring her dad got in the house okay, they went through the back gate to his SUV. He buckled Brayden in his car seat. If he was anywhere near as tuckered out as he looked, he'd be asleep before they left the driveway. The sight of him compressed around Cooper's chest again. He brushed Brayden's slightly damp hair to one side and kissed his head.

Turning, he caught a smile fixed on him that seemed to brighten and then dim with thoughts he'd pay to hear. "What?"

Quinn lifted a nonchalant shoulder. "Nothing. You're just getting really good with him. It's sweet to watch."

His face fell. Sweet maybe, but not enough. Thankfully, his cell interrupted them and cut off a conversation that would end up going nowhere. Cooper heaved a sigh at Drew's name on the screen. On to another conversation he didn't want to have.

He turned and answered. "Sorry I couldn't take your call earlier, hoss. What's up?"

"I hope you have a guest room ready."

"Why?"

Audible anticipation pulsed through the phone line. "'Cause we're coming for a visit."

CHAPTER ELEVEN

Walls

Under the lamplight on his dock, Cooper scooted the two-by-four he'd just cut against the previous board until their edges were flush. He sat back on his heels and pushed his hair off his forehead with his arm.

What was Drew thinking, springing a visit on him like this? He didn't have time to listen to whatever lecture was bound to be the reason his brother was coming. He had a deadline approaching whether anyone wanted it to or not. An in-person argument wasn't going to change that.

Cooper withdrew his hammer from his tool belt and drove a nail through the wood with more force than necessary. The blunt echo shuddered across the still water and disappeared in the rustle of tree branches waving in the wind.

A *creak* from the boards closest to his yard brought Quinn into focus, walking barefoot across the planks. She pointed the baby monitor behind her. "He conked right out."

"He had a long day."

"Didn't we all," she mumbled. Sitting on the bench at the end of the pier, she set the monitor beside her and lifted one of the boards he'd propped against the seat. "Nothing like the smell of cedar." She twisted it on its edge in slow, mindless circles.

Going to her parents' had been more taxing on her than he'd expected. But he'd caught glimpses of a homesick girl tonight. One who wasn't willing to admit she missed parts of what she'd left behind. How could he help her lower those walls?

Above them, a clear dark sky showcased the stars in the kind of summer night stories were written about. He'd sat out on this lake hundreds of times since he moved in, admiring the serenity in every season. But something about seeing Quinn in the lamplight against a backdrop that'd been home for him this last year made it the kind of story he wished wouldn't end.

She ran her fingers along the smooth grains he'd sanded before she'd come out. "Chase and I used to race to Dad's workshop whenever he was in there, so eager to help him." A sad laugh tugged at her lips. "I'm sure he had to go back and fix everything we messed up, but he never said anything about it. Never complained. He always seemed happy to have us nearby." She set the wood aside. "Even made us feel like we'd helped make something special."

A wistful gaze gravitated across the shore and into memories he could almost feel from here. Truth be told, they could've been his own memories. Their fathers sounded very similar.

An unbidden lump built in his throat. Forcing it down, Cooper checked the time on his phone and unbuckled his tool belt. It was too late to be out here making noise. But he'd been doing what he did best—pushing limits.

He stood and gathered the rest of the boards into a pile. "You two seem close."

"We were."

Cooper didn't miss the ache in those words. "Until the dementia?" No one had labeled her father's illness, but it wasn't too hard to guess.

Another splintered look passed her eyes. "It started out with little things at first. Forgetting where he'd left something, missing appointments. But then ..." Her voice trailed into the wind, taking his heart with it.

He sat beside her. "It must be hard to watch someone you love deteriorate in front of you. Is that why you left?"

"More the other way around."

He searched her face, but her thoughts seemed to keep her focus on the gentle ripples lapping against the bank.

"You should've seen him when I got engaged. He was so happy for me. So proud. Like life was finally complete." She coiled a pine needle around her finger. "Honestly, I was happy too."

"What happened?"

"Things changed. *I* changed. After Brian and I broke up, I moved to Hatteras, thinking I could do something with my writing." Dejection plagued her voice as she chucked the needle into the water. "Guess you could say I needed to start over. Away from the disappointment I would've seen if I'd stayed."

Had they been looking at the same man tonight? "I only saw love in your dad's eyes."

She swept a glance away from him. "The more someone loves you, the more you can disappoint them."

The words drilled into him with reminders of the last conversation he'd had with Dad. If you could even call it that. Cooper letting his father down was one thing. But Quinn? No chance.

The bench's top edge creased into the bottom of his shoulder blades as he stretched backward. "I get it, QT. Trust me. But if I was you, I'd take the risk before it's too late."

"*Were* you," she said after a quiet moment.

He turned and caught an untamable and entirely too cute grin.

"When using the subjunctive, it's were, not was."

"Right. Because now's the perfect time to bring up a random grammar rule."

Her sweet laugh tumbled past her scrunched lips. "Sorry. I told you I was lame. I can't help it."

He shook his head. "You, Quinn Thompson, are anything but lame. And I have no doubt that includes your writing."

A gorgeous shade of pink tinted her cheeks. But rather than look away, intuitive eyes studied him underneath the glow of the pier's light.

One of the neighbor's boats passed by them. Tiny waves swelled toward the shore, drawing in the solemnity of the earlier moment.

"You lost your dad, didn't you?" she asked.

Cooper rose and loosened his neck instead of answering. Facing the clear water, he leaned an arm against the light post. "He was a good carpenter. Taught me what I know."

"About boats too?" Quinn stood beside him now and motioned to his speedboat.

She didn't miss much, did she?

"He was in the Coast Guard before opening a souvenir shop in Ocracoke." Countless hours spent with him on the ocean garnered a smile. "Not that retiring kept him off the water. The man was out in his old skiff whenever he had the chance."

"If you don't mind my asking, how'd he die?"

Cooper kicked a splinter of wood into the water, wishing the dark memories still haunting him would sink with it. "He drowned while trying to rescue a family caught in a storm."

"I'm so sorry." A gentle hand smoothed over the back of his shoulder.

He breathed in at her soft touch. Words weren't usually hard for him, but this topic … Or maybe it was something about her, the things she stirred.

"That's why you're opening a boat shop, isn't it? To honor him."

Why he bothered to withhold anything from her, he had no idea.

"I owe him that much." He backed against the pole and ran a knuckle down his jawline. "My brother was always the golden child. Walked right in his footsteps like second nature." And he was good at it, made for it even: awesome dad, responsible business owner, admirable husband. "Drew took over the souvenir shop when we lost him."

"You didn't want it?"

He wrinkled his nose. "Not my scene."

The slightest touch of her arm grazed his. "But?"

"But nothing. It worked out exactly as it should've." He rolled his flip-flop back and forth over a loose nail. "Drew was always the one Dad counted on to take care of things."

"Does that bother you?"

"Only if I let it." Which he had no right to. He was the one who'd played into the reckless little brother label people had given him. He'd learned long ago it wasn't worth defying people's assumptions. They would believe whatever they wanted anyway, so why not prove them right?

He picked up the nail and crammed it into his pocket with thoughts better left buried.

"Seems ironic," she said slowly. "You want to move across the world to open a boat shop for your dad, but you won't get in the boat sitting right here."

Cooper followed another nod to the speedboat he'd left untouched all summer. "That has nothing to do with my dad."

"You sure about that?"

A tendon on his neck constricted. "Save your psychoanaly-sis, okay?" The harsh words rebounded into him with regret the moment they'd rushed out. "I'm sorry. I didn't mean—"

"No, I shouldn't push." She swept her long hair over her shoulder without looking up from the dock. "I just don't understand your urgency to leave. It's fine if you really want to move, but why not wait? At least long enough to give yourself some time to sort through things with Brayden." Eyes of yearning met his. "You might even decide to stay instead."

His heart sank at her hopefulness. Because, truthfully, part of him longed for her to be right. But it didn't matter. Whether he stayed or moved, he'd be letting someone down. At least Brayden still had time left to one day understand.

He steeled himself. "I already told you. I have to leave the Fourth."

"But why?"

"Because." Cooper turned and thrust his fingers through the back of his hair until a labored exhale gradually released them. He could withhold the answer all he wanted. It wouldn't change it.

"Dad and I were supposed to take a cross-country trip the summer he died. I'd been begging him since I was ten. Had this whole epic journey planned out—just me and him, you know? Something neither of us would ever forget."

"Starting on the Fourth?"

"I said it was going to be epic, didn't I?" A wave of guilt absorbed his laugh till it felt like he was trying to breathe under water. "But I was too busy that summer. Too caught up in my new job offer at Shore Corp and my chance to get out of Ocracoke." His voice dissolved to a whisper. "And then it was too late."

A storm like the one from the night Dad died raged inside him. "I should've been there, Quinn. I could've helped Drew. Could've saved him."

"It's not your fault."

Shaking his head, he smiled sadly. "You know, I got in a car accident the night of his funeral. Being reckless, angry. I could've died or been paralyzed. But nothing, not even a broken bone." He dug his fingers through his hair. "I did everything wrong, while he—"

"Coop."

"I've been nothing but selfish for years, putting off this trip because it wasn't convenient. This is my last chance to do it. If I cancel again, it's never gonna happen." He swallowed before facing her. "I need to do this for him, Quinn." For both of them, if he was being honest.

"Are you sure that's really what this is all about?"

Cooper released a long breath instead of responding. Truthfully, he didn't have an answer. At least, not one he was ready to face.

A damp breeze rolled off the west end of the lake and swirled around them. Rather than press further, she simply rubbed her arms and gave him the space he needed.

Minutes drifted in the quiet. Though time never fully healed wounds as deep as his, something about the time he spent with Quinn lessened the ache. Even in the silence.

"What you were saying about your brother," she said slowly. "The comparisons ... Is that why you're upset he's coming?"

"Nah." Cooper swatted a mosquito away. "I just don't want to deal with him trying to change my mind about leaving."

"Maybe he only wants the chance to say goodbye." Chin lowered, Quinn tucked her hands in her back pockets. "You said you lived with them last year. That you were close with your niece."

One sting followed another. "We spent a lot of time together while Drew was working to keep the shop open."

"Hence your knowledge of teen girls and tans."

He chuckled, grateful for the reprieve. "Maddie loves to paddle board. Loves anything to do with the ocean, really. And don't get her started on sea turtles." Thoughts of her soothed and ached at the same time. Saying goodbye wouldn't be easy. "She has this way of looking at the world. Brave, accepting. Tackles life's setbacks like they're nothing but a bump in the road."

"Setbacks?"

"She started to get real sick a few years ago. Turns out she has an autoimmune disease. She's doing much better," he quickly amended when Quinn's eyes filled with concern. "But Drew had a pretty rough go of it the first two years."

"Sounds like it was a good thing you were there to help."

"Help?" He shrugged. "Drew's too prideful to ask for help. I'm not sure how much I did anyway."

"I have a feeling Maddie might argue otherwise." She raised her shoulders. "In fact, I bet she even thinks you make a great father."

"Quinn."

"I know. I know." A small wrinkle furrowed between her brows. "But you have as much love to offer Brayden as you do for Maddie. Don't you think he's worth your time too?"

"Of course I do." He pushed off the pole. "That's the whole point. He deserves time. *Quality* time from parents who won't disappoint him. Swooping in to play the fun uncle card for a while isn't the same as being a father, but that doesn't mean I don't wish I could be what Brayden needs."

He pinched his forehead and blew out a breath. "You act like this is easy for me, Quinn, but it's not. I don't want to walk out of his life."

"Then don't."

"What choice do I have?" Brayden's best shot at the future Cooper wanted for him would require them to cut all ties.

She lowered his hand from his head and took it in hers. "You can choose love over fear."

He held her tender gaze, breathed. As misguided as her belief in him was, he couldn't help wanting it to be real, valid. "Quinn—"

Someone behind them cleared his throat.

They both turned toward Brian, of all people, standing at the top of the pier.

He pointed a thumb over his shoulder. "I saw your car parked out front. When you didn't return my call, I thought …"

That he'd come trespassing on Cooper's property? And what was he doing calling her when he was married to someone else? "You might try taking an unreturned call as a hint, hoss."

Quinn set a hand to his broad shoulders that had moved into a protective stance in front of her. "It's okay." She eased around his arm and faced Brian. "I'm actually glad you came. We should talk."

She had to be kidding.

She motioned that she was good, evidently reading his thoughts.

Jaw tighter than it had any reason to be, Cooper nodded at Brian and picked up his tool belt from the dock. "I'll just be in the house." He brushed past her ex, making sure he knew "in the house" meant close enough to haul him back to his car if he tried anything.

Not that Quinn couldn't hold her own. Tall and confident, she stood at the edge of the pier like she was ready to withstand any storm that came her way. He didn't doubt she'd be the last one standing.

In the house, he rinsed off in the bathroom and then eased in to check on Brayden. Moonlight cast a small glow throughout the room and onto his son's peaceful silhouette in the crib. *His* son. The attribution caught him low and deep, followed by an even worse realization. Brayden wasn't the only one he was getting attached to.

The view out back showed Brian hang his head at something Quinn had told him. He pulled her into his arms, and the nail in Cooper's pocket might as well have twisted in his gut. After a moment lasting too long, Brian pressed a kiss to Quinn's cheek and turned to leave.

She crossed her arms as though holding herself together, and the urge to go out to comfort her almost drove him past the one barrier keeping him in place. She didn't need another guy in her life who'd end up hurting her.

She'd said it herself—the more someone loves you, the more you can let them down. Getting attached only bred heartache. He'd walked through it before. Had seen it so many times, even in Drew's life. Quinn deserved more. He redirected his focus from the window to the crib, heart heavy. "So do you, buddy," he whispered. "One day, you'll understand."

Cooper had made enough mistakes in his life. He wasn't about to add these next two weeks to the list. He'd do what was best for them both. Starting with figuring out how to convince his brother not to come and make things worse.

CHAPTER TWELVE

Enthralled

Slow, lazy blinks brought a venti cardboard cup into focus on Quinn's nightstand where the baby monitor usually was. Quinn sat up in bed and looked from her stack of novels in the corner chair to her laptop on the modern dresser against the side wall. The guest room was as still and quiet as it'd been when she'd cut the lights off last night.

"Cooper?" she called.

No answer. No movement. Only the delectable aroma of what could only be one thing.

She picked up the warm cup, lifted the lid, and breathed in steamy, frothy, heavenly perfection. Her lips indulged in a smile and the sweet taste of vanilla. Despite living in the middle of nowhere, Cooper had found her a latte.

The man truly was something else. She was the one who should be buying him drinks after enduring a day at her family's. Okay, he'd had his share of amusement yesterday, too, but he was doing her a favor she didn't deserve.

As if eager and waiting to second the thought, the Cruella De Vil song roared into the silence. Quinn wiped the streak of coffee running down her chin while scrambling for her cell.

"Hello?"

"I'm loving the story, Thompson. Who knew Cooper Anderson was such a troubled bachelor?"

Quinn hadn't written everything Cooper had shared with her, but she'd obviously painted enough of an idea for Cruella to run with it.

This was exactly why she wanted the executive editor position to begin with. So she could choose the right stories for the magazine, match them up with the best writers for the job, and start printing inspiring articles without the gossip and slander.

She scooted against the headboard and bunched a pillow under her arms. "You know, I was thinking. Why not do a different piece on Cooper? I really don't think anyone's interested in his past. Even if there was something going on with …"

A thought tied itself around her vocal cords and yanked them to the pit of her stomach. Fragments fused together a breath at a time: Cooper's sudden departure from Shore Corp, his niece's illness, his brother not wanting to ask for help. There never was a big scandal. Cooper gave up his job to help take care of Maddie, and the only reason he'd kept it so secretive was to shield his brother's pride. No wonder he'd turned down every interview.

The coffee churned in her stomach.

"Forget the scandal," Cruella said. "This single-parent, wounded-hero angle is far juicier. Readers are going to eat it up."

"That's not really the angle I was going—"

"You'll write this piece, Thompson. And you'll get Cooper's permission to print it, or you can forget about coming back to this magazine."

"What?" The coffee turned to lead, her insides cracking.

"I expect to see the full feature on my desk by Monday."

In only a week? "Wait." Quinn flung her legs over the side of the bed, her mind reeling as fast as her pulse.

It didn't matter if Cruella lost her job in a month or not. She was her boss right now. Even worse, Corporate had them both under scrutiny. If Quinn cracked under the pressure and messed up this feature, she'd lose her one shot at everything she'd spent the last four years working toward. "If we can just talk about this, I'm sure we can—"

"Monday morning, Thompson. And by the way, I'd look for a new roommate if you don't follow through on this. Two jobless girls won't be able to keep a roof over their heads in Hatteras for very long."

Ava.

The second Cruella hung up, Quinn scrolled for her best friend's number, knowing full well she wouldn't be awake yet.

"You've reached Ava Constello. If this is Ryan Reynolds, I'll call you back in five. Anyone else? Take your chances." *Beep.*

"Ava, please tell me Cruella hasn't fired you. Call me back, girl. This is important." Quinn ended the call, tapped the phone to her forehead, and tried not to freak.

No, she could handle it. *Had* to handle it. It'd be fine. She'd come up with a game plan—something that'd make things right for everyone involved. She just had to clear her head.

With a purging exhale, she traded her cell for the cup of deliverance waiting for her and got out of bed.

Her clothes from last night lay in a heap on the floor, tangled with images of Brian hugging her on the pier in an attempt to glue parts together that would always be broken. At least she'd finally told him why she left. Now, she had to find a way to tell Cooper why she'd come back.

She walked straight to Brayden's room on instinct. Sunlight seeping through the closed blinds lit a path to his crib. With damp hair and red cheeks, he lay asleep in a onesie he was already outgrowing. Her heart cinched.

Cooper shouldn't miss watching every little change take place in his son's life. To see him take his first steps. Hear his first full sentence. She'd give anything to have that chance. Did he really not realize how lucky he was?

And what about Brayden? Would he accept love from adoptive parents the way he did from Cooper? Would he grow up feeling unwanted?

The possibility nearly bent her in half as she took in this precious, perfect baby boy.

A song she hadn't thought about in ages swelled inside her. Maybe it was from visiting her childhood home yesterday. Or maybe it was so ingrained in her after all the times

Dad had sung it to her, it had become a reflex. Whatever the reason, Quinn knew she had to sing it over him. She set her coffee down and leaned both arms on the crib railing.

He woke up to her singing, and she would've sworn he smiled at her as if understanding.

"That's a beautiful song."

Quinn flung a hand to her mouth to squelch a gasp. She turned toward Cooper, leaning into the doorjamb with eyes on her like he was admiring a confounding art piece.

Her hand slid to her chest. "You really need to stop sneaking up on me like that."

"Maybe if you stopped leaving me standing in doorways, enthralled, I'd have a chance."

Heat climbed her neck at his compliment. Even more at the sight of him in his chic dress clothes, looking like a confident power executive.

She swiped at her coffee and a plausible excuse for the stupid flush reaching her cheeks now. "Thanks for the latte. Don't tell me you flew this in from Hatteras."

"You don't think I would?"

"To impress a girl?" She snorted. "Probably."

The corners of his mouth reached for his dimples. "Who said I was trying to impress you?"

She coughed through a swallow. "No one. I didn't mean... I was just..." And there went any chance of extinguishing the heat soaring clear past her hairline. She snagged Brayden from the crib. "I need to change him. Unless you want to do the honors." She held him out.

Palms raised, Cooper backed up. "I have to get to a meeting with a client."

"Good." She exhaled.

"Good?"

Shoot. "Not that I want you to leave or anything. I mean, it doesn't matter one way or another. I was just thinking it's probably good for you. You know, to take care of business … stuff." Yeah, that sounded intelligent all right.

"Uh-huh. Well, I should be off then." His lips quirked. "Taking care of *business stuff.*"

For all his money, the guy really should've built a secret chamber in this place so she'd have somewhere to escape to right now.

Still grinning, he disappeared around the frame, and Quinn's chin sagged to her chest. *Classy, Thompson.* Even Brayden seemed amused. She looked from him back to the door, Cruella's call slithering to mind. "Wait!" She whirled around the trim. "Can we talk?"

"Would love to." By the front door, Cooper shucked on a suit jacket and pushed back the cuff to check his watch. "But I only have a few minutes."

"Right, yeah." She tried to play it cool. "Of course. We can talk whenever you get back."

He studied her, probably reading everything she was supposed to keep hidden. "You sure? 'Cause if it's important …"

With a practiced smile secured, she adjusted Brayden on her hip. "It's nothing that can't wait. Besides, little man and I have a date of our own."

"If you're positive." Cooper hesitated a moment longer before opening the door. "But call me if you need anything. Anything at all, okay?"

"We'll be fine. No rush." In fact, the sooner those piercing hazel eyes were behind that door, the better. She took Brayden's hand in hers and waved a happy goodbye.

The expression on Cooper's face as he waved back gutted her down the middle. He could deny it if he wanted to, but he was falling for his son. She'd been watching it happen every day.

No sooner had he left when a knock at the door echoed into the foyer. Relief swept through her as she whisked it open. "Good, I wanted to say—"

"There he is." Instead of Cooper, a grandmotherly woman stood on the porch, red lipstick curving in a bright smile fixed on Brayden. "How's my surrogate grandbaby doing?" She reached for him. "You mind?"

Not that it mattered if Quinn did, because the woman already had Brayden up in the air. She lowered his belly to her mouth and gave him a loud raspberry.

Quinn pulled on her ear. "I'm sorry, and you are?"

She lowered Brayden to her hip, while his pudgy fingers went straight for her glasses. "Just look at me, forgetting my manners. I'm Cooper's neighbor, Sheila." Extending her free hand, she looked Quinn up and down. "And you must be the reason he hasn't called lately."

"Excuse me?"

Sheila gestured toward the inside of the house in a silent request to come in. Considering she still had Brayden hostage, what was Quinn supposed to say? She held the door back to let the woman pass and grimaced at the cloud of perfume ambushing her.

"Cooper's been a lifesaver to the neighborhood. He helped mend my fence this past fall." She slid her glasses down as though getting ready to tell her something she shouldn't. "Refusing to accept payment in return, of course. But when this baby of his showed up ..." She bounced him on her hip. "Well, I just knew it was my chance to return the favor."

Quinn's arms came uncrossed. "*You're* the one who's been coming over to change Brayden's diapers?" And here, she'd accused him of luring bimbo girlfriends over to do his dirty work. Guilt wormed through her rib cage.

"Can't blame a single father for being a little overwhelmed. And I certainly understand him wanting to keep his privacy. People treat you differently when they know you have money. Believe me, I know." She tugged Brayden's fingers free from her necklace with a jewel-clad hand. "So, I help out wherever I can. Even make some dinners on occasion."

Meanwhile, Quinn only made assumptions—ones Cooper was consistently breaking.

"He does better than he thinks he does, though." Sheila finally surrendered her glasses, which ended up straight in Brayden's mouth. "One day, he'll see it. Just needs to give himself a little time."

Time. The one thing they were running out of. But she was right. Quinn had been watching Cooper become more and more connected to Brayden.

Hope rose through the ashes of her own problems and formed an entirely different plan than the one she needed to be working on. Maybe she couldn't save face with Cooper, but she could at least save a son's relationship with his father. They both deserved that chance. She just had to make Cooper see it before it was too late.

CHAPTER THIRTEEN

Home

At his front door, Cooper loosened his tie while holding his phone to his ear. "What exactly constitutes 'good cause'?" And how had he even ended up in a position to be talking about terminating parental rights. It all still felt surreal, like someone had thrust him into another person's life without giving him the slightest forewarning.

It sounded like Jim thumbed through a stack of papers. "In North Carolina, 'good cause' could be anything from abuse to neglect, the inability to provide proper care, even abandonment."

He rattled off the list like everyday events—probably ones he was accustomed to seeing more than anyone should.

"So, basically, you have to be a crackpot father." Now, there was a legacy.

Jim wheezed through the line. "Parents often want to get out of their financial obligation. The courts see it all the time."

"Is that what they think I'm doing?" Financial support was the only thing he *could* offer Brayden.

"It's nothing personal, Cooper."

He tugged his collar away from his sweaty neck. "Well, maybe it should be." If they knew him, they'd understand.

Cooper exhaled. He shouldn't be taking his frustrations out on his lawyer. "Listen, I'm just getting back from a meeting and need to take care of a few things. Why don't we talk later?"

Four hours with a high maintenance client had been draining enough. Sure, Cooper might've missed a few aspects of corporate life. But never-ending meetings? They were definitely supposed to be a thing of the past—a glorious perk of being a one-man operation.

After hanging up, Cooper rotated his tense shoulders, relieved to be home.

Home. The word sent a pang tightening across his chest. He stretched a palm against the siding, hung his head, and released another lengthy breath. This heat must be getting to him. Otherwise, he wouldn't be thinking …

Cutting off that train of thought, Cooper slid his phone into his pocket and pinched the bridge of his nose. His last coffee had obviously worn off one too many hours ago.

Through the door, a burst of cold air whirled around his collar onto his overheated skin, trailed by a sweet aroma of something honey-like. He smiled. Quinn must be baking again.

He stopped in the entryway at the sight of Brayden in his high chair, eating a concoction that looked almost gourmet, while Quinn sat crisscrossed on the couch, writing voraciously on a notepad.

Brayden flailed his chubby legs and slapped his sippy cup on the tray in front of him, face alight. "Dada." He waved orange-coated fingers at him.

A warmth like Cooper had never experienced spread through him as he returned Brayden's wave. And just like that, the weight of the morning lifted.

Quinn obviously noticed. She looked from Brayden to Cooper, a thin sheen forming over her eyes at hearing him say "Dada" for the first time.

An onlooker who didn't know any better might've thought he was a husband and father coming home to his family. Was this what it was like for Dad?

Shaking off the unsolicited emotions, he dumped his briefcase on the narrow table in the hall.

"Put that away." Quinn's expression shifted back to whatever had been weighing it down before he walked in.

His lips quirked. "Yes, dear."

She twirled her long hair into a twist and jimmied a pencil through it. "I did some cleaning today."

"So I see." The place was practically spotless—no clutter, all boxes organized and out of the way. His forehead pinched. "You know that's not part of the deal, right? I mean, I don't expect you to be my maid."

She met his eyes then. Soft, genuine. "Busywork helps me think."

"Like baking." His stomach growled on cue.

"Guess so." She wiped Brayden's face and hands and sat him on the floor by his foam blocks. "Though, I didn't get around to baking today."

"Really?" He jutted a thumb toward the kitchen. "But that smell ..."

"What smell?"

He started toward her. "You don't ...?" The honey-like scent swirled around him with the answer to his own question. The scent wasn't Quinn's baking. It was *her*—subtle, sweet, and dangerously alluring. Even worse, it was beginning to smell like home. The one he was getting ready to walk away from.

An errant strand of hair slipped loose from her twist as she tilted her head at him. "Are you all right?"

Hardly. "Fine." He undid the second button on his dress shirt and loosened his collar even more.

Quinn slipped her fingers through the handle on her coffee mug and moved to sit on the very tip of the opposite couch arm. In an old Button Your Fly T-shirt she must've brought back from her parents' house, she looked like the teenage girl in the photos lining her parents' living room walls. All she needed was that cowgirl hat.

He suppressed a laugh. Before this was all said and done, he'd get her to admit she missed that part of her life.

Quinn closed her eyes, visibly lost in her own thoughts, and stretched her legs into a sunbeam while balancing her mug in one hand.

Cooper laughed. "You know, the coffee table's over here, right?"

"But the sunshine's right here."

Glowing, she looked more at home in that one spot than he'd ever felt anywhere.

Man, that smile. He turned before she caught him reciprocating it. Doubtful it held her finesse anyway. He scratched
his cheek. His five-o'clock shadow was getting out of control.
As were his thoughts.

A text chimed from his phone. He glanced at a message
from his realtor about needing his appraisal paperwork. He
ignored it, not in the mood to duke it out with Ray, but the
interruption had already changed the atmosphere.

With a long sigh, Quinn plopped back into her spot on
the couch among stacks of notes. Apparently, he wasn't the
only one who'd had a rough morning.

"Long day?"

She flung a magazine over top of her notepad as he
neared. "I've been working on the party for Ginny," she rambled off a little too quickly. "The band she wants is too expen-
sive. She's going to be crushed when I tell her. Since it's so
close to the Fourth, maybe doing fireworks would make up
for it. Ooh, and sparklers." She shook her head. "Or is that too
lame for kids her age? It is, isn't it?"

She tapped the end of a pen ferociously against her thigh.
"You have way too many pens, by the way. Seriously, if the
stockbroker thing doesn't work out for you, you could start a
business selling refurbished office supplies."

"Uh-huh." The girl's rambling stress mode was more than
a little cute, but it didn't compensate for the underlying ache
behind it. He sat on the arm of the chair beside her. "Quinn,
listen, if money's an issue, why don't you let me—?"

"No." She curled the corner of the magazine in her lap back and forth. "I appreciate it, really, but I can't ask you to do that."

"You aren't." He leaned down to meet her gaze. "I'm offering."

The hints of amber in her eyes brightened but only for a moment. She looked away. "All the same, I'll figure something out. You've been generous enough already," she added so softly, he almost didn't hear her.

"If anyone owes something, it's me." He scooted forward to the edge. "Money doesn't come close to what you're doing for Brayden and me. You know that, right?"

Her brow furrowed, the pen falling from her fingers into the crease between the cushions.

He reached for her hand without thinking. "Quinn?"

When she finally faced him, a glimpse of the fractured girl inside that she strained so hard to hide looked back at him. She slid one leg out from the other and smiled that girl away. "Do you need more coffee as much as I do?"

More like he needed a sledgehammer if he was ever going to break through her walls. Resigning for now, he took her empty mug, stood up, and ruffled Brayden's soft hair on his way to the kitchen. "I'll make us a pot."

Once the coffee finished brewing, Cooper shuffled back into the living room with two filled-to-the-brim mugs in tow. He handed her one. "Hey, while you were cleaning, did you happen to see a paper about the appraisal I had done a few weeks ago?"

"I put it in a folder with the other house sale paperwork. It's in your office by your laptop." The corner of her mouth curled above the rim of her mug. "Where it should be."

Of course it was. He headed to his office. "You sure you don't want me to start calling you Pepper?"

"Try it once and see what happens," she called.

Laughter tipped his head back. Title or not, she definitely made things easier around here. At least, when it came to business. His heart was another story.

He turned to his study. "I'll be in my—Whaaat is that?" Briefcase against his stomach, he tried not to spill his coffee and whipped a glance from a random black cat rubbing its cheeks on the doorframe back to Quinn.

She lifted a shoulder. "Most people call it a cat."

"Thanks for clarifying." He gave her a stiff smile. "What's it doing in my house?"

"She's not yours?"

The cat trotted over and brushed up against his pant leg. Cooper shooed it away. "That would be a negative."

The moment Quinn called it, the cat ran for her and settled into her lap like it was a favorite vacation spot. "I found her out on your deck the other day."

"So, you decided to let her in?"

"She seemed at home." Quinn nuzzled her nose to the cat's. "Figured she'd been here before."

If she'd been around the yard, Cooper had never noticed. "Yeah, well, she can feel at home back outside. I don't do strays."

Quinn feathered two fingers over her scarred ear. "Aw, come on. She's adorable."

"She's missing half her whiskers."

"She's scrappy." Quinn stroked a hand down her back as it nestled the top of her head under Quinn's chin. "I'm gonna call her Trooper."

He coughed to drown out his snicker.

"You don't think a girl can be a trooper?" With her arms crossed, she wriggled up the back of the couch an inch taller with each punctuated word. "Maybe she's tough and smart and resilient." She glowered at his growing smile. "What?"

"Nothing." If she admitted she was talking about herself, he'd add downright attractive to the list. "I'm sure the cat can hold her own ... outside where she belongs. No use in her getting attached here. We'll all be gone soon."

The words nearly sawed him in half with their pressing reality. He'd do good to heed them himself.

Backing up, Cooper bumped into the table behind him and almost spilled his coffee again. Smooth. He pointed to the doorway. "I'm just gonna ..." Pretend she wasn't getting to him.

Quinn gave him a thumbs-up, unaware she didn't give him even half a chance.

In the safety of his office, he lowered his briefcase to the floor, set his mug on his desk, and slumped into his leather chair with a heavy exhale. What was wrong with him?

A yellow sticky note sat beside his laptop with a message from a girl he'd gone on two dates with a month ago. Nice girl, but after the second date fell flatter than the first, he politely ended things before they ever started. She shouldn't still be calling.

He dropped a folder over the note and wrenched backward in his chair. Why did he get himself in these situations?

A glance up intersected another sticky note—a bright pink one that read *You're Welcome* adhered to an overflowing cup of pens Quinn must've collected from around the house. He tore it off, laughed. She may be right, but being a pen hoarder was the least of his problems.

The calendar on the wall waved under the A/C like a shot clock. The days were moving the same direction his heart and focus needed to go. Forward. There was no point grounding roots he'd only have to pull up in a matter of days. He peered at a framed photo of Dad and him on his old skiff. "I'll make things up to you, Dad. Promise."

Productivity swept the minutes by until a shriek from the living room propelled him out of his chair. He swung around the trim toward a hint of embarrassment tingeing Quinn's forehead.

She covered her face with her magazine. "Sorry." Lowering it, she batted apologetic eyes at him. "Didn't mean to distract you."

His gaze fell over Brayden, half asleep against a pile of blocks he'd stacked together. "Everything all right?"

"No." She dropped the magazine to her lap and smacked a finger to an ad. "Someone please tell me why anyone would name their coffee shop Xpresso Café? That's only going to perpetuate the common mispronunciation. Do you know how annoying that is? It's almost as bad as ex-cetera. Ugh, or real-a-tor." She shuddered. "I better never hear you call Ray that."

He reined in a laugh, but the honest exasperation tinting her eyes pulled it right back out of him.

She rolled up the magazine and chucked it at his stomach. "I'm serious."

"I see that." He picked up the evidently disgraceful magazine and peeked into her empty coffee mug. "Maybe you should add a couple shots of Kahlúa to your coffee next time."

"Funny." She fell backward on the couch. "I'm trying to write up something to say at the party. A tribute to the family, I guess."

"Like your old blogs."

"In ways, yeah." She grabbed the scribbled-over notepad beside her. "But I keep hitting this wall. I just thought..." She smacked the page to her head and sighed. "I used to be so sure I was meant to be a writer. That I had something to say that'd matter, but lately... I don't know. Maybe this is a stupid idea."

He pulled the paper away from her face. "Or maybe you just need a break." He knew the weight of stress, the roadblocks it could create. Just like he knew the solution.

Cooper helped her to her feet. He might be leaving in a couple of weeks, but he could at least leave her with something worthwhile.

The notepad fell to the floor and sent her pen rolling under the coffee table. She resisted his pull. "Where are we going?"

"To take a leap of faith."

CHAPTER FOURTEEN

Leap

It was official. Cooper had lost his mind. Quinn obviously had too, or she wouldn't be shimmying a life jacket over her head right now.

From the dock, she peered at Ginny and Brayden sitting under the shade of a huge oak tree up shore and then back at Cooper. "How'd you even get my aunt's number?"

He stopped wiping down his WaveRunner and faced her, his blasted dimples already answering. "She gave it to me."

Of course she did. Quinn exaggerated an eye roll. "Just because most women are putty in your hands doesn't mean I am." *Says the girl about to get on the back of a death machine with him. Stupid.*

He tossed the rag on the bench and sauntered close. Too close. With hazel eyes dismantling her resolve a layer at a time, he grazed a cool hand along her ear while pulling a string of moss from the trees out of her hair. "Then what are you doing here right now?"

Trying to remember how to breathe? "I'm ..."

"Being a wuss," Ginny shouted.

Quinn whipped around. "Am not." No, instead she was acting like a five-year-old. Nice. She turned toward Cooper's simpering grin and swiped the keys from him. "A kayak's too much work for you?"

"Too slow."

Great. Quinn kept her fears from wrangling her play-it-cool expression.

Obviously, not well enough.

Cooper laughed. "Don't worry." He took the keys back and straddled the WaveRunner. "I'll drive this first round. All you gotta do is hang on."

To his shirtless waist. Sure, no problem. Tempering her nerves, she reluctantly climbed on. But as soon as the runner rocked, she dug her fingers into his arms.

He unclasped her death grip and wound her arms around his defined stomach. "Ready for some fun?"

Ready or not.

They took off, soaring across every rise and dip in the water. Wind coursed through her hair as cold mist sprayed her skin from all directions.

He picked up speed, and Quinn buried her head in his back, her grip tightening with each squeal the race against the water elicited.

Cooper finally slowed around the middle of the lake and looked behind him. "If you live with your eyes open, you might be surprised what you've been missing."

"I live with my eyes open plenty wide, thank you." And saw the world exactly for what it was. She could thank her past for that. Not to mention this job debacle she'd gotten herself into. Thankfully, Cruella hadn't fired Ava yet, but that didn't mean it wasn't coming. For all of them.

She untangled her arms from Cooper's waist. This whole thing was probably one giant mistake.

"C'mon, QT. I'm not talking about skepticism. I'm talking about possibilities, adventure, taking chances."

She toyed with the clasps on her life jacket. "I'm not very good at that," she mumbled.

"You gotta start somewhere." He rose to his feet, the WaveRunner swaying. "Don't overthink it. Just leap." With one flash of a smile over his shoulder, he dove into the lake.

Quinn stretched to grasp the handle bars and waited for the runner to steady.

A splash brought Cooper's head popping to the surface. He pushed his wet hair off his face and beamed at her like he'd just made the sanest move possible.

"You're crazy."

"At least I'm having fun." He jutted his chin at her. "What are you gonna do?"

"Run you over?"

His laughter gave way to a look in his eyes rivaling the lake's expanse. "I'll get you out here sometime."

"Time's not exactly on your side, buddy." She cocked her head, expecting a returned dig, but Cooper only exhaled.

"I know," he whispered. Before she could interpret his expression, he swam back over to the WaveRunner and climbed on behind her this time. "But I'm at least getting you in the driver's seat."

Backed against his firm chest, Quinn breathed in. But when his cool fingers smoothed over hers along the handle bars, all breath disappeared with the wind that seemed to have gone on strike out of nowhere. So much for not being putty.

"Just go easy at first." He turned one bar slowly, his low voice in her ear.

Easy. Sure. She swallowed and increased the gas a little at a time until they were flying across the lake top. The wind, the freedom, the adrenaline—it swept through her like a fire reigniting feelings she'd long ago written off. "We're doing it."

Cooper's husky laugh clung to her with the misty water. "*You're* doing it, QT." He released the bars, circled his arms around her waist, and kept his mouth beside her ear. "Just takes a little faith to let go."

Sunlight poured over her skin, his words over her heart. Her gaze gravitated to the white water churning beside the runner. If only taking leaps came with a guarantee you'd never drown.

Cooper slid his hands over hers again. "But in case you still need a little help ..."

She knew that tone, knew it couldn't be good. "Coop—"

Speed stole her voice. One wave, one jump, and they spun through the air. Her heart didn't find its way back to her chest until the runner hit the water again.

Ginny cheered as they approached the dock. "That was awesome. Can I go next?"

Brayden clapped. "'Gain. 'Gain."

Quinn eased off the WaveRunner like a city girl dismounting a horse. "You want to fly, huh, Dimplestiltskin?" She took Brayden from Ginny and twirled him up in the air.

His laughter sent her heart soaring almost as much as that ride had. "'Gain," he repeated.

She pinned him to her side. "Why don't we leave the water tricks to Daddy."

"Dada."

Cooper came over with water still dripping from his hair down his body. He shook his head, dotting both of them in drops of water. Quinn shoved him away, while Brayden ate it up. "Boys," she mumbled.

Cooper took an incoming call on his return to the dock. "It's not a good night, Ray ... Yeah, I know, time's running out ... Look, I'm almost finished with the deck. Everything else is set." He cut a glance at Quinn and rolled his eyes at his phone. "What's that? Sorry, hoss, I'm losing you. Yeah, let me call you later." Hanging up, he shook his head and then winked at her. "Real-a-tors."

She shoved him.

All joking aside, she couldn't help half pitying Ray for trying to work with such a confounding client. Cooper was quick to troubleshoot other people's problems. But his own? Sometimes, he seemed bent on making things happen right away, like the powerhouse executive he was. Other times, it was like his laid-back, free-spirited side took over. No wonder Ava called him Mr. Elusive.

He mussed Brayden's hair and kissed the top of his head before helping Ginny onto the WaveRunner.

"Be careful," Quinn called.

Not that Ginny was listening. Caught up on the Cooper dream boat, her cousin eagerly roped her arms around his waist, and all Quinn could do was laugh.

"I don't blame you, girl," she said once they took off.

Alone with Brayden, she moseyed to the shade and sat on the grass. Brayden held onto both her hands and bounced up and down, clearly ready to go for a few rides of his own.

"You're going to be an adventure junkie like your dad, aren't you, mister?"

A devilish grin answered for him.

"Oh, you think you're cute. I see. Give me that chunkamunka leg."

As soon as she let go, he squirmed to crawl away. Like that was happening. She scooped him up and pretended to gobble up his thigh, releasing a round of giggles that were beginning to take up permanent residence in her heart.

Quinn smoothed back his damp hair from his red cheeks. "Don't worry. We're gonna get you walking in no time." Her earlier comment to Cooper about time being the enemy speared through her with the reality that she might never see Brayden walk. Even more gut-wrenching, Cooper might not either. Unless she hurried up and did something to change that.

Another arrow trailed the first. Would telling Cooper the truth about why she was here ruin her chance to change his mind about his son?

Brayden grabbed onto the front of her shirt, pulled himself up, and landed an almost-kiss smack to her chin. She took one look at the sweet hazel eyes beaming up at her, and she was head over heels lost.

For the next twenty minutes, she failed miserably at reeling her heart away from the electric fence called hope that'd burned her too many times.

But when the purr of the WaveRunner's engine signaled its return, and Cooper's smile came into view, she knew the chance to walk away unscathed had passed a long time ago.

"That was the coolest." Ginny adjusted her windblown ponytail. "Quinn, would you take a picture of us?"

She rose, resituated Brayden, and snapped a photo of Ginny crowding Cooper at the dock like a groupie.

Her cousin took her cell back and inspected the picture, face still glowing.

Just as Quinn was turning, Ginny stopped her. "Now one of us."

Brayden almost slipped out of her arms. "You want a picture with me?" She must've swallowed too much water out there.

She shrugged. "Why not?"

Alrighty then. Quinn passed off Brayden to Cooper and slid an arm around her cousin's back. The camera snapped, and memories flashed of all the time they used to spend together. She couldn't fault Ginny for being mad at her for leaving. She hadn't even said goodbye.

She blinked back a sudden rise of emotion and reached for Brayden again.

"I got him." Ginny intercepted him. When Quinn eyed her, she perched a hand on her free hip. "I'm not the same kid you left four years ago. I'm sixteen now. I know how to babysit."

Quinn lifted her palms. Hard to argue with that. Quinn used to babysit at only ten years old. Not to mention, she'd known Ginny all her life. Trusted her.

Halfway up the slope to the back of the house, a squeal whirled her around. "Wait till my friend Bethany sees these pics. She'll be so jealous." Ginny disappeared up the steps to the deck in a bubble of adolescent excitement.

"Forewarning, that picture might show up on your Facebook page," Quinn said to Cooper.

"Good thing I don't do social media."

Seriously? "Even my mom does Facebook."

He shrugged. "I prefer to keep a low profile. It's too easy for the media to invade your privacy. I'm not about to voluntarily give them something to distort and smear across the tabloids. I already have to field enough presumptions about my life."

His confession jabbed like an ice pick dead to her gut. Her stomach churned at the possibilities of what would happen when he found out she was part of the media he hated.

"You're lucky," he said. "We haven't had to dodge any reporters since you came, but I probably should've warned you to watch your back when we're out in public."

She would dig out the ice pick if she could. Instead, it only twisted deeper. "All the drama that went down with Shore Corp ... You didn't leave because of that, did you?"

"There was obviously stuff going on while I was still there, but I didn't know what. I left before any of it came out."

Cooper finished locking up his WaveRunner. "But as long as the media thinks there's a story there ..."

"They'll keep digging." She clutched her elbows, even more so when a streak of weariness slipped through his usual carefree exterior.

He cleared his throat and straightened. "It was cool of Ginny to take a picture with you."

Evidently, she wasn't alone in wanting to shift the conversation.

Quinn turned a skeptical stare on him. "Seems kind of odd to have a change of heart all of a sudden, don't you think?"

"She's sixteen." He scratched his jaw. "Do you really need another explanation?"

"Mm-hmm." More like he was at it again, trying to find solutions to all her problems.

Cooper tugged a T-shirt over his sun-dried skin. "You know, after getting so close to my niece that year I lived with them, I was pretty nervous about how she'd respond when I moved away again."

"And?" Quinn sat on the bench and tucked her hands under her legs.

"She extended the same grace she always does." A wistful expression lifted his cheeks. "That doesn't mean she hesitates to put me in my place when I need it, but I wouldn't trade getting to keep that relationship for anything."

"Mm." Quinn slid her toes in and out of her flip-flops. "I don't suppose you mentioned any of that to Ginny while you had her out on the water."

He pulled on his ear, dodging her question. "Life's too short to live with regrets."

His brow furrowed at the underlying meaning, and so did her heart. She'd lost her dad in ways, but not like he had.

Cooper dusted off his hands. "So, you wanna tell me what's up with your fear of the water? I thought you grew up on this lake. Something happen?"

"Billy Finley. That's what happened."

Amusement coalesced with the intrigue in his eyes.

"Summer of sixth grade, this annoying boy in my class told me all these stories about the Loch Ness Monster."

Quinn threatened to swat Cooper with her flip-flop when he snickered. "Hey, you try not freaking out as a little girl when something swims up against your legs after you just heard a horror story. I was scarred for life." The silly memory settled across her face in a smile but evaporated a minute later.

She moved to the edge of the dock and wrapped a hand around the light post. "A few years later, a kid here on vacation drowned. I never went in again after that."

"I'm sorry." A consoling hand caressed the top of her shoulder.

Despite knowing she shouldn't, Quinn gently leaned into Cooper's secure body behind her.

"You know, one person's fate doesn't determine another's."

She turned and looked up at him. "But one person can change another's."

Cooper held her gaze with such intensity, her heart rate pulsed in her ears. She breathed in, held it. Too afraid to release it or the moment, but equally as afraid to press in.

He diverted his focus to the dock, then sat on the edge with his legs dangling above the water.

After stealing a moment to regroup, Quinn joined him. "Tell me about her."

"Who?" He picked up three acorns on the board beside him.

"Brayden's mom."

His body stiffened. "Not much to tell." He chucked one of the acorns across the water. "I was in Ocracoke helping my brother. Megan was there for a summer escape. We hit it off, had the kind of summer you'd read in one of your books, and then she left."

"You never saw her again?"

"Once," he said slowly.

Quinn ran her fingers along the grooves in the wood. "Did you love her?"

"I thought I did. Turns out it was just a fling." He spun the two acorns 'round and 'round in his hand. "Hard to blame her. People vacation in Ocracoke to get away from everyday life, not to get tied down to more obligations holding them back."

"Back from what?"

"Living unattached."

"Unattached." Her muscles tensed. "You mean, to a son?"

"You're the one who said the more someone loves you, the more you can disappoint them, remember? The one who left to avoid hurting her family."

But what happened when cutting yourself off from everyone turned out to bring nothing but emptiness?

"Why do you think Megan kept him from me, Quinn? She knew I'd let him down as much as I know it."

Her voice grew small. "You can't really believe that."

Still staring across the lake, Cooper skimmed the last acorn over the placid water. He clutched the edge of the dock. "We've already been through all this."

"But you're not listening."

He pivoted toward her then, eyes laden with beliefs they were never meant to carry.

"Can't you see it?" she pleaded. "He loves you, Cooper."

"And one day he'll understand how much love motivated my choice to give him a reliable home to grow up in."

Quinn clamped her lips shut, but the question broke through anyway. "Are you sure you're not mistaking fear for love."

He angled his head at her. "Are you?" With a flick of his chin at the lake, his mischievousness chased away the gravity he obviously wanted to avoid. "If you're not ruled by fear, then jump."

Of course it had to come back to that. She wasn't going to win this argument. Not today.

She breathed in the fresh cedar and redirected the conversation to his dock project instead. If nothing else, maybe he'd at least recognize he had things to offer besides just money.

"You've really done a great job on this, you know? At some point, you should check out some of my dad's woodwork. Working with your hands like that … creating something new … it's kind of an art form."

"Sorta like writing."

She made a face. "They're just words."

"Words that matter. If you don't share them, who will?"

"Anyone can tell a story, Cooper."

"But maybe someone needs to hear yours." He walked to the bench, opened it, and pulled out a small bag.

"You make it sound like I have some big gift to share or something."

Cooper strode back over and handed her the bag. "I'd wager you're the only one who believes you don't."

Torn between caution and curiosity, Quinn slowly unfurled the bag to find an embossed leather journal inside. She was supposed to be helping him see what he had to offer, not the other way around.

"If writing's your passion, you should pursue it." He nudged his shoulder into hers. "Even if that means taking a leap."

"A leap."

"Sure." He shrugged. "Pick up your old blog again or start a new one. An online magazine, a book—anything." Genuine belief looked back at her. "You never know who your words will reach."

Quinn willed down the tears clawing to the surface at his unexpected thoughtfulness and sincerity.

Instead of pressing, Cooper returned to his spot beside her and seemed content to wait for her to respond.

Start her own business? It wasn't that she hadn't thought about it, maybe even had wanted to a long time ago, when it was safe to dream. But things had changed.

She held the gift to her stomach and watched distant dragonflies glide along the top of the water. "My dad used to say God whispers our destiny to us through little moments every day." Shaking her head, she pulled her knees up to her chest. "It sounds cheesy now, but I used to listen for them."

Cooper pressed his warm arm into hers. "Seems like you had it figured out once."

She thought she had. "Have you ever felt like you knew for sure you were supposed to do something—go in a certain direction, make a specific choice—only to end up on the other side, feeling like you must've gotten it completely wrong?"

"More than I want to admit." He rubbed his stubbly chin.

"I don't know. I'm probably not making any sense." She twisted toward him. "It's just ... do you think you can be afraid of losing something you've never found?"

His eyes searched hers with such depth, her pulse quickened. "I think I'm starting to."

Neither of them moved. Still half wet, his hair lay flat against his forehead in an image of the tender boy trapped beneath a persona few people saw past. Her hands slid from her knees to her ankles, wanting so much to reach for him. To show him—

What did she think she was doing? She was supposed to be writing a news article, not a romance novel, for crying out loud.

Breaking the connection, she pushed on the boards and shot to her feet. "I should, um, go get something started for dinner." And give herself a solid head slap for being that vulnerable with him, while she was at it.

"Why don't we go out tonight? My treat."

Her head nodded on its own, succumbing to his impossible-to-turn-down eyes. At least in a public restaurant, maybe she stood a chance at thinking clearly enough to talk to him about the feature.

A whack to the back of her leg whirled her around to a nonchalant-looking expression.

"Did you just swat my thigh?"

Cooper hopped up and wiped his hands. "Nope. You didn't see that? The Loch Ness Monster's tail just swept up and almost got you. It was close. You're lucky I'm here."

"More like you're lucky I don't shove you into the lake right now." She hedged him backward, welcoming the distraction from the earlier intensity. "Keep laughing, and you'll get to meet that monster personally."

His feet teetered on the edge, and he roped his arms around her waist. "If I go, you go."

Her hands linked around his neck, panic spiraling. "You wouldn't."

"Oh, c'mon. You wouldn't be going in alone. I've got you."

This close, panic escalated for a whole different reason. Fear of drowning in the lake was nothing compared to drowning in those hazel eyes. Problem was, she'd been sinking since day one. Unless he was blind, he saw it too. Felt it. Even now, her pulse surged.

But instead of letting go, her insubordinate hand slid from his neck across the whiskers on his cheek. In a mirrored dance, his hand found her cheek in return. The rhythm of their breathing deepened, the cadence of the breeze drawing them closer. His gaze roved to her lips, already parted. Ready, waiting. Full of yearning and fear and—

"Awkward." Ginny giggled from the top of the deck.

Quinn flinched away, and Cooper had to catch her hand to keep from falling backward into the lake. Once stabilized, they both looked in about every direction but at each other.

"Sorry to interrupt," Ginny called on her way across the lawn. "But my mom's here."

Quinn's erratic gaze finally landed on Ginny and Brayden. "Is it six already?" She hurried up the dock to take Brayden from her. "Thanks for coming out today. It was fun."

Ginny leaned in and whispered, "I think you mean electric." She bobbed her brows just when Quinn thought the mortification couldn't get worse. At least Mama hadn't been there.

Once Ginny disappeared around the side of the house, Quinn turned. "I should probably..." *Go crawl under the house.*

"Here." He reached for Brayden. "I'll take him while you get changed."

"Changed?"

"We're going out to eat, right?"

"Right." She shook her head as if it would cause sense and dignity to magically regain a foothold. "I should probably put some clothes on. Not that I'd ever be around you without clothes on. I just meant *fresh* clothes." And was clearly aiming to win an award on how many times she could say clothes in one breath.

Cringing at Cooper's amusement, she closed her eyes and gestured behind her. "I'm leaving now."

She made an awkward about-face and half jogged up the hill. Almost to the deck, her cell buzzed from her pocket. Mama. Perfect. The woman's timing was almost as attuned as Cruella's.

"Hey, Mama."

"Oh good, I was hoping I'd catch you. How'd you all like to come over for supper tonight? Just the four of us."

"Sounds lovely, but Cooper and I already have plans." Thank heavens.

"Really?" she said in a simpering voice. "Well, then, you two have fun on that date."

"It's not—" Quinn cut herself off. No point. "Thanks. We will."

"Be careful driving. It's going to be a real gully washer to-night."

Quinn craned her head toward the clouds moving in. "Thanks for the heads-up. We'll be fine."

"Okay, sugar. But make sure you're free on Friday. We're having another cookout."

Massaging her forehead, Quinn plastered on a compliant smile. "Wouldn't miss it."

The doorbell rang from Mama's end of the line. "Nurse Murphy just got here, honey. Let me go. Your daddy's got a real burr in his saddle today."

Quinn wasn't about to ask. "See you Friday."

"If the good Lord's willing and the creek don't rise."

Right. Quinn overlooked the flood of crazy southernisms while stopping at the bottom of the stairs. "Mama?" She swirled her toes in the grass and tried to untangle her voice. "Tell Daddy I said hello."

"I will, sweetheart. Bye."

Quinn stayed in place after hanging up. Maybe Cooper wasn't the only one confusing love and fear.

She peered behind her to the dock where he was dangling his keys in one hand while holding his son with the other. Brayden planted two pudgy palms to Cooper's scruffy cheeks and leaned in to kiss him as he'd done with Quinn earlier. The moment he nestled his head under Cooper's chin, Quinn's insides split in two.

How could she tell a guy who wanted no roots that they already held her heart?

CHAPTER FIFTEEN

Storm

Cooper dragged a hand along his face after trimming his scruff. He rolled up his shirt cuffs, took one last glance in the bathroom mirror, and then flipped the lights.

It didn't matter what he looked like. This wasn't a date. Just a guy giving a girl a break from making dinner for the night. If he really wanted to get technical about it, Quinn was actually an employee.

Yeah, and when did employers ask their staff to dinner? *Smart move, Anderson.* He hadn't exactly meant to ask her out. The question just sort of came out on its own.

Around the door to the nursery, Cooper stopped and grinned. Brayden was standing up in his crib, holding the railing.

"You ready to eat?"

"Eat." He bounced up and down the closer Cooper neared. "I sweam!"

"Ice cream?" He laughed. "Wow. Loraine really did spoil you, didn't she?"

Brayden extended both arms to him, and Cooper's chest tightened at the open trust and acceptance Brayden offered him so easily.

Curbing his reaction, he hauled him out of the crib. "I'll tell you what. You'll get some ice cream if you help me get through dinner first. I need you on your game tonight, hoss. No letting me slip up and almost make a move like I did on the dock today. Deal?" He couldn't afford to complicate things.

Brayden swung both hands over his mouth.

"Uh-huh. Don't even act like you haven't fallen for Quinn too. I saw you earlier, smacking that kiss on her chin."

Brayden flung his hands away and blew his lips in a blubber sound.

Cooper laughed. "Yeah, well, let's hope I at least didn't look like that."

He kicked his legs in excitement. "I sweam! I sweam!"

"You're gonna be a lot of help, aren't you?" Shaking his head, Cooper got him dressed and carried him into the hall.

Two steps into the living room, he halted at the sight of Quinn coming down the hall in the same outfit she had on the day she first arrived. She'd caused a double take then, but now, he couldn't look away.

Long brown waves flowed over her shoulders and onto a cream blouse that shimmered in all the right places. She bent her leg behind her and adjusted her heel, the simple pose causing an unjustified spike in his pulse.

Brayden squirmed in Cooper's arms, obviously wanting Quinn.

She turned and smiled at him. "Look at you in your cute polo." She smoothed her hands down her skirt and met Cooper's gaze. "I wasn't sure what to wear. Is this too much?"

For him? Right now? Maybe. "You're perfect."

The implication behind those two words zinged inside him like a pinball. He started forward to hide it. Surely, movement would help.

Fat chance.

Brayden practically soared from his arms in an attempt to settle into hers, and whatever acrobats his insides were doing, seeing his son's affection for Quinn upped the intensity tenfold.

What was his problem tonight? Nothing had changed. So, they'd almost kissed. And something in him came alive while watching her thrive on the WaveRunner. And the way she viewed him—believed in him—left him more than a little undone. And—

Stop, just stop.

"Cooper?"

He snapped his head up. "Sorry?"

"I asked if you're ready to go."

"Of course." He opened the door for her. Behind them, he eyed Brayden's bubbly grin above her shoulder. *Way to help me out, hoss.*

Outside, wind tunneled up from the backyard and whirled Quinn's hair in a beautiful mess. Cooper clicked the fob to his SUV. While she fastened Brayden in his car seat, Cooper peered toward the shadowy sky. A single raindrop splattered onto his forehead. He looked from the clouds to Quinn's unassuming smile, knowing full well he'd already lost to the one storm he'd never seen coming.

By the time they turned onto the street for Watersview Restaurant, an all-out downpour was assaulting the pavement. Quinn darted a glance from the sheet of rain cascading down the windshield to her open-toed shoes as Cooper pulled into the full parking lot.

A Ford pickup backed out of a spot directly across from the entrance.

"Go! Before someone else scoops it up," she said in response to the hesitation on Cooper's face.

"I can drop you off at the door."

"It's fine. We can run for it." She slanted a brow. "You should really take more leaps in life, you know."

One dimple reached for the other. "I'll try to work on that."

Meanwhile, she'd better work on not blushing when he looked at her that way.

Parked, he flipped the locks and handed her his jacket. "I'll get Brayden. Ready? On three."

Quinn tossed the jacket over her shoulders and grabbed the door handle. On cue, she sprang into the rain, squealing at the cold pellets beating onto her hair. Puddles engulfed her shoes, but she kept running. At the entrance, she wiped down her legs while laughing.

At least Brayden had a blanket draped over him. Cooper, on the other hand, got as drenched as she did. His white button-down clung to his skin, accentuating muscles defined through both work and play.

"Good job, QT." He shook his wet hair back from his face. "See? A little water isn't so bad. We'll get you in that lake yet."

She lifted on her toes to pull a leaf from his hair. "Don't hold your breath." Her hand slid down to his collar as her heels eased back to the ground. The look in his eyes deepened, and holding her breath was about all she could do.

A hostess opened the door. "Welcome to Watersview."

Quinn flung her hand back to her side, where it belonged, and slipped inside. "Thank you," she said on her way past the young girl.

Goose bumps peppered her skin from head to toe under the waves of A/C circulating mouthwatering scents throughout the restaurant.

Once seated, Cooper set a pen with Watersview's logo on it beside his silverware.

"What is that?"

He looked from the pen to her and shrugged. "They were giving them away up front."

"Because you needed one more to add to your endless collection?" She picked up her menu. "You know there are steps for overcoming addiction, right?"

While he laughed, she tried to ignore the way her toes were sliding over her wet shoes.

"What's wrong?" Cooper asked, surveying her face.

"The rain. My shoes are all slimy now."

He reached under the table, cupped a hand to her ankle, and slid her shoe strap off. "There's an easy remedy to that." He unrolled his silverware and shook out the cloth napkin.

"Cooper, don't you dare."

"They have to wash it anyway."

Solving problems, once again.

She covered her face. "I can't believe you." But worse than embarrassment, a sensation far more dangerous followed his gentle touch to her ankle. With the way he was tending to her foot, she was going to need an entire carton of napkins to mop herself up off the floor when he was finished.

Brayden waved the menu in the air and swatted it against the tray on his high chair, rescuing them from yet another moment she couldn't keep letting herself get drawn into.

They both turned to Brayden and laughed. He'd teepeed the menu over his head as though expecting applause.

She stole the opportunity to collect her focus and scanned the menu.

A waiter, probably in his early forties, stopped by the table. After a quick introduction, he turned his attention to Quinn. "Can I get a drink started for the lovely lady? A red wine, perhaps? Something to complement her natural beauty."

Cooper coughed.

"Just a water, please." She returned the drink menu to him.

"Same for me," Cooper added. "And a milk for the little guy."

"My pleasure."

When he left, Quinn met an unreadable grin from across the table. "What?"

He ran a knuckle along his brow. "Nothing."

Rather than press, she let it drop. Probably better not to get sidetracked. The talk they needed to have tonight was going to take every ounce of strength she had as it was.

No one there could've known the anticipated conversation was already choking her, but chatter throughout the noisy restaurant seemed only to heighten the silence at their table.

The waiter returned to take their orders. As soon as Quinn got her drink, she sucked down a third of her water like she would find the words she needed at the bottom of her glass.

Cooper stared across the table. "Are you all right?"

Of course he'd notice. She set her fidgety hands in her lap. "Cooper, I ... I need to tell you something." Except, that required intelligent sentences, breath—things failing her in every way right now.

She twisted the straw wrapper around her index finger and looked up to face the consequences of letting things go this far. "I wasn't completely honest with you about why I came back."

"I know."

The wrapper unfurled. "You do?" Her pulse spiked.

"Cooper Anderson?" A guy in a short-sleeved white dress shirt and loose tie approached their table with a drink in his hand. "Tonight must be my lucky night."

Cooper looked him over. "I'm sorry, do I know you?"

"Chad Peters with the *Hatteras Tribune*." He withdrew a business card from his pocket and held it out for him. "I've been trying to secure an interview with you for months."

When Cooper stared without taking the card from him, Chad set it on the table instead. "Maybe we could get some drinks. Even talk off the record if you want."

Cooper's hand clenched around his water glass. "I realize you may have missed it, but I'm in the middle of a dinner date."

Chad's focus strayed to Quinn long enough for assumptions to swirl. He looked behind him to the woman he'd left at his own table. "Me too." He pitched an insinuating brow. "But I wouldn't mind introducing you to my date. We could always hook up afterward. Go down to that beach around the lake I hear you enjoy taking the ladies to, eh?"

If Cooper's jaw got any tighter, it would be stiffer than that drink Chad was about two seconds away from getting poured over his head. No wonder Cooper held such a distaste for the media. What gave this guy the right to infringe on Cooper's privacy, waltzing over here like he had him all figured out, when all he was doing was insulting him?

Quinn shot to her feet before she thought better of it. "I think you need to leave. Now."

Chad studied her then. When something too close to recognition flitted across his eyes, her knees buckled. Quinn sat right back down. If he was a journalist from Hatteras, their paths had probably crossed at some point. He didn't look familiar, but that didn't mean the opposite wasn't true.

Defying the A/C, sweat beaded under her shirt. One word, and the jerk could expose her for being more of a fraud than he was. Guilt seared into her. How could she judge him when she was even worse? She'd weaseled into Cooper's life with the same exact presumptions and gall Chad had. The only difference was, a guy like Chad didn't hide behind pretenses or rationalize his motives.

Quinn strained to swallow, strained to pretend he didn't unnerve her. But his silent appraisal felt like a floodlight drilling heat onto every hidden nook and crevice she'd tried to ignore since stepping foot in Lake Gaston again.

A screech from Cooper's chair legs grinding against the floor jerked Chad's attention back to him. The second Cooper rose, Chad's smug demeanor wavered.

"I think you heard her." He jutted his chin toward the table Chad had abandoned. As usual, Cooper's commanding presence rendered words unnecessary.

Chad sent one last look over Quinn, nodded in submission, and backed away. "You have my card if you change your mind."

Their waiter came over, his brow knitted with concern. "Is everything all right, sir?"

"Fine." Cooper returned to his seat and pulled his chair to the table.

When the waiter still looked uncertain, Quinn offered him an assuring smile. They didn't need any more attention drawn to themselves.

"Fresh bread will be up in a moment."

"Thank you," Quinn managed. Once the waiter left, she tried to gauge Cooper's mood. How they'd go back to having a normal dinner now, she had no idea. But maybe it wasn't fair to hope they could. If anything, running into Chad only fueled the urgency to get the truth out in the open before it reached the point where Cooper would never forgive her.

"I'm sorry," she said. *For so many things.*

"I'm used to it."

"That doesn't mean you should be." She straightened the silverware on her napkin and inhaled. "Cooper, the reason I came home ... I'm not proud of the way I—"

"It's nothing to be ashamed about." He sat back. Traces of his frustration with Chad receded behind a look of tenderness Quinn couldn't reconcile with the conversation. If he really knew why she was here, how could he hold anything but animosity toward her? Especially after how he'd reacted to Chad.

He leaned both arms on the table. "I know you don't want to admit it, but it's obvious you want to reconnect with your family. I saw it that day at your parents' place. The way your face lit up around your brother, your dad. You miss them, Quinn. And who wouldn't? You have a great family."

It was a good thing he kept talking, because whatever she had planned to say lodged itself halfway up her throat.

"I know it wasn't easy for you to come home. You needed an excuse to be nearby without it coming off as if you're the one waving the white flag. I get it."

Cooper reached across the table and rested a compassionate hand over hers. "But why not? Why not go all in? If you admit you were wrong in leaving, they'll admit they shouldn't have let you go." His thumb grazed the top of her hand. "Love instead of fear, right?"

Her eyelids finally moved in a single blink. Another. But her mouth wouldn't budge, words still trapped.

"You've already taken a bunch of leaps today. Just keep going."

His cell vibrated on the tabletop. Before he dismissed the call, Quinn caught a flash of the name on the screen—Livy.

So much for his not giving out his cell number to girls.

A twinge of reprimand broke through her momentary lapse in jealousy. Stupid. He'd already made it clear he viewed relationships as baggage that weighed him down. Sure, maybe they had some chemistry, but it didn't matter in the end. She shouldn't let misconstrued feelings get in the way of what she needed to do.

Quinn wriggled up in her seat. "Cooper, this isn't about family. It's about business."

The waiter's uncanny timing returned him to their table with a basket of freshly baked bread. He faced Quinn again. "I'll have your food out in another few minutes. Anything else I can get for you?"

A do over?

"This is great for now," Cooper answered. "Thank you."

Quinn ran her fingers along the condensation on her glass. She just needed to come out with it. Shoot straight. He'd be mad at first. But if anyone could be levelheaded about business, it should be Cooper Anderson. She placed her hands on the table, looked up.

Her cell rang inside her purse, but she didn't move. One more interruption, and so help her ...

"You gonna get that?"

"No."

He fed Brayden a piece of warm bread the waiter had brought. "What if it's your mom?"

Even more reason to ignore the call.

"QT."

"Fine." She withdrew her cell. Mama, of course. Reluctantly, she dragged her thumb across the screen and covered her opposite ear. "Hey, we're in a restaurant right now. Can I call you—?"

"Quinn, honey?" The tremor in her mom's voice traveled through the line and up Quinn's spine.

"What's wrong? Are you okay?"

The heavy pause dragged Quinn's free arm down to her lap. She wrapped it around her middle, her voice shrinking to a whisper. "Mama?"

"Baby, it's your dad."

CHAPTER SIXTEEN

Breakable

Aunt Loraine met Quinn and Cooper at the hospital entrance and reached for Brayden. "I'll look after him. You two go on."

They rushed into the waiting room at the same time Nurse Murphy came through the door leading to the wing Dad was in.

Quinn examined the woman's expression for any indication of the prognosis. "Is he ...?" She couldn't even get the words out.

"He's going to be okay. They'll likely keep him overnight for observation." She patted Quinn's forearm. "It's completely normal protocol any time there's trauma to the head."

"Trauma?" The room started to slant.

Next to her, Cooper gently drew her to the safety of his side.

Nurse Murphy's warm smile emitted waves of assurance Quinn wished she could grasp on to. "Your dad took quite the fall off those back steps. But I tell you what. If there's anyone hardheaded enough to get the better of those rickety things, it's George Thompson."

A small laugh escaped Quinn's tight diaphragm. "You're probably right about that."

Cooper ran a hand up and down her arm, strong and comforting.

Nurse Murphy's eyes softened while looking them over. "You remind me of your parents. George may be losing portions of his mental capabilities, but his love for his wife? I reckon it's as strong as the day he married her."

She reached for both their arms. "You two hang on to that kind of love. It's what'll carry you through moments like these." With a quick pat, she offered one more nod and headed past them to leave.

Quinn brought her hands around her elbows, but her insides still crumbled.

A love like her parents had. Is that what people saw? What they believed? Guilt closed in on the tails of an even greater sorrow. She'd wanted that kind of love most of her life. Turns out the closest she could come was nothing more than a charade.

It was one thing to let herself start to rely on having Cooper in her life, but to drag her family into getting attached to him too?

"Quinn—"

"Don't." She couldn't bear the apology in his voice, the tenderness. Stepping away from the false security, she met Cooper's eyes for the briefest moment. "Please, don't say anything." She walked through the door from one lie toward another.

The sound of machines led her down a cold, sterile hall. In the doorway to Dad's hospital room, she held the trim, grasping on to what little composure she had left. She couldn't deny this was part of why she'd moved away. To avoid seeing him like this, asleep in a hospital bed with probes and tubes tethered to his body while monitors chimed their anthem of uncertainty. It was too much, too hard.

"Quinn." Mama let go of Dad's hand, crossed the room, and bundled her in a hug. "He's going to be fine, sugar." She rubbed circles over Quinn's back.

"Why didn't you tell me things were getting this bad?"

The circular motion stopped. Mama leaned back and draped Quinn's hair over the front of either shoulder. "Now, don't you be fretting over this. Your daddy's as strong as they come. And with everyone praying, I just know—"

"Stop. Mama, will you just stop." Still cradling her arms to her chest, Quinn paced inside the small room. "He's not okay. Look at him. He's falling apart day by day." A blurry image of her infallible father looked back at her. He'd been her hero growing up, her rock. But she couldn't keep holding on to what she'd already lost.

She staved off the beginning of tears and faced her mom. "At some point, you have to stop lying to yourself."

"Me?" Mama's cheeks burned a fiery red. "That's rich coming from you, dear."

"What's that supposed to mean?"

"You know darn well what I'm talking about, and I'm not having it, Quinn Mary Beth. Not here. Not right now." A hard breath wrenched her shoulders up as she turned.

After stealing a minute to recollect her proper southern poise, Mama returned to Dad's bedside. "Your daddy needs you, and you're here. That's all that matters."

She was right. Arguing wasn't doing anyone favors right now. "I'm sorry." She took Mama's hand in hers. "Would you mind giving me a moment alone with him?"

Mama's eyes warmed in return. "Of course. I'll be in the waiting room if you need me."

"Thanks."

Once she disappeared around the doorway, Quinn took her place holding Dad's hand and watched him breathe in an unconscious flow. How many times had she listened to that same soothing rhythm? From early years all the way through high school, she could always lay her head on his chest and know she was home. That she was safe, loved. And when he'd needed her to do the same for him, she'd run away.

Raw emotion tainted her whispered voice. "You gotta hang on for me, okay? I've been working hard for a promotion at work." She swallowed, the fear of losing her chance never so prevalent. "I know it might not be where you saw me ending up, but I think you could be real proud of me if you saw what I could change as executive editor. The difference I could make."

She rubbed a hand over his, careful to avoid the IV. "I need you to keep fighting so you can see everything's going to work out and that I'm going to be taken care of. I know that's what you always wanted for me, and I need you to have that peace. Dad, please, I ..."

So much more than that, she simply needed her dad to be okay.

He stirred but didn't wake. Even if he did, he'd always be asleep in many ways.

The ache of already losing part of him throbbed with the heart monitors as tears fought a battle she was sure to lose if she didn't leave soon. She pressed a kiss to his forehead. "I love you, Daddy."

"He loves you too, you know. More than anything."

She turned toward Chase, leaning a brawny arm into the doorframe. Not caring how long he'd been there or how much he'd overheard, she barreled straight into her brother's embrace.

"The doc came back with the most recent X-ray. The swelling's gone down. Looks like he's going to make a full recovery."

"But what if he falls again? Or he's in his workshop with no one around and ..." Quinn gripped his sleeve. "I can't lose him."

"Hey." He lifted her back with a hand to each of her shoulders. "Look at me. Dad's not going anywhere. And you have nothing to prove, Quinn. You hear me?"

She hung her head to the floor and smiled sadly. "You're wrong." She rushed through the doorway and down the hall without giving him a chance to argue.

On the other side of the waiting room, Cooper caught her in his arms. "Hey, easy. Slow down."

When she trembled against him, he cradled her head under his chin and stroked her hair. She balled the back of his shirt in her fingers, wanting to lose herself in his tender affection. Wanting it to be real, to last.

He brought his lips to her ear and whispered, "It's okay not to be okay."

"But what if it's never okay?" She untied herself from his arms. "Some things are too broken to fix, Cooper. Even for you." Emotions beyond her control launched her out of the hospital to catch a cab. She needed to get away from there. Out of Littleton and away from a mistake she was only making worse every day she stayed.

Back at Cooper's lake house, she got straight in her Altima, cranked the engine, and swerved into reverse. No more than five feet out of his driveway, she slammed on the brakes. The intensity she'd been carrying—the guilt and expectations, the fear and hope—crashed into her and drove her tears past their longstanding barriers.

She folded her arms over the steering wheel and dropped her head to them, letting her emotions run freely for the first time since she'd moved away. But no matter how many tears she let escape, they couldn't tell her where in the world she was supposed to go from here.

In his kitchen, Cooper poured his third cup of coffee for the morning. If the caffeine didn't kick in soon, working on his dock was going to be more than a little interesting.

Quinn's bedroom door opened at the same time he entered the living room. Still in her clothes from yesterday, she lowered her cell to her side and stared at him.

"Morning." He tipped his head.

"My mom just called."

"Mm-hmm."

"Mm-hmm? Cooper, I can't believe you stayed up last night to fix my parents' back steps. After everything, I ... I don't know what to say."

He set his coffee on the end table and picked up his toolbox. "Nothing to say. It needed to be done, and it wasn't a big deal. Chase and I banged it out together." Grabbing his coffee again, he straightened. "Not everything's too broken to fix."

The slightest blush tinted her cheeks as she curled her disheveled hair over one shoulder. "I'm sorry about how I acted, the things I said. It's just ..." She heaved a breath and slowly lifted her eyes to his. "Thank you, Cooper. For all of it. You're really sweet." A half smile finally found her lips. "When you're not being ornery."

There was the girl he missed. "Sure you didn't used to blog on complimenting skills?"

Her long lashes fell the way they always did when he brought up her writing. Little did she know how attractive her unassuming beauty was.

Cooper swallowed the thought with another sip of coffee. "Brayden's already been up once, but he's napping again. Should be down for a while."

Quinn's pink cheeks drained of color. Wide-eyed, she clasped her forehead. "I'm so sorry. I wasn't thinking last night. I just ran out and—"

"There's nothing wrong with needing space, QT. Don't worry, Brayden and I did just fine. He even has on a fresh diaper, and no, I didn't call the neighbor."

Her brow shot up, and he couldn't help laughing. Catching her by surprise never got old.

When he picked up his toolbox, her gaze darted to the wall clock, and the momentary breach in tension retreated as quickly as it came.

Quinn fiddled with the corner of her blouse that'd come untucked from her skirt. "I'm sorry. I didn't mean to sleep in this late."

"You don't have to apologize for being human." He crossed the room and stopped in front of her. "Being tired isn't a weakness."

The bashful look on her face had him straining against the urge to hold her close again. That had clearly gotten him in enough trouble last night. He backed up instead.

"There's coffee in the kitchen." Once across the room, he peered over his shoulder. "I left you a sticky note. In case you miss it."

"Very funny." She visibly fought a smile. "Don't get too cozy outside. As soon as Brayden wakes up, I want to see those diaper changing skills firsthand."

A round of laughter led him onto the back deck. Wherever that girl ended up after this, she'd have no problem holding her own. That he was sure about.

The unsolicited realization that she'd be moving on soon slammed into him with the day's already-building humidity. This whole arrangement with Quinn had an expiration date from the beginning. The idea of it ending shouldn't be getting to him now.

He polished off his coffee, leaving his mug and any un-checked feelings on the patio table, and trekked down to the dock with his tools.

An hour into replacing the boards, Cooper wiped off the sweat running into his eyes with his sleeve and sat back on his heels. Loraine had been so good to watch Brayden last night. She'd make an awesome grandma. She and Mrs. Thompson both.

He tossed his hammer in his toolbox and buried the thought. Aside from both women having their hands full with their own family members, Brayden needed more than a doting grandma.

When an incoming call flashed his lawyer's name on his cell, Cooper reached for his phone and the hope that he'd found an answer Cooper wasn't thinking of. "Jim, what's the latest?"

"Like I advised you earlier, the courts are more likely to grant termination in order to facilitate adoption. You'd have a greater chance of the petition falling in your favor if you al-ready had an adoptive family lined up."

When Cooper didn't respond, his lawyer went on. "But if there are no family members you can ask, we can contact the Division of Health and Human Services and connect with a caseworker."

Pressure began to build between Cooper's eyes, a headache on the verge of following. He dragged a hand down his face. Though he already knew the answer, the question twisting inside him came out anyway. "Will I get to be in contact with the potential parents?"

Jim didn't respond at first. "Cooper, maybe you should take a little more time on this."

"Time for what?"

"To decide if you want to stay in Brayden's life or not."

The choice burned into him with the early afternoon sun. "I don't have time."

"Then you better make a decision soon." Another line beeped in the background. "I need to go, but give it some thought. We'll touch base when you're ready."

What if he never would be?

The minute he hung up, his brother's ringtone went off with the answer Cooper had fought from the beginning. Drew was the better man. Always had been. As hard as it was to admit it, Cooper knew Drew and Ti could give Brayden the nurturing upbringing he couldn't. More than that, he wouldn't trust anyone else. It was time to let go of his pride.

He rose, raked his damp hair off his face, and cleared all traces of emotion from his voice. "What happened to your surprise trip?"

"Hello to you too." Drew chuckled. "If it were a surprise, we'd show up without warning. Be glad I talked Ti into letting me actually plan the trip."

Grinning despite himself, Cooper lifted a foot to the bench and hunched over his knee. "I bet she loved that idea." His sister-in-law was the queen of spontaneity.

"I might've had to promise she could drive on the way home … and stop wherever the wind blew her." He laughed through the line, a sound Cooper missed more than he realized. But when his niece's sweet voice rang in the background, his heart begged him to end the call.

"Is Maddie coming too?" he managed to get out.

"You been swallowing too much lake water up there? I'm not about to stand in the way of my daughter getting to say goodbye to Uncle Coop."

His foot slid off the edge of the bench, his voice all but tanking into the water. "You guys really don't have to make the drive. I'll try to be back for Christmas. There's no need to—"

"Cooper. We're coming. Get over it."

He bit back a response and rotated his neck.

"No one likes goodbyes, all right, but that doesn't mean you avoid them."

Cooper shook his head. "You sound like Dad."

A pause passed between them. "The man usually knew what he was talking about."

Same way Drew did. They were so much alike. The ache of missing Dad wedged itself between his ribs. He would give all the money in the world to have his father here again. To hear his advice. Would he be disappointed in his choices again? He had to know Cooper was trying to do what was right for everyone.

He switched the phone to his opposite ear, strolled to the end of the dock, and peered across the horizon into a decision it was past time to make. "Listen, Drew, there's something I want to talk to you about when you're here."

"We'll be there Saturday." An audible smile filled the line. "So, don't be staying out late with Tabitha Friday night."

"Tabitha?"

"Tiffany, Tanya? Sorry, man, I lose track. Who are you dating right now?"

His stomach curled at the insinuation. "I haven't been on a date in weeks."

Again with the weighty pause.

"Really? So, who's the girl?"

Cooper strode back to his toolbox. "What girl? I just told you—"

"That you've fallen for someone."

He shoved his hammer to one side of the box. "And you talk to *me* about swallowing too much lake water. The salt there's obviously getting to you, hoss. I'm moving out of the country. I'm not looking for a relationship."

"Love doesn't usually care whether you're looking or not. Trust me."

Sunlight drilled into his neck and burned with irritation. He dragged the front of his shirt over his face while pushing off the box to stand. "We're not talking about you and Ti."

"No one said we were. Doesn't mean you can't fall in love too."

He let out a sardonic laugh. "What's the point?" He'd either end up hurting her or getting hurt. That's how it worked. "You're the family man, Drew. Not me. Why do you think I'm selling this place? I don't need anything tying me down."

It didn't matter that Drew was six hours away. Even over the phone, Cooper could feel the impact of the look he knew was on Drew's face right now.

"Then you better make sure the girl you're with knows that too."

His words steered Cooper's gaze up to the back of his house, and his thoughts to moments he'd spent with Quinn these last couple of weeks. Despite all the warning bells blaring in his head half the time, it was like logic disappeared when he was with her, overriding everything he'd tell himself only minutes prior.

A flicker of the *For Sale* sign out front flashed to mind. Steeling himself, he pulled his shoulders back. "There's nothing going on between us."

"Uh-huh." A weary exhale seeped through the line. "We'll see you Saturday, Coop."

If he made it till then.

He tossed his phone in his toolbox and matched Drew's heavy exhale.

He couldn't blame Quinn if she was reading more into his actions than what he had to offer. Honestly, he was too. Ignoring it wouldn't make it go away. Drew was right. He had to clear the air and make sure she knew where they stood before this next week ended in nothing but casualties.

CHAPTER SEVENTEEN

Games

A rich chocolaty aroma stopped Cooper by the nose the minute he stepped through the sliding door. His legs moved on their own, drawn under a spell. The sound of music, laughter, and clanging drew him around the doorway to the kitchen and into a scene he'd pay to have on film.

While Quinn was entranced in her usual baking-slash-dancing routine, Brayden sat in the middle of the floor, surrounded by pots and pans he must've dragged out of the bottom cabinet. He looked up from his makeshift instruments and expanded a chocolate-coated smile at Cooper. Shrieking in delight, he banged a wooden spoon over the back of the nearest pot.

"Nice beat, hoss." He rubbed Brayden's hair.

Quinn turned from the counter where she was using a spatula to smooth out a decadent looking mixture in an aluminum pan. "Oh good. I have something I need to talk to you about, but give me twelve minutes or so." She opened the oven and slid the pan inside. "And you can try these cheesecake brownies I'm testing out for Ginny's party first."

"Looks like you guys have been taste testing without me." Cooper sauntered across the tiles and wiped a dollop of batter from her bangs.

A coy smile spread flour smudges across her cheeks. "Maybe a little."

Loose wavy strands of hair falling from her ponytail fluttered under the vent, and Cooper simply stared. He'd come in to make sure they both knew where things stood between them, but all he could do was stand there like a speechless idiot.

"What's wrong?" The faintest collection of freckles wrinkled on her nose. "You look like something's on your mind."

More like tearing his mind apart. He pulled on his ear, downplaying. "Just surprised to see you okay with a big mess like this." A panoramic glance around the disheveled kitchen ended in a sideways smirk. "All without a single sticky note, no less. You're really taking this leap stuff seriously, aren't you? I'm not sure if I should be impressed or nervous."

The stiff grin she doled at him morphed into something almost devilish. "Making a mess can be kind of fun." She unrolled a bag of flour on the counter. "When someone *else* gets to clean it up." With the last word hanging in a laugh, Quinn flicked a handful of flour at his face.

Cooper didn't move except for a single blink. "You did not just start this."

"Oh, more than start." She grabbed the beaters and turned them on high speed, splattering chocolate batter across his face. "I just finished it, *hoss*."

Giggles erupted from the floor as Brayden waved his giant spoon in the air like a conductor. "'Gain. 'Gain."

Quinn backed up, her pinched lips barely restraining a laugh.

Nice try. Cooper lassoed her at the waist before she got more than five steps away. "You think that's funny, do you?" He whirled her around and wedged his head past her flailing hands to smear the chocolate from his face to hers. "It's on now, girl."

She squealed while reaching for more flour to dust his hair with.

He intercepted the bag, flung a scoop at her, and caught her wrists when she tried to retaliate. "You're right. It *is* fun when someone *else* is cleaning it up."

"Don't think you're getting out of this one, buddy." She squirmed harder, but Cooper backed her into the corner by the sink with no way to escape.

"I'm sorry, *who's* the one needing to get out of something?"

Quinn braced her palms against his chest. "You're lucky Brayden's here."

That made two of them. With her backed against the counter, bookended between his arms, his pulse jack rabbited past the adrenaline of horsing around into a sphere far more uncontrollable.

Emotion shifted in her eyes as she reached a thumb to a smudge of batter that'd ended up by the corner of his mouth. "The kitchen isn't the only thing that's a mess."

She had no idea, and he was only making it worse. But instead of listening to reason, a yearning he couldn't douse kept him in place. His pulse drowned out the music coming from her phone and hedged all logic back to the dock where he'd obviously left it.

On instinct, he let go of the counter and cupped the back of her neck. Breaths passed between them, each one anchoring him in eyes drawing him deeper. The sweet fragrance of chocolate mingling with honey consumed his senses until nothing else mattered.

Quinn held his gaze with earnest, and the spell that'd lured him in from the beginning overtook his heart. He lifted his free hand to her cheek and pressed in till his lips barely grazed hers.

She leaned back, looking torn between two opposing emotions. His heart sank. What did he expect? He'd crossed a line they both knew needed to stay intact.

The doorbell blared from the entryway, but he didn't move at first.

Quinn pulled the hair band out of what was left of her ponytail and stared at the grout between the tiles.

Good job, Anderson. Instead of clearing things up, he'd made them even more convoluted and uncomfortable. He kneaded his shoulder, stalling. If he found the right pressure point, maybe he'd unlock something half decent to say.

Not even close.

When the doorbell rang a second time, he shuffled backward. "I should go..." *Put an end to the awkwardness overtaking the room?* Stretching it even further instead, he made a clumsy about-face and almost smacked right into the edge of the open doorway. He tapped a hand to the trim. "Nice and sturdy."

Really? Forget awkward. How about pathetic?

Cringing, Cooper made a beeline to the hall and opened the front door.

On the other side, his realtor stood with a middle-aged couple beside him, looking like they'd just come from a country club. The blatant once-over they cast down the brownie batter left on Cooper's face joined Ray's mortified stare.

Cooper ran his hands across his cheeks and through his hair, as if there was any dignity left to salvage. "Ray, why didn't you tell me you were stopping by?"

His realtor's phony laugh filled the stagnant air hovering on the porch. He splayed an arm between the couple and Cooper. "Businessmen. We'd all be lost without our secretaries. Am I right?" He clamped a hand on Cooper's shoulder and pitched his suave smile at his clients. "Give us just a quick moment."

Ray steered him through the door. "Since when aren't you answering your phone? I left you two messages."

Cooper patted his empty pockets. Clearly, his head wasn't the only thing he'd lost recently. "I'm sorry. I got caught up in—"

The oven timer went off.

"I know exactly what you're caught up in." Ray's line of sight ricocheted down the hall and landed on Quinn, setting the pan of brownies on the counter. "This isn't the time for games, Cooper." He pointed to the closed door. "You have potential buyers expecting a tour today. Do you want to sell this place or not?"

"Of course I do."

"Then start acting like it." Ray adjusted his tie. "Listen, I want to help you out, but you've gotta decide whether you're leaving or staying."

A tendon on Cooper's neck flexed. "There's nothing to decide."

"You positive?" He flicked a glance at Quinn again. "'Cause that sure looks like a complication to me."

First Drew, now Ray. His phone call with his brother stormed to mind, sparking his frustration with people's perceptions of him and his lifestyle.

"She's the nanny, all right? There's nothing holding me back from leaving. Certainly not a temporary employee." The heated words came out louder than he meant them to. When he caught a flash of hurt move past Quinn's eyes, complication didn't come close to covering it.

His shoulders slumped. Releasing a hard breath, he started toward her without thinking, until Ray cut him off. Cooper glared at the hand on his shoulder.

Ray let go. "The ball's in your court. When you're ready to make a move, you call me." He backed up and showed himself out while Cooper just stood there. Lost.

What the heck was wrong with him?

Back in the kitchen, Quinn dabbed a washcloth to the corners of Brayden's chocolate mustache.

His heart tanked again. He wasn't playing games, but Ray was right about one thing. He had to start living like his choice was the one he truly wanted. No more getting side-tracked by feelings that didn't matter. No more giving in to spells. Just truth, facts. They'd be parting in a week. It was time he made it clear what that meant.

A knock at the door stopped him mid-step down the hall toward Quinn. Ray couldn't really think he'd cleaned everything up in two minutes.

He hustled back to the door, swung it open, and froze. Not Ray. "Livy?"

His good friend from Ocracoke raised her delicate shoulders. "Surprise."

After Livy had a chance to settle in and meet Quinn and Brayden, Cooper got cleaned up and then gave her a quick tour of his place. Out on his dock, he nudged his toolbox beside the bench to clear the path. "I still can't believe you drove up here without telling me."

"Correction. I tried to tell you. Someone isn't answering his phone very often these days." Livy tossed him a pointed look.

If she didn't know him better than most, he would've tried to dodge it. "Yeah, guess there's been a lot going on around here." He scratched his jaw, expecting her to dish out an intuitive comment about Quinn.

When it didn't come, he angled to catch her gaze. "I'm sorry for losing touch lately. It really is good to see you, Liv." He raised a suspicious brow. "But Drew didn't happen to put you up to coming, did he?"

Saying everything and nothing at the same time, an evasive smile clung to the sunlight as she turned toward the lake. "I can see why you like it here. It's beautiful."

He'd let her sidestep the question. For now. "It's nothing like the ocean, though."

"It has a different kind of charm. You can feel the peacefulness here, you know? The seclusion, serenity. It's almost… freeing." She watched an osprey glide across the water as though wishing she had wings of her own.

Cooper sidled up beside her at the end of the dock. "Something going on you wanna talk about?"

"Just feeling like I'm ready for a change, I guess." She slipped her hands into her back pockets and rocked on her feet. "I don't know, Coop. This past year, things have been… different. You're gone. Seeing Grandma Jo and Mr. Fiazza together is just plain weird." She laughed. "And Drew and Ti are adorable as ever."

"They're not making you sick, are they?" Grinning, Cooper grabbed a chisel from his toolbox along with a file.

"I've never seen Drew and Maddie so happy." Her expression turned wistful. "Or Ti, for that matter. They're so perfect together. It still amazes me—last summer, I mean. After everything they went through, now look at them."

"As Grandma Jo would say, things have a way—"

"Of working themselves out. Yeah, I know." Livy twisted her long blonde hair up and fanned her neck.

"I take it you don't believe that."

"Do you?" Tilting her head, she let her hair fall and studied him. Avoiding the question obviously didn't disable her ability to read between the lines. "Drew would take Brayden, you know. If you asked."

Cooper stopped filing and stared at his chisel, wishing the truth wasn't as sharp. "I know he would."

"But that doesn't mean it's your only choice." She twiddled her fingers, head down. "Being able to raise a son … It's a special gift not everyone's lucky enough to have." She looked up with eyes carrying the same brokenness in her voice. "I just don't want to see you throw something away out of fear. You'll end up regretting it all your life."

Instead of pressing it further, she left the comment hanging in the thick air and returned her focus to the backdrop surrounding them.

The same bird from earlier skimmed across the water in the opposite direction. This time, Cooper wouldn't have minded being the one with wings. Maybe in the sky, he'd find perspective. Or at least escape.

Livy steadied his fidgety hands. "I admire you, Coop. Always have. And I think opening the boat shop in honor of your dad is really courageous, I do." Squinting, she jabbed a pointer finger in his chest. "As long as you're not running away."

"From what?" He strode to the bench, probably sounding about as nonchalant as that blasted osprey, squawking for its mate.

If Livy's chuckle meant anything, she obviously agreed. "You know the problem with being good friends? I know when you're lying. Even to yourself."

Cooper peered at the house and heaved an exhale. "There's nothing to run from, Liv. Brayden needs a solid family, and Quinn's ..."

"Different?"

He chucked his tools on the bench. "I know what you're gonna say, all right? Everyone assumes I'm just playing games, but—"

"Actually, I was *going* to say, I think there's something there worth giving a chance." She crossed the boards and leaned a shoulder into his. "C'mon, Coop. It took me all of two minutes with you guys to see it's more than a fling."

"It doesn't matter."

"You're so infuriatingly daft sometimes, you know that? You're as bad as your brother." She punched him in the shoulder.

"Dang, GI Jane." He rubbed his arm. "When did Mr. Fiazza start tacking weights onto those trays you carry around all day?"

"You're lucky we're not in the restaurant, or I'd dump one of his specials right on your head. Maybe then you'd wise up."

He matched her sassy brow. "Wow. Looks like *someone's* been spending a little too much time with Grandma Jo lately."

"For your sake, I won't tell her you said that."

Their shared laugh drifted into the breeze careening along the dock, leaving a sense of gravity in its wake. Gentle laps against the shoreline hovered in the quiet.

Livy's arms came uncrossed with a sigh. "Listen, you know I'm the last person to give advice on life, especially relationships. So, all I'm going to say is this, and then I promise I'll leave it alone."

She turned him to face her. "I've watched you carry the weight of loss for a long time. You've covered it up for years, pretending to be the free, unattached bachelor without a care in the world. But I know you. You want more than that."

When Cooper's forehead scrunched in defense, her smile softened all the more. "You're a terrible liar, remember?"

Apparently, worse than he thought.

"All I'm saying is, look what Drew and Ti would be missing if they kept running instead of risking a second chance?" She squeezed his hand and turned toward the lake again. "Maybe Grandma Jo's right about things working themselves out, but I can't help wondering how much we mess things up by getting in our own way."

The deep-seated tenor in her voice held a palpable ache as familiar as his own. Cooper brought his longtime friend into a hug. "I'm glad you came, Liv."

His gaze roamed toward the house again, his thoughts toward the girl inside.

Livy must've noticed. "What are you waiting for?"

"The courage you seem to think I have."

"To tell her …?" She waved a hand, prompting.

With a deep inhale, Cooper raked his fingers through his hair. "The truth."

CHAPTER EIGHTEEN

Assumptions

Quinn pinned her cell to her ear while stretching two blinds apart in Brayden's room. If she weren't holding a cupcake in her other hand, she might've pulled it off with a little more stealth. Not that Cooper or Livy would notice her from out back. "She's been here four days, and I swear they've been glued at the hip since the minute she got here."

Ava took a sip of something. "I thought Cooper told you they were just friends."

"He did, but it's obvious they were more than that at one point. Did I tell you she used to be a model?"

"Only ten times."

"She worked a runway in London, Ava. She and Cooper's sister-in-law both."

"So."

"So?" Quinn let the blinds snap back together, paused to make sure she didn't wake Brayden from his nap, and lowered her voice to a whisper yell. "Those are the kind of women Cooper's used to being around. Drop-dead gorgeous models."

Then there was her—a country bumpkin, wearing decade-old clothes. Ugh. If she didn't need this promotion to prove to everyone that leaving four years ago wasn't for nothing, she would've left last night. But with Dad's health declining faster than she thought, she was running out of time. And now, with Brayden in the picture, could she really just walk away?

"What does it matter who Cooper hangs out with if you don't like him?"

"I ..."

"Mm-hmm."

Quinn peeled off the cupcake wrapper a corner at a time on her way into the living room. "What are you mm-hmming about? There's nothing mm-hmm worthy here."

"How many cupcakes did you just bake?"

"I don't know. A dozen or so." She bit into the chocolate top of one and tossed the wrapper into a trash can.

"Just *one* dozen?"

"Maybe two," she mumbled with her mouth full.

"Quinn."

"Fine. More like six. So what?"

Ava's laugh sang through the phone line and practically bounced off the high ceiling. "You just turned the guy's kitchen into its own bakery shop. What does that tell you?"

"Nothing. You know I bake when I'm stressed. Between planning Ginny's party and trying to get Cruella off my back, what do you expect?"

"Mm-hmm."

Quinn marched into the kitchen and the mess she hadn't cleaned up yet. Like she hadn't made a big enough mess of life already. She tore another piece of cupcake top off and stuffed it in her mouth.

"Girl, just admit you like Mr. Entrepreneur of the Year. What's the big deal?"

Quinn almost choked on a swallow. The big deal? Was she kidding? "I can't like him. When he finds out what I'm writing ..." She couldn't even finish the thought. Wiping crumbs from her hands, she straightened her spine. "It doesn't matter anyway because I don't like him. And trust me, the guy might be a flirt, but he made it perfectly clear I'm nothing but the nanny." The hurt of hearing him say that to his realtor flared inside her again.

"Mm-hmm."

Man, she hated when Ava kept doing that. "Have you been listening to anything I've been saying?"

"I'm not the one who isn't listening."

Quinn slumped against the counter. "What's that supposed to mean?"

A loaded laugh answered for her. "Give it a few more days, girl. You'll get it eventually."

The only thing she needed to get was Cooper Anderson out of her mind. If he lived unattached, so could she. That's what journalists did, right? She had to get back to focusing on the original piece, get it done, and move on. Plain and simple.

"No peach cobbler?" he said from behind her.

Quinn spun toward a ridiculously attractive half grin. Simple. Yeah, right.

He stood in the doorway with his thumbs in his belt loops. His T-shirt tugged slightly to the left, unveiling a sliver of tan skin at his waistline.

Get him out of her mind? Sure. Like she wouldn't be picturing *that* for the next umpteen days now.

The chocolate cupcake turned to cotton in her mouth.

"He's standing right there, isn't he?" Ava said in a singsong voice.

"Yes. No." Quinn scoured for a steady tone. "Let me call you back."

"I want details—"

She hung up, set her cell down before she dropped it, and leaned into the counter she was now gripping like a life jacket. *Just the nanny. Nothing more.*

"You ready for tonight?" he asked as though genuinely caring. He was as good of an actor as he was a businessman. Truthfully, she had no right to be mad at him for that. She'd spun her own web. It was past time to unravel it.

"About that." She released the counter and turned again. "I just want you to know I'm going to set my parents straight tonight. So, don't worry. You'll finally be off the hook."

He started toward her, face creased. "Are you sure tonight's the best time?"

She wasn't sure of anything anymore. Especially when he looked at her like that.

Right in front of her, the earnestness in his eyes overtook the kitchen until she couldn't breathe, let alone speak.

"Hey, I think Brayden's up." Livy circled the doorway, stopped, and swung a glance between them. "Oh. Sorry to interrupt."

"Not at all. I was just about to go check on Brayden anyway. A nanny's job is never done." Quinn folded up her apron and laid it beside an empty muffin pan.

The lines on Cooper's face deepened. "I can get him."

"No, it's fine. You have a guest." She maneuvered past him. "Besides, that's why I'm here, right?"

"QT."

She cringed at the immaturity and hurt seeping through every word, but she wasn't about to turn around. In fact, she didn't allow herself to slow down until it was time to head over to her parents' for the cookout.

With a blissfully ignorant Brayden on her hip, Quinn closed the front door and stopped halfway to Cooper's SUV, where he and Livy stood waiting. She looked from her own capris to the ones Livy had on. They might've been similar if Quinn had half the same curves to hold hers up. Seriously, who made a flowy tank top look like it must've cost a thousand dollars?

Cooper met her on the walkway and took Brayden. "I'll get him buckled in."

"You know, maybe you should stay. Keep Livy company. She did come all this way to see you. It'd be kind of rude to leave her."

"Why do you think she's coming with us?" Cooper flashed her a no-brainer stare.

"Oh, I don't think that's a good idea." She could hear her parents' questions already.

"Is your brother bringing a date?"

Quinn raised a brow. "Not that I know of."

"Good. Livy can fill in. If we're pretending, so can they. It'll be fine."

Pretending. Right. The reality of that truth should've lost its sting by now. Her focus wandered toward his model friend again.

"QT?"

A blink brought him back into focus. "Sorry. I'm, uh … I'm just gonna …" She motioned behind her to the house. "Can you give me a minute?"

Once behind the safety of the front door, she tapped her head against it. She'd be lucky if she passed off her brisk walk for anything other than looking like a toddler without training pants making a mad dash to the bathroom.

She shoved off the door, strode to the kitchen, and downed a cupcake in one minute flat. Pacing, she dug her phone from her pocket and pulled up the last grueling message she'd gotten from Cruella.

Nothing like a little motivation to get herself in gear.

"I'm a successful editor. An up-and-coming leader who's perfectly capable of being professional in any setting." The icing on her fingers glared in the sunlight. She licked it off. Okay, maybe not in *any* setting, but she could handle this. It was just another part to play.

After changing into a dainty sundress and flattering heels, Quinn held her head high while walking out this time.

Cooper turned and dropped his keys.

The more ground she gained, the more he seemed to lose. He reached for his keys without taking his eyes off her but fumbled them again a second later.

Livy bit back a grin. "You look great, Quinn." She slapped Cooper on the back. "As soon as Mr. Smooth, here, catches his breath, he'll tell you the same."

Still bent over, he glared at her, and a wave of self-consciousness rushed over Quinn with the hot breeze. Sure, maybe nice clothes gave her a boost in confidence, and maybe girls like Livy brought out irrational insecurities. But what was Quinn really trying to accomplish?

"You know what? Maybe I should change again. Give me two more minutes. Promise." An awkward turn brought her only two strides forward before Cooper slid in her path.

"Quinn, what's going on?"

"Nothing." She swept her gaze to the pavement, away from eyes capable of turning her brain to mush. "Just have a lot on my mind. You know going to my parents' always drives me a little crazy. Speaking of which, we need to run by the farmer's market to pick up some peaches on our way."

He adjusted his Tar Heels hat. "Maybe we should talk first."

"There's nothing to talk about." She met his eyes long enough to force a smile. "We should get going." Forget changing. At least in the car, she wouldn't have to face him head-on. Maybe then she'd have half a chance believing her pep talk. Not to mention Livy would be there as a buffer.

Of course, that hope went out the window once they made it to the farmer's market. Livy stayed in the car with Brayden while Cooper insisted on walking with Quinn.

She busied herself with feeling and smelling each peach before deciding which ones to get.

Beside her, Cooper picked up a plum and turned it around in his hands like a Magic 8 Ball he hoped would tell him what to say. "I didn't mean what I said to Ray. It's just that people's assumptions—"

"Are right?" Regretting the words, she looked away from the brokenness on his face and added another peach to her basket. "Cooper, you don't have to apologize. You've been up front with me from the beginning. Nothing's changed."

He followed her toward the register. "But that's just it. I—"

"Howdy." A young guy behind the counter dipped his straw hat at her. "My mama always tells me I'll find a girl as pretty as a peach one day, but I didn't expect it to be today."

"Dude, seriously?" Cooper edged beside her. "In case you didn't notice, hoss, we're together." The words weren't out more than two seconds before his face turned a shade darker than the plum he was still holding. "I mean, not *together* together. Just, you know, together."

Great, and now Quinn's cheeks were probably the same color too. Why was he making this so awkward?

The market worker looked like he was about to open his mouth, but Cooper grabbed the basket from Quinn and set it on the scale without giving him a chance. "How much do we owe you?"

While he pulled out his wallet, Quinn hurried back to the buffer zone in the car. Cooper got in a minute later, set the peaches between them, and shifted into drive without a word.

She risked a glance to the quiet seat beside her every few minutes. His tight jaw didn't override whatever was tugging at the corner of his eye. She sank in the leather seat, a sense of dread escalating with each mile that passed. Being honest with her parents tonight might end up giving her an ulcer, but that had to be better than what it would cost her to be honest with herself.

CHAPTER NINETEEN

Blind

The peaches rolled around as the tires dipped and bounced along the dirt driveway leading to her parents' house. Parked under an oak tree, Quinn grabbed the basket of fruit and stole a minute to breathe in her last chance at conjuring up any shred of self-confidence before opening the door.

Cooper was already getting Brayden out of his car seat when Quinn joined him and Livy outside. Instant sweat turned her dress into a suction cup against her skin. Classy.

Livy must've agreed. She swept her long hair to the side and wove it into a quick braid to keep it off her neck. "Did it get even hotter since we left your place?"

"It's always cooler by the lake," Quinn answered for Cooper, whose voice still seemed to be on strike.

Footsteps sounded behind them. "Olivia Hensley. Now there's a face I never expected to run into again."

They all turned toward Chase strolling up from his Chevy pickup with a wide-eyed expression that took less than thirty seconds for Livy to match.

"Wow, Chase Thompson. Talk about long time, no see."

They stood across from each other, looking almost star-struck.

Quinn ping-ponged a glance between them. "Um, you two know each other?"

"Knew." Chase twisted the tip of his cowboy boot in the dirt. "I mean, it's been a while."

"Chase went to college with my brother. Jack brought some of the guys home over a few of the breaks." Livy gave him a playful shove to the arm. "And they used to drive his *little sister* crazy."

"Hey, now, those pranks were all Jack's idea."

"Sure they were."

What was up with Chase's goofy grin?

Cooper moved Brayden to his opposite arm and reached for Quinn's free hand. "We should probably see if your mom needs any help."

Apparently, actor mode was back in full swing.

A little way ahead, he let go of her hand but held on to a growing grin.

"What?"

He raised both brows. "You didn't see the way your brother looked at Livy?"

"Like a sixteen-year-old groupie? Yeah, I saw. Guess he was pretty shocked."

"That was more than shock." Cooper nudged her with his elbow. "At least we don't have to worry about them pretending to be a couple."

"Because they know each other?"

He laughed. "You really are blind when it comes to guys, aren't you?"

Quinn stopped, peaches rolling in the basket. "Excuse me?"

"C'mon, QT. We can't go anywhere without guys hitting on you, and you don't even notice."

When she tilted her head in rebuttal, he cocked his right back. "The waiter at Watersview, Mr. Peaches at the market just now."

She waved him off. "Southern guys can't help being friendly. It's in their DNA." She headed toward the backyard again. "Just because you enjoy leading girls on, doesn't mean every guy on the planet does."

He drew her to a stop by the hand. "Is that what you think I'm doing?"

Gaze averted, she sighed. Did they have to have this conversation now? Here? "You are the way you are, Cooper. I knew that coming into this. I shouldn't have turned it into a big deal."

"The way I am." His jaw ticked in and out. "Well, I guess it's good everyone's assumptions are right, isn't it?" He strode past her.

"Cooper, I didn't mean ..."

Mama met them both around the corner of the house. She spread her arms out, smile equally as wide. "How's my favorite couple doing?"

"Fine," they both blurted out gruffly. So much for acting.

Her face scrunched. "Who peed in your cornflakes this morning?"

"Mama!"

She raised her palms and redirected her attention to Brayden. "Well, now, I hope my favorite munchkin is doing a little better than these two grumps." She scooped Brayden into a grandmotherly hug.

"Nanna."

She squealed with delight. "Ha. See that? He remembers me." She wiggled a finger in his belly. "What a smart boy you are. I bet you know what's going on between these two, don't you? You just tell Nanna all about it."

"Mama, really?"

"Oh, all right." She perched Brayden on her side and flashed a smile brimming with southern hospitality. "Cooper, honey, can I get you some sweet tea?"

"That'd be perfect, ma'am. Let me help you with the drinks."

She fanned her face. "You keep up that charm, young man, and you'll be needing to fetch me a pail of ice instead of a drink."

Oh, dear Lord. Eyes shut, Quinn pinched the bridge of her nose and shook her head. A little tug to the basket in her other hand drew her eyes open again.

Mama's peek inside turned into a quizzical stare. "Well, dang, sweetheart, did you bring the peaches and forget the cobbler?"

"Fruit has plenty of sugar by itself. It won't hurt us to eat them plain every now and then."

"Plain?" She spat out the word as if it were foreign.

Chase and Livy strolled up behind them. "I always wondered if you were adopted."

"Funny." Quinn shoved him, egging on his already-obnoxious laugh.

While he introduced Livy, Quinn aired out her dress. "Mama, don't you think we might want to eat dinner inside tonight? It's hotter than blue blazes out here." She almost tried to retract the random country phrase but didn't bother. No point in fighting a dying battle.

"A cookout inside? Honestly, sugar, you sure you're feeling all right?"

Just peachy.

"We can bring out the sprinklers." Chase lounged an arm around Quinn's shoulders. "I'm sure Mom can find something for you to wear."

"You so want to die, don't you?" she whispered at him.

Still laughing, he held out an arm to Livy and tipped his head at Quinn. "We're gonna go check in on Dad. You coming?"

Quinn trained her focus on the basket of peaches. "In a bit," she finally said. After seeing him laid up in the hospital, she wasn't quite ready for the emotions seeing him back home would stir.

As Chase and Livy moseyed over to the barn, Cooper motioned Mama toward the house. "Guess we should get those drinks."

"Make sure a few are spiked," Quinn said under her breath once they were out of earshot.

Mama reluctantly passed Brayden off to Aunt Loraine's hungry hands before disappearing inside, and Quinn simply shook her head. At least Brayden didn't have to question whether he was loved.

A few minutes after she reached the picnic table, Ginny meandered over and picked up one of the peaches.

Quinn smiled at her. "Cooper was right. You got some color the other day on the lake."

"Yeah, I guess."

She knew that tone. "Clay wasn't impressed, huh?"

"I don't know." Ginny shrugged. "He's cool one day, and then it's like I don't exist the next. Boys are so hard to read."

"Tell me about it," Quinn mumbled.

"Whatever. I'm over it." She dropped the peach back into the basket. "Besides, I'm gonna have the coolest band in North Carolina at my party, right? I mean, they're too old for me, obviously. But one of them might have a younger brother."

"Oh, hon, about that." Quinn traced her nail along the patterned tablecloth, stalling for the right way to say it. "I'm really sorry, but we can't afford that band. With it being last minute, too, it's just not going to work this time. But we'll figure something out," she added quickly. "It'll be—"

"Lame." Ginny tucked one arm into the other across her chest. "Driveshaft was going to *make* the party. Now, what am I supposed to tell my friends?"

"We'll make it just as fun without them. I promise, all your friends will have a great time."

"Yeah, whatever." She sulked toward her mom, probably to fill her in on how much Quinn had let her down.

"Anyone else I can upset today?" she said to the empty table. "I'm batting a thousand here." She bit into a peach while plopping onto the picnic bench.

The back screen door squeaked open. "Quinn Mary Beth, look what I found," Mama said like she was standing at the end of a rainbow.

Midway into another bite, Quinn froze. No telling what she'd see when she turned around. Repressed laughter from the barn steered her gaze toward Chase instead. Great, like she wasn't worried enough already. He pulled off a straight face and feigned a shrug like it was no big deal. Yeah, right.

Slowly, Quinn inched around on the bench. Her peach dropped into the dirt. "Oh my word."

Cooper came down the steps behind Mama. Carrying his drink, he seemed oblivious to the faded yellow bikini she was dangling in the air.

She stretched the bottoms between two fingers and stared like it was some mystifying contraption. "I think I *might* be able to fit this thing over one thigh, if I had my Spanx on."

Cooper looked from Quinn's mortified face to Mama, who'd switched to analyzing the bikini top next.

"Now, *this* I'd have no problem filling. You sure you used to wear this, sugar?"

When Quinn begged the ground to open up and swallow her whole, Mama shot her an understanding look. "Don't you worry yourself, dear. I bet I have some extra stuffing in my sewing kit. We'll make it work."

If the blood weren't already draining from her face, she would've blushed. A mounting geyser rocketed her up from her seat instead. "What are you doing going through my old stuff?"

"No need to get your knickers all in a knot. You were the one complaining about how hot it is. And it's not like everyone here hasn't seen you in a bathing suit before. Except maybe this boy of yours, and I'm sure he won't mind," she added with a wink.

Shoot me now.

Quinn stormed over and swiped the ancient bikini from her. "He's not a boy, Mama. He's a grown man who's probably dated swimsuit models. He doesn't need to see some dry rotted suit on a girl who can't even fill it out."

In case her mom's blank stare didn't tell her what was coming, the added pinch to her arm left little doubt. Without a word, she dragged Quinn inside, down the hall, and into her old bedroom. She plopped her down at the paint-chipped vanity and stood behind her like she'd done a thousand times while Quinn was growing up.

"Mama, I'm too old for this."

"You're never too old for the truth." She motioned to the mirror. "Go on, now, before I have to tan your hide."

Sighing, Quinn faced her reflection and began the words of affirmation Mama had ingrained in her since she was old enough to remember. "I'm not only loved, I'm cherished. I'm unique, made with a purpose only I can fulfill. Equipped with hands to accomplish it, gifted with a voice to share it, and strengthened with courage to live it. This—"

"Is my story," Mama joined in at the end as she always did.

She gave Quinn's shoulders a good squeeze. "I better never hear you saying nothing different neither. None of this, 'I'm not good enough' nonsense. You hear me?"

"Yes, ma'am."

She'd spent most of her life wanting to live up to those words. To make both her parents proud. But at the rate things were going with this feature, she might lose her chance of advancing—maybe even lose her job altogether—and then what? Without being able to give them the family they wanted for her, becoming executive editor was her last shot.

Mama gave a firm nod. "Okay, then. Now that that's settled, your *boy's* awaiting."

Quinn set her hand over her mom's before she could walk away. "Wait. There's something I need to tell you." Since she was on a roll today, she might as well keep it going.

Staring at her lap, she toyed with her sundress's rope belt. "Cooper's not *my boy*. He's not my anything. That day at the parlor, he was just trying to make me feel less like a loser in front of Brian and Cindy Mae. Then you and Aunt Loraine showed up, and it kind of got out of hand." She lifted her eyes to her mom's in the mirror. "I'm sorry for letting you think we were a real couple."

"Don't be silly, sugar. That young man's more real than all your book boyfriends, now isn't he?"

Quinn's hands fell to her lap. "You knew about that?"

"Don't look at me like I'm as lost as last year's Easter egg. Of course I knew. I told you I may be old, but I'm not blind. What I don't know is why you felt like you had to tell your daddy and me you were dating someone all those years when you weren't."

"C'mon, Mama. You know neither one of you will rest until you get me hitched." She rose and ambled over to the tie on her bedpost. "I guess I thought it'd be easier than seeing you both so disappointed. I thought maybe Dad would finally ..."

"Oh, sweetie, come here." She drew Quinn into a hug. "You've been away from home too long if you think your dad and I could be anything but proud of our little girl."

She might change her mind when the rest of the truth came out about what she was really doing back in Littleton. Everyone would. Especially Cooper.

CHAPTER TWENTY

Unspoken

Cooper took one look at the basket of peaches on the table and scoured the yard for a safer bet. He strolled up to Quinn's grandpa, who seemed to be manning an empty grill. "How we doing today?"

"Less drafty." Her grandpa whacked him in the chest with the back of his hand and motioned to his zipper, which Cooper ardently avoided veering his focus to at all costs. "Eh? You remember?"

"Sure do." Unfortunately. He took a swig of his sweet tea and stared aimlessly until his line of sight grazed across something stuck in her grandpa's overgrown mustache. Cooper rubbed his chin. "You, uh, have a little something ..."

He followed Cooper's finger toward a crumb caught in his 'stache. He plucked it out, sniffed it, and popped it in his mouth. "Paula's fried okra. The best you'll ever have."

"Uh-huh." Cooper took another sip of tea and eyed her grandpa's grease-covered fingers. "Thanks for the heads-up. I'll remember to avoid that dish at dinner." No doubt, he'd blame the raccoons again for rummaging through the food while no one was looking.

Her grandpa smiled widely, clearly missing the joke along with a handful of teeth.

"I should probably go check on Brayden." Cooper clapped him on the shoulder. "Good talking with ya."

Halfway across the yard to the picnic table, Cooper peered behind him toward the sound of her grandpa's delayed reaction.

"Avoid that dish," he mimicked through a raspy laugh. "You're a fast one, son."

Not fast enough, or he wouldn't be left speechless half the time he was around Quinn. Though, maybe it was better that way. Less chance of digging his hole any deeper.

When he caught Brayden stretching out his arms toward him, his chest constricted without warning.

"Nothing beats a boy loving his daddy," Loraine said as Brayden wiggled from her arms into Cooper's.

He latched on to the rim of Cooper's hat and smiled like he was in the safest place in the world.

Seeing his own eyes looking back at him was hard enough. Seeing Brayden trust him, even love him? It was too much, too raw. His throat tensed until the grip matched the unrelenting grasp Brayden had on his hat.

Ginny sauntered by the table. Brayden took one look at her long brown hair and reached for her instead.

"Oh, I see how it is." Laughing, Cooper held him out for Quinn's cousin. "Only loved till someone who smells better comes along."

"A boy after your own heart, huh?" Loraine dished a knowing grin at him while Ginny and Brayden made their way toward the sprinkler.

Cooper stuffed his hands in his front pockets. "Meaning?" Like he had to ask. He already knew what most people thought of him and his perceived lifestyle.

"Even out in the country, people hear things, darlin'."

His jaw ticked. "You can't believe everything you hear."

"Ain't that the truth." She dragged the basket of peaches across the table and brought one to her nose. "I prefer to believe what I see."

"And what's that?"

"A guy lucky to have found a girl to change his mind."

Cooper pulled his hands free and leaned one on the table. Why he was following this loaded conversation, he had no idea, but the responses came out on their own. "Change his mind about what?"

Loraine rose and patted the top of his hand. "Everything."

Before Cooper's defiant jaw could draw him farther down this dead-end road, Nurse Murphy sailed around the corner of the house with a stack of foil-wrapped trays.

"Let me help you with those." He took the top two and set them on the table.

"Thanks." She wiped her brow with her sleeve.

"You all right, dear?" Loraine asked.

"Fine. Long day is all."

"Your mama?"

Head down, Nurse Murphy re-secured the foil that'd come loose on a corner of one of the dishes. "The hurtful words ... I know it's not really her saying them, but sometimes ..." She swallowed.

A crash from inside the house whipped all their attention toward the kitchen window. "Loraine? I could use a hand," Mrs. Thompson called through the screen.

Loraine brandished a teasing expression toward them. "She'd never survive without me." She squeezed Nurse Murphy's arm and smiled warmly before trekking off to the kitchen toward whatever catastrophe there was to clean up after.

Nurse Murphy set a thatched bag on the bench and withdrew a group of serving utensils. "My mom has Alzheimer's," she said in response to Cooper's unspoken question.

"I'm so sorry." He cast a glance behind him toward the barn. "It must be hard coming here to work with Mr. Thompson too."

"Actually, it helps." She laid a wooden serving spoon across each of the covered trays. "This family gives me a lot of strength. All the families I work with do. It's one of the reasons I switched from Cardiac Care to Geriatrics."

Cooper picked up his glass of tea. "To better help your mom?"

"In a way." She leaned against the table edge. "When I was in nursing school, I fell in love with this one blog. I don't know, maybe I just needed some distraction from all the pressure of school, but it became a little safe haven for me. A reminder of what was important."

Staring off into the field opposite them, she must've been peering into memories vivid enough to relive. "Every week, the author shared a recipe along with the funniest family stories." She laughed. "I don't know who they were, but I tell ya what. They sounded almost as entertaining as this bunch. The blog even had 'crazy' in the title."

Cooper cut a glance at her, perception zeroing in on that last part. She didn't mean …

Her amusement gave way to a sense of gravity, reverence. "But no matter how crazy things got, they always came back to each other. They never lost sight of the importance of taking care of family, you know? Of nurturing those bonds, no matter how much circumstances strain them sometimes." She straightened. "I realized that was something worth dedicating my life to."

"Sounds like that author made a real impact on you."

Her eyes warmed as she turned toward the table and tapped the dish closest to her. "Taught me a few good recipes too."

"I'm sure she did." Cooper couldn't help grinning.

"It's too bad she stayed anonymous. It would've been nice to tell her the difference she made."

The back screen door squeaked open from across the yard. Quinn shuffled down the steps, carrying a small ceramic bowl. She stopped at the sight of him taking her in but then continued slow strides toward them.

Cooper looked at Nurse Murphy. "Maybe you'll still get the chance to thank her one day."

"I hope so." After greeting Quinn, she gestured toward the house. "I better go see if your mom needs any more help."

"Enter at your own risk," Quinn called after her.

Left alone, a round of uncomfortable silence settled between them.

She set the bowl down and nodded to the glazed topping inside it. "Can't have peaches unless they're drizzled in sugar."

"Lost that battle, huh?"

"Always do."

"Yet you never give up." He returned his glass to the table. "Real trooper, right there."

A laugh snuck through her lips.

Man, that smile. He ran his tongue against the inside of his cheek as if that would keep him from reciprocating. He should know better. He obviously couldn't stay upset with her if he tried.

"It's kind of hard to be a trooper when I'm acting like an angsty teenager." Her smile waned. "I'm really sorry, Cooper. Truth is, Livy showing up sort of brought out some insecurities I thought I'd laid to rest a long time ago."

He stared at her. "Livy?"

She pitched a brow at him. "And you say *I'm* blind."

That's what all this was about? Amusement dismantled any attempt to keep a straight face. He edged in. "You weren't jealous, were you?"

She rolled her eyes. "Don't let it go to your head."

"Oh, I think it's too late for that." Giving his smile free reign, he inched a step closer.

"Yeah, well, don't hold your breath. Apparently, I'm pretty good at dishing out insults too." Though pained, her smile held a smidge of humor in it. "A girl of many talents. What can I say."

"Mm." He looked her up and down. "Too bad wrestling isn't one of those talents." He swooped her over his shoulder before she could respond.

Caught between laughing and yelling, Quinn fought to escape. He secured her by the legs before he ended up with an unpleasant knee jab and started for the sprinkler.

"If you don't want to die, you better put me down."

"You're the one who said you needed to cool off, right?"

She slapped his back. "Don't you dare."

The sight of Mr. Thompson coming out of the barn jerked him to a stop. Quinn slid down the front of him, but Cooper grabbed her waist before she fell to the grass. Just centimeters away, she lifted her fiercely gorgeous eyes at him. And for an isolated second, he forgot where he was. Along with who was watching.

The minute it reregistered, he flung his hands free from Quinn's waist like she had the plague. *Way to make it worse, Coop.*

Each step bringing her father toward them seemed to echo across the open yard.

Or maybe that was just his pulse. Cooper leveled his shoulders and nodded. "Mr. Thompson. Good to see you."

Without releasing Cooper from an intense gaze, he wiped his hands on a faded rag.

Nothing like being transported back to high school on prom night.

Quinn slipped through the invisible tension line between them and wrapped her arms around her dad's neck. "Are you sure you should be back in your workshop so soon after the hospital?"

"Hospital?" He waved it off. "I haven't been in a hospital for over fifteen years."

Quinn stepped back slowly. "No, Daddy. You fell off the back steps and had to spend the night at Community Memorial. Don't you remember?" She searched his eyes. If she was looking for humor, she would've been disappointed.

A pained sense of confusion streaked his face as though he were seeing the effects of his illness reflected in his daughter's eyes. "Is that so?" He toyed with his rag. "Well, I'm just fine now, aren't I? But I could use a hand on something before dinner." He redirected his attention to Cooper. "Son?"

He shot an uncertain glance at Quinn, who mouthed, "Trooper."

No getting out of it now.

With a little more trepidation than he wanted anyone to sense, he followed Mr. Thompson over to the barn. Chase and Livy passed them on their way out.

Cooper made a face at him. "Get lost?"

"Nope." Chase flaunted a grin right back.

Livy ignored them both. "You have a fantastic shop, Mr. Thompson."

"Thank you …"

"Livy," she reminded him.

Chase landed a hand to the top of his shoulder. "Dinner should be about ready, Pops."

"We'll be along in a minute." He shuffled toward the back of the barn.

Cooper sent off one last silent flare for intervention, which Chase obviously found as amusing as Quinn had.

Chase patted him on the back. "Whatever he gives you, just keep sanding it," he whispered.

"Wait, what?" What the heck did that mean?

Instead of an answer, a laugh trailed them as they rounded the barn door and disappeared into the yard.

So much for being bros. Cooper turned to find Mr. Thompson had already reached the far end of an otherwise mostly empty barn. He hustled to meet up with him.

At a workbench, her dad turned the rod handle on a mechanical vise 'round and 'round.

Cooper surveyed the spread of tools—some old and well scuffed, others still carrying the shine of little use. "This is a great setup you have here, sir."

The slow squeak of the vise's jaw opening served as the only response.

Did Mr. Thompson forget he was there? Based on what he'd seen so far, his coherence seemed to come and go.

Cooper ran a finger along the beveled edges of a carved rail slat that looked halfway finished. Maybe he should let himself out, give her dad some time alone doing what he loved. This was obviously a special place for him.

He turned, ready to bail. But instead of a clear escape route, a scrap of sandpaper waved in his path.

Mr. Thompson kept his hand out, waiting.

Cooper looked from the paper to the rail he'd been admiring. Just keep sanding, right. He took the paper from him and started in on the slat.

"You know what I like about wood?" Mr. Thompson's low, calm voice reverberated throughout the quiet barn.

Cooper faced him. "What's that, sir?"

He picked up a small block of wood, maple from the looks of it, and gave it a rap with his knuckle. "It's sturdy, durable." He set it in the vise and began rotating the handle again until the jaws clamped securely around it. "But just 'cause it can handle pressure doesn't mean it can't break." The squeaky rod strained as Mr. Thompson circled it yet another time.

Good thing he had a block of wood in that jaw instead of Cooper's hand. Though, something gave him the impression he wouldn't have minded demonstrating on the latter.

When he looked up, Mr. Thompson stood right in front of him. Cooper tried not to flinch as he helped him sand the rail along the grains of wood in slow, graceful movements.

"Even with the right tools, nurturing wood takes care and patience. You have to respect its natural beauty while drawing out its potential to build something that'll last a lifetime."

Mr. Thompson returned to his workbench and loosened the vise. "But you have to be careful." He removed the block, gave it to Cooper, and tapped a weathered palm over his hand. "Without boundaries, that pressure can leave marks forever."

Cooper stroked a fingertip over the grooves burrowed into the grains by the vise's clamp. When he met Mr. Thompson's gray eyes, there was no second-guessing his lucidity. Same way there was no questioning what they were really talking about here.

Loraine obviously wasn't the only one who saw things. Even someone only half cognizant could see Cooper would eventually hurt Quinn in the end.

Indignation flared until a slow burn eroded behind the truth left in its place. Resenting assumptions didn't make them wrong.

Before he could summon a response, a shriek from outside shuddered into the barn. Cooper dropped the wood without thinking. *Quinn.*

CHAPTER TWENTY-ONE

Boundary

Cooper didn't hesitate. He sprinted. Over by the sprinkler, Quinn had Brayden swaddled in her arms. The look on her face lodged his heart in his throat.

Ginny stood beside them, her skin a pale version of her new tan. "I only looked away for a second," she eked out when he approached.

A wide scratch on Brayden's forehead began to swell. Cooper ran a hand over his son's hair, but Brayden pushed against Quinn's chest, not wanting to be comforted by either of them. With his face as red as the bricks he'd obviously scraped it on, he wailed as if he'd fallen onto a bed of nails instead.

"Shh. It's okay, baby." Quinn bobbed him in her arms while walking back and forth, but inconsolable sobs kept him squirming restlessly to break free. "Brayden, calm down. We're both here. Everything's all right."

The harder she tried to comfort him, the louder he cried.

Not knowing what else to do, Cooper set a hand on Ginny's shoulder and gave it a reassuring squeeze. The last thing she needed was to feel guilty over an accident.

"Give him here." Loraine came charging up to the scene with outstretched arms.

"He doesn't want anyone."

As if Loraine would listen. She scooped him up, turned him sideways till he was cozied against her middle, and rocked him from side to side. "That's it, dear. Just relax now. Aunt Loraine's got you."

His sobs gradually tapered to a slow fizzle.

The rest of Quinn's family had already flocked over to see what was going on while Loraine sent Ginny inside for a wet washcloth.

When Ginny returned, Loraine smoothed back Brayden's hair and set the cloth to the bump on his head. "There we go, sweetie. You're all right."

Cooper looked from Quinn, who was cradling her empty arms, back to Loraine. "Thank you. That was kind of amazing. How'd you know what to do?"

She fluttered a hand at him. "Don't you worry yourself about that, dear. Some things only a mama knows how to do."

The second the words left her mouth, she looked like she would've given her right arm to take them back. Her eyes filled with regret as she reached for Quinn. "Oh, honey, I'm so sorry. I didn't mean ..."

Cooper's gaze bounced from person to person in their cramped semi-circle, all bearing expressions of visible discomfort. Clearly, he was missing something. "Didn't mean what?"

"Nothing." Quinn's arms came undone, and her stoic expression shattered down her face like broken glass. "Excuse me." She pushed through the line of family members and jogged to the back door.

Cooper started after her. "Quinn?"

Mrs. Thompson stopped him by the arm. "Let it be."

"I'm sorry. I can't." He might not know what was going on, but one thing he was sure of. The hurt in Quinn's eyes drove his feet past any reason to stay behind.

In the house, he hurried down the hall, not slowing until he reached her old bedroom. Cautious yet resolute strides led him around the open doorway.

Quinn stood in the corner by a bedpost with her back facing him.

The oak floorboards creaked under his footsteps. Startling, she wiped her cheeks. He'd been in such a hurry to get to her, he hadn't thought of what to say.

After a long moment, she traced her fingers down a blue and silver textured tie hanging from the top of the post. "It's sharp, isn't it?" she said randomly. "A present from my dad on my sixteenth birthday."

Despite the gravity of the moment, Cooper cracked a grin. "It'd look good on you."

A soft laugh sent a glance over her shoulder. "It's not for me, smart aleck."

"But you just said..."

"It was for my future husband—the guy Dad's been praying for since before I was born." She straightened the loose knot. "It was supposed to be a reminder for me to pray for him too. For our family, the life we'd build together." The tie slid through her hands. "Turns out Dad and I both lost a lot of time on our knees for nothing."

"Quinn—"

"We should go." She turned, resolution once again coloring over the hidden aches trapped in her eyes. She passed him in the doorway. As much as he wanted to stop her, he sensed he shouldn't.

By the time he reached the kitchen, Quinn had already gotten in the car. Chase came through the back door with Brayden in his arms. "You guys go on. I'll take Livy home."

"Thanks." Cooper took Brayden and clasped Chase's hand. "Tell your folks I'm sorry for leaving so abruptly."

"Don't worry about it, man. They understand."

Good thing someone did.

Cooper half hoped he'd figured it out on the way home. But when Quinn stared out the passenger window the entire ride, the chance of talking faded with the sunlight.

Maybe her mom was right about letting it be for now. Considering Quinn went straight to her room when they got home, she obviously agreed.

Cooper took his time getting Brayden down by extending their bedtime reading, maybe more for himself than for Brayden. That fall would leave a mark on his head for a few days, but like most kids, his resilience had already relegated the memory to a thing of the past. Too bad adults couldn't do the same with their own pain.

He kissed Brayden good night, eased the door closed, and started down the hall to the opposite end. But when he noticed the light coming from Quinn's room, he couldn't bring himself to pass. He tapped a knuckle to the unclosed door and cracked it open far enough to see if she was okay.

Still in her sundress, Quinn sat on the bed with a pillow buried in her lap.

He dropped his hat on the dresser and sat beside her, not sure what to say or if she wanted him to say anything at all. His mind wandered back to the way Loraine's comment had driven her to the tie in her room and the disappointment in what she thought she'd missed out on.

The veins in Cooper's hands tightened. "If this is about Brian—"

"It's about me, and don't worry, I feel nothing. Because a woman who isn't whole couldn't possibly feel anything, right?"

The dejection in her voice splintered through his chest. "Not whole? What are you talking about?"

She coiled a stray thread from the hem of her pillowcase around her finger—one direction, then the other—until she finally looked up. The entire lake couldn't hold the amount of grief in her eyes. "I can't have kids, Cooper."

Her words almost knocked the wind from him. "I don't understand."

"Neither do I." She let the thread unfurl, but the resonance of bitterness coiled even tighter. "I started having these symptoms a few months after Brian and I got engaged. I knew something was wrong, but I wouldn't let myself think the worst, even after I got the results."

She compressed the pillow to her stomach as though trying to cauterize a fresh wound. "I begged my doctor to give me more options, prayed for another solution. But there was only one."

The yearning to comfort her overrode the urge to brace himself for whatever she was about to say. He stretched a hand over hers and smoothed his thumb across her skin.

"I had a hysterectomy two months later." She withdrew and caged in her shame behind her long lashes. "I didn't want to. I swear, I searched for an alternative, but I ..." Her voice broke, and so did his heart.

Cooper took her hand again. When she didn't retreat this time, he brought it to his lap and cradled it in both of his. "Quinn."

"I know I act like I don't want this life, but you're right. I do." Sorrow bled down her cheeks. "Growing up, it's all I ever wanted: a family home like my parents have, a heritage my children could build on. I can't offer anyone that now."

"That's not true."

A broken smile looked up at him. "You haven't lived here long, Cooper. Family is everything. If you can't have kids, you're ..."

The look on his face must've told her not to finish that insane thought. This wasn't the Stone Age.

Their conversation about Loraine and her husband leaving her soared to mind, chased by the image of Brian standing beside his pregnant wife.

Was that why they broke up? So he could go find someone who could bear his children? Seriously, what century were they in? The tendons in Cooper's arms pulsed. What a world-class jerk. If the loser were half a real man, he'd see how amazing Quinn was with kids and what a great mom she'd make if given the chance. There were other options.

His heart raced a dangerous mix of emotions.

She wiped her cheek. "It's one of those things that never crosses your mind growing up."

The soft, vulnerable tenor in her voice shut out everything else around them. "You always think you'll have a choice. That you can start a family whenever you want."

A slow blink lifted her eyes toward his. "No one prepares you how to feel when you find out you failed at being a woman."

Sitting with her and hearing the damage in her heart poured out so vulnerably, Cooper could hardly breathe for how much he wanted to take her hurt away and make her see she was more of a woman than any girl he'd ever met.

Heart pounding, he stood and pulled her to her feet.

"What are you doing?"

"Getting you off the bed."

The skin between her eyes wrinkled. "I see that. Why?"

"Because." His fingertips glided over her cheek, his eyes deep and earnest. "If I kiss you on that bed, I won't be able to leave."

Her breath quickened under his touch. He leaned in, never releasing her gaze, until his lips brushed hers. He'd imagined kissing her more times than he should admit. But the moment her mouth softened against his, an all-consuming desire to love her overtook every part of him.

Breath, time—lost. Heartbeats replaced seconds. His free hand slid around her waistline to her back and brought her tighter.

Secured against him, Quinn stretched her hand up his chest and into the hair behind his ear. The more she gave herself to him, the deeper he lost himself in all she was, all he wanted to share with her. Until fragmented conversations sprang to mind with clear reminders this was a mistake.

"She's more fragile than she lets on."

"Without boundaries, that pressure can leave marks forever."

He'd wanted to help her heal, but here he was, proving her parents right that he would hurt her.

A feather-soft moan separated his lips from hers and ignited short, shallow breaths in the space between them. At least one of them could breathe.

Eyes closed, Cooper covered her hand with his and drew her wrist to his lips. For what felt like an indefinite amount of time, he held it there, waiting for the strength to let go.

"Trust me, you haven't come close to failing." Without saying anything else, he set her palm on his chest, framed her cheeks in his hands, and kissed her once more with the kind of tenderness she deserved from a guy who'd treat her right. "Good night, Quinn."

Her eyes seemed to beg for an explanation, but he couldn't answer. Couldn't stay.

He hesitated at the door for another second before leaving her behind a boundary he knew needed to be in place. For both their sakes.

Three steps down the hall, he stopped and turned right back around. With one hand on the knob and the other braced against the trim, Cooper released a tense breath. It was too late to take back that kiss. And honestly? He didn't want to. But this wasn't about him or his selfishness.

Shadows flickered underneath the door. The knob turned but then stopped, and everything in him wanted her to open it so he could go back inside, tell her what he felt.

Yielding to resolve instead, he rested his forehead to the door and prayed his heart had the courage to surrender what wasn't his to keep.

CHAPTER TWENTY-TWO

Family

Quinn dabbed concealer under her eyes and examined her reflection in the bathroom mirror. Between a hot shower and fresh makeup, she should at least somewhat be able to hide the remnants of last night's fiasco. Yeah, because she was so great at keeping things to herself. Right.

Her shoulders caved. What was she thinking, breaking down and spilling her guts in front of Cooper? Of course Mr. Fix It would kiss her after she told him she felt less than a whole woman, and sure, it had more than worked. But what now? How were they supposed to keep things from being completely awkward after crossing that line?

Then again, it probably wouldn't even faze him. Who knew how many girls he'd shared casual kisses with. She was the one who would end up acting like a schoolgirl around him now if she didn't find a way to muster up a fraction of his laid-back smoothness.

She tightened the towel across her torso, flipped her hair over, and dried it with a second towel. When she straightened, a rush of feelings from that kiss flooded over her again as it'd done for most of the night.

Yep, definitely a schoolgirl. But who could blame her? Cooper's movement was saturated with charisma and confidence—the kind she could give herself to, get lost in. His touch had been even more captivating than she'd imagined it would be. And when he'd kissed her the second time with a tenderness that surpassed the first, she might as well have seeped through the floorboards.

If she could've talked, she would've replied. If she could've moved, she'd have followed him through that door. Paralyzed on both accounts, she'd simply stood there with her breath and heart tangled in her ribs.

The alarm on her cell roared from the bathroom counter. Flinching, Quinn knocked her makeup bag onto the floor and almost lost her towel in a scramble to grab the phone. *Way to be smooth.* She silenced the alarm but couldn't ignore the reminder that she had to finish her feature no later than tomorrow, or everything she'd fought for could be over.

The moment she set her cell down, the doorbell rang. Quinn held her breath. It'd taken her almost an hour to get Brayden down for a nap this morning. If that bell woke him up, she'd make whoever it was deal with his cranky tantrum.

She poked her head through the bathroom door. "Cooper," she called.

No answer.

The doorbell echoed through the house a second time. She darted a glance to Brayden's closed door. "Cooper," she called again.

Still answerless, she traded her towel for the oversized bathrobe hooked behind the door, practically skidded down the hall, and whirled open the front door before the stupid bell could sound yet a third time.

A guy resembling Cooper stood on the porch with an arm raised, about to knock. Beside him, another model lookalike in a fringe-edged dress and trilby hat removed her sunglasses.

Panic rumbled in the bottom of Quinn's stomach. This had to be Drew and Ti. Running out of the shower, in Cooper's bathrobe no less, wasn't exactly how she'd envisioned meeting his brother and sister-in-law.

She clutched the top of the robe together at her neck. "I'm so sorry. I didn't realize you were coming this morning. I would've ..." What? Hightailed it out of here on Cooper's WaveRunner? She looked behind her, giving it serious consideration.

Drew ran a hand through his hair like Cooper often did. "Don't worry. We're used to it."

Ti whacked him in the chest with the back of her hand. While he shot her a what-was-that-for stare, she smiled a look of apology at Quinn. "What my husband meant to say is, it's good to meet you."

Right. A dime a dozen. That's what they must've thought she was. Just another girl on the list of casual relationships Cooper was so well-known for, even his family expected it. A flush of competing emotions climbed her face.

The couple exchanged an uncertain glance like they weren't sure whether to invite themselves in or keep standing there, waiting for her to gain her wits about her.

"Is Coop around?" Drew finally asked.

"Um, actually, I'm not sure where—"

"You guys are early." Cooper's voice sailed around the corner of the house right before he did.

The door to the Jeep in the driveway opened, and a preteen girl hopped out. "Uncle Coop!"

He knelt in time to catch an incoming hug, swooped her off the ground, and spun her around. "Man, I've missed you, Freckles."

It only took a single look at the two of them caught up in each other's arms for the walls Quinn had just resurrected around her heart to crumble to dust.

When Maddie's feet touched the grass again, her face glowed. "I brought my paddle board."

"I see that." He peered from the Jeep's roof rack to the open windows. "No Jasper?"

She frowned. "I wanted to bring him, but someone had to stay and mediate between Grandma Jo and Mr. Fiazza."

Cooper laughed while rustling the top of her hair. "No doubt about that. It's probably a good thing. Apparently, we have a stray cat wandering around here."

Her eyes widened. "Really?"

"Don't get too excited."

"You know better than that," Drew said from the porch. "She probably already has it named."

"Dad."

Cooper tossed an arm around his niece and strolled up to the porch to greet the rest of them. "What happened to no surprises?"

Ti gave him a hug. "Sorry, that was my fault. I might've gotten a little foot heavy with the gas pedal."

"New Yorker," Drew mouthed to Quinn.

Her shoulders relaxed until she met an open and curious expression from Maddie. A breeze of self-consciousness rippled across her face. She pointed into the house. "Excuse me."

Once around the corner to the hall, Quinn scurried to her bedroom and leaned against the back of the door. *Great first impression.*

Confined to her room, the polo scent from Cooper's robe engulfed her like a comforting embrace. For a minute, she nestled into it, absorbing the feeling of being wrapped in his arms.

Her eyes blasted open. *Oh my word.* She had serious problems. She chucked the silly robe in her hamper and hustled to put actual clothes on. Once presentable, she wandered out to the living room where everyone had gathered while she'd taken longer than necessary to get herself ready.

Livy must've been out earlier, on a jog from the looks of it. Joined with the rest of the Anderson clan now, she looked like one of the family.

Cooper sat propped against the couch on the hardwoods next to a basket of party favors Quinn had just barely started making for Ginny's party.

Beside him, Brayden stood on wobbly legs while latching on to Maddie's two pointer fingers. Either he was still in the not-quite-awake stage, or he was a bit overwhelmed at the number of unfamiliar people in his living room. Quinn resisted the urge to scoop him up. At least he wasn't fussing.

Maddie giggled when he almost toppled over. "You think he's gonna be a surfer like you, Uncle Coop?"

He gave one of Brayden's chunky legs a squeeze. "Maybe with time. You'd be surprised what you can accomplish with a little practice." He flaunted a wink at Quinn. His and Brayden's dimples quirked at the same time, and she had to smile at their inside joke about needing to practice flirting.

A lot of good all their practicing was doing either of them. About the only thing it'd accomplished was getting her heart further into trouble.

Her smile faded. Something about having Drew and his family there wrenched reality back into the gear it never should've stalled out of. They'd come to say goodbye. Because the truth of the matter was, Cooper was leaving in four days, Quinn had a story to submit, and they'd both be walking out of Brayden's life for good.

Her heart cinched.

"You've got a gorgeous view, Coop," Ti said from the windowed wall overlooking the lake. "Seriously amazing. You mind if I go down to the dock in a bit? You know I brought my easel."

"Of course you did." Cooper laughed. "I just replaced the boards. Feel free to set up your paint stuff anytime. It's all yours."

"Sweet." She wrapped her arms around Drew's waist and smiled contentedly.

"And where's this painting going to go?" he asked.

She shrugged. "I'll find a spot for it."

Shaking his head, he leaned in to kiss her. "You always do."

The obvious love between them was so tangible it almost ached.

Livy sidled up beside Quinn. "You all right?"

"Hmm?" She blinked toward her, embarrassed she'd dazed off. "Oh, sorry, fine. Must need some coffee." Quinn strode for the kitchen toward the chance to escape the family bonds taking over the living room.

At the counter, she opened the coffee Cooper had coerced her into falling for—like everything else. She gave herself a pat on the cheek before another thought like that could weasel its way to the surface. *Enough with the sappy already.*

"QT!" Cooper's voice boomed from the other room. "Get in here. Now."

She dropped the coffee scoop on the counter and barreled around the doorframe and into the living room. "What's wron—?"

Brayden stood on his own in the center of the floor with his face beaming at her.

Her hand moved to her chest. "Is he …?"

"Just wait," Cooper said with so much enthusiasm it almost drew her focus toward him instead.

One shaky step followed another until Brayden had tottered halfway across the room. Quinn met him the rest of the way, just before he fell, and scooped him up.

Cooper joined her, cupping one hand to her lower back and the other over Brayden's. It didn't matter if a room full of eyes were on them, she wanted to kiss Cooper right there. Let him embrace them both like a real family would.

The unsolicited desire speared into her chest.

Cooper held her gaze, and she almost couldn't breathe. Did he know what she was thinking? What she wanted?

Tears burned in her throat. Her arms tightened around Brayden for fear she'd crumble if she let go. She kissed him right on the dimple. With an inhale of courage, she gave him to Cooper so she could retreat to the seclusion of the kitchen before he saw even deeper into her heart than he already had.

Quinn flexed both palms over the counter and grappled for composure, but questions kept winding together without beginning or end. How much would she miss in Brayden's life after this weekend? How much would she miss in Cooper's?

The ache of what she'd always longed for sank into her gut with a realization she'd been too blind or stubborn to fully admit until right now. She didn't just want a family with anyone. She wanted it with Cooper.

She swung the basket on the coffee maker and gripped the counter. Here, he was just looking for a little fun before moving on to the next adventure, and she was falling in love with him. No, this wasn't happening. This couldn't—

"Hey." Livy strolled into the kitchen. "I can make a pretty good cup of coffee. Thought I'd check if you need any help in here."

Only if that help involved knocking some sense into her head with a two-by-four. "I've already got a pot going."

Livy nodded and pointed to the cabinet with a sticky note labeled *MUGS*. "You got Coop organized. I'm impressed."

"I didn't exactly ask."

She laughed. "I knew I liked you." She set two mugs on the counter and reached for the next set. "For real, getting him to bend is a big deal. He tends to be a little on the take charge side."

"You don't say." Quinn pressed the On button on the coffee maker for the third time in hopes that would speed it up.

"It'd take an equally strong girl to balance him out." Livy collected the four mugs by their handles. "You two are brilliant together."

Quinn almost dropped the sugar bowl she was taking out of the cabinet. "Oh, we're, um, we're not together." She glared at the blasted coffee maker. If it had any sense of how uncomfortable she was right now, surely, it would cut her some slack and hurry it up already.

The group of mugs clinked together as Livy slid them beside the coffeepot. "Listen, I know how Cooper can get with the whole *carpe diem* thing. But trust me, it's more of a show than anything."

She risked peering in Livy's direction. From the look on her face, there was no question. This was definitely some kind of pep talk. For the love of Pete, why did this coffee maker hate her right now?

The doorbell rang, and Quinn exhaled. Hallelujah, someone loved her.

"Would you excuse me for a minute?" She rushed out of the room. The last thing she needed was dating advice from Cooper's model ex-girlfriend, of all people.

Or maybe not. As soon as she opened the door, her arm slid down the trim to her side. Leave it to today to prove her wrong. The real last thing she needed was seeing one of Cooper's bimbo dates at his door right now.

Malibu Barbie sized her up. "Sorry, I'm looking for Cooper."

It took a minute for Quinn to force her jaw to work. Why she was fighting it, she'd never know. She slapped on a smile. "*Carpe diem.*"

The blonde tilted her head. "*Carpe*, what?"

"Never mind." She held the door open and swung her arm down the hall. Trailing behind her, Quinn bypassed the kitchen and maneuvered to the back door, but not before catching the awkward look passing Cooper's face.

She opened the sliding door. "I'll be back in a bit," she said in response to the silent question Ti shot her.

Outside, she trekked down the deck steps toward the dock where she could finally breathe again. Well, sort of. The mixed feelings surging through her pressed in where the thick wall of humidity left off.

She kicked the tip of her Converse against the bottom of the bench. Stupid. So incredibly stupid to get sucked into a fantasy.

Her phone rang. Cruella, great. She hovered a thumb over the answer button.

"QT?" The back door closed, and Cooper jogged across the yard.

She stuffed her cell in her pocket.

His strides slowed over the wooden planks separating them. "You okay?"

Facing the lake instead of him, she ran a finger under her nose. "Fine. Just stressed about wrapping things up for the party. I have all those favors left to finish and—"

"Quinn." When Cooper turned her around, his gaze cut right through her rambling.

Tires peeling away squealed from up front.

"Barbie didn't want to stay?"

He squeezed the back of his neck. "I have no idea why Tanya showed up here like that. We went on a couple of dates weeks ago. I haven't called her since."

She turned toward the water again—away from his hazel eyes. "You don't owe me an explanation."

"Yeah, I do."

"No, you really don't." She started to pace, jumbled thoughts zapping through her head a mile a minute. "I'm not that kind of girl, Cooper."

He ran a knuckle over his jaw. "And what kind is that exactly?"

"The kind who melts when you look at her. Who sinks into your bathrobe because it smells like you and makes her feel safe." *Stop talking.* "The kind who pretends she's smooth enough to be okay with casual kisses, but who'd show up at your doorstep if you never called her again. I can't be one of those girls, Cooper. I—"

If his swaggering stride didn't show he was amused at her blabbering, his lopsided grin made up for it.

Quinn laced her arms across her chest. "What?"

"I make you melt?"

"Not the point."

He crossed another board. "You sure?"

"Yes. Maybe." She shook her head. "The point is, I'm not the no-strings-attached girl you usually date. I'm not a model or some country club trophy you can carry on your arm at business functions. I wear Fruit of the Loom underwear, for Pete's sake."

The corner of his mouth quirked.

Fabulous. As if letting the other confessions spew from her mouth wasn't mortifying enough, she had to go and blurt that out in front of him, while he was only a foot away. Make that less than a foot. Three inches.

She sucked in a breath.

"Fruit of the Loom, huh?"

"Shut up." She smacked his arm. "And seriously, I just spilled my guts, and that's all you have to say?"

Still smiling, he weaved his fingers through her hair. "You didn't let me finish."

His lips met hers, and his presence overtook the air. Everything that'd just transpired vanished. Slow, tender, and irrevocable, his touch beckoned her deeper into the yearning to explore him, know him. To cut through the lock on her heart and give him the residence he already had.

When he leaned back, she had to curl her fingers around his collar to keep standing. "You can't keep doing that," she whispered.

"You don't make it very easy on me."

A knot overran her throat. "I … we …" Unable to speak, she turned away, but he held on to her hand and drew her back around.

"What if I don't want that kind of girl, Quinn? What if I only want the one right in front of me?"

The knot expanded. "For four more days?"

His brow pinched. But when he met her gaze again, the earnestness in his eyes almost drained every bit of resistance out of her. "Come with me."

"To Indonesia? You can't be serious."

"Why not?" He brought her closer.

"Cooper." She set a palm to his chest. "I have a life in Hatteras to get back to. And you don't want to be tied down, remember?"

Head lowered, he released a slow breath. "I shouldn't be asking you. I know what you think of me, and you're probably right about most of it." He closed his eyes and rested his forehead to hers. "But you're wrong about how I feel about you." He pressed the lightest of kisses to the top of her head before breaking away.

Shuffling backward, he fixed torn eyes on her. "And you're wrong about the kind of wife and mom you'll make one day."

He turned as Livy, Ti, and Maddie were coming down the steps.

Quinn didn't move. She roped her arms around her sides to hold the pieces together while watching him walk away. Of all the things she was wrong about, why couldn't falling in love with Cooper Anderson be one of them?

CHAPTER TWENTY-THREE

Lost

Carrying Brayden, Livy followed Maddie to the shoreline while Ti headed toward them. Quinn held her breath when Cooper stopped at the end of the pier to let Ti pass.

"Sorry to interrupt." She cast a piqued glance between her and Cooper, propped an easel against the bench, and lowered a canvas bag to the dock. "We were so focused on the lake, we didn't notice you two were out here at first."

"No problem," Cooper said. "I was just going to find Drew."

If Quinn interpreted Ti's half smile right, she seemed to read about a hundred different meanings into that single sentence. "He ran out to the Jeep to grab the rest of our bags. Give him a sec, and you can meet him back inside."

"Good, good." Cooper's gaze strayed toward Quinn for the briefest moment. With his chin down again, he looked like he was pillaging an emotional reserve for a passable smile. But when he looked up, only the ghost of one emerged. "Excuse me."

"Uncle Coop." Maddie's call from the bank stopped him only a few steps across the lawn. "Can we search for turtles today?"

A glance from the house back to her lowered his shoulders. Something in his eyes shifted as he headed toward her. The visible tug-of-war vying for his attention clearly wasn't a match against his affection for his niece. "We sure can, Freckles."

At the edge of his property, he drew Maddie into a side hug. She squeezed her skinny arms around his waist in a bear hug anyone could see she didn't want to release. He kissed the top of her head before stretching over to kiss Brayden's too, and the feeble stitching across Quinn's chest unraveled a thread at a time.

She ran her hands up and down her arms. "He's great with her, isn't he?"

"With Maddie?" Ti set up her easel at the end of the pier. "She couldn't ask for a better uncle. Loves him like you wouldn't believe."

Quinn knew the feeling. She blinked away from the scene breaking her heart and focused on Ti instead. "You have a special family."

"They're a gift, that's for sure. One I definitely don't deserve." Her pensive expression deepened as she withdrew a palette from her bag. "I'm still trying to wrap my head around the whole grace thing."

Grace. Quinn's insides hardened at the word. What good was grace if it couldn't take away pain?

Her phone rang from her pocket. She pulled it out, about to take Ava's call, when a glimpse of Cooper's silhouette drifting up the yard caught her eye. Was he going to talk to Drew about Brayden? She kicked herself for not talking to him first.

Maybe he and his brother had their differences, but there was no denying Cooper admired Drew—as a father if nothing else. Surely, if anyone could change Cooper's mind about giving up his parental rights, it would be him.

She mindlessly spun her cell in her hands while tapping her Converse against a nail not hammered in all the way. "Can I ask you something?"

"If Cooper's in love with you?"

Almost tripping, Quinn juggled the phone like a hot potato to keep from dropping it into the lake. "Um, no. That's not ..."

"No need to be embarrassed." Ti squeezed a rich blue colored paint onto her palette and set the tube aside. "It's obvious in how he interacts with you."

Quinn swept her bangs off her lashes. "So obvious, your husband's seen it enough times to be used to it, huh?"

Ti barely let a pause linger before mixing two shades of blue and white with a painter's knife. "We all have pasts. Things we hide behind, run from. Trust me." She exchanged her knife for a thin brush and swirled the bristles around her blended color. "That doesn't mean we can't have new beginnings."

Not everyone was so lucky.

Quinn peered over to Maddie, Livy, and Brayden under the canopy of an oak tree. "Is there something so awful in

Cooper's past that he feels like he has to run all the way to Indonesia to get away from it?"

Ti stroked her brush along the blank canvas with the kind of vision only an artist could wield. "Maybe he's running to something instead of away from it."

"To what?"

"I think he's still trying to figure that out." Ti set the brush and palette down and thumbed through some prints in her bag until she found the one she was looking for. With tangible reverence, she withdrew a piece that obviously held sentimental value to her and turned it around.

An artistic quote painted in water colors shined in the sunlight: *We'll never find where we belong until we're willing to admit we're lost.*

Ti's eyes held a mixture of affection, gratefulness, and hope. "It's something their dad used to say. I'm planning to give it to Cooper as a gift before he leaves." She turned it around again and traced a thumb along its edge. "A reminder of a truth he once shared with me when I needed to hear it most."

The two brothers came through the back door and sat at the patio table on the deck. Quinn's chest hollowed at the torn expression shadowing Cooper's face.

She'd wanted to use the little time they had together to help him believe in the kind of father he could be if he gave himself a chance. But like so many other times, the clock had run out. Instead of the breakthrough she'd hoped for, disappointment bound her with ties so familiar, they were hemmed into her identity.

Was there nothing she could do to change things?

"Dada." Brayden must've caught sight of Cooper up on the deck. Livy held his hands above his head as he took wobbly strides across the lawn toward a dad he needed in his life.

Ti followed her line of sight. "He made a lot of sacrifices for Maddie when she really needed him. I'm willing to bet he's trying to do the same for Brayden. Just in different ways."

Her words joined the entire scene closing in around Quinn, and she somehow knew right then what she needed to do. She breathed a breath of assurance. This wasn't over yet.

She pointed her cell behind her shoulder. "I'm sorry to cut things short, but I have something to take care of. We'll talk more later?"

"Of course." Ti waved her on. "I'll be up in a bit. As soon as this painting releases me."

Ti's connection with her art ignited Quinn's desire to recharge her own. Once in her bedroom, she locked the door, opened her laptop, and erased everything she'd written for the piece on Cooper so far.

The cursor blinked on the blank page in a call to her heart. For the first time since she'd gotten here, the words flowed without hindrance. It wasn't about trying to gain Cruella's respect or impress the bigwigs at Corporate anymore. This was about showcasing the real Cooper Anderson with no assumptions skewing the truth—not even his own. He needed to see himself through the eyes of people who loved him. Including her.

She'd be risking more than just her job, but Cooper wasn't the only one who thought he'd been acting out of love instead of fear. The only trouble was, choosing real love might cost her the very thing she finally understood was worth running to.

The summer afternoon stretched into early evening like a song transitioning from verse to refrain. Except this was one of the last times Cooper would get to watch the sunset play across the lake's quiet waters.

Refrain? He shook his head. Ti had hardly been here a day, and her artistic flair was already rubbing off on him. If he started spouting off sonnets next, he was in big trouble.

He hauled his board onto the dock and closed his paddle under the bench seat, tucked away with these random emotional ties to his property sprouting to the surface.

Maddie heaved her board next to his. "It's a lot easier to paddle out here than in the ocean." Her brows peaked into her bangs. "Lake life hasn't turned you soft on me, has it?"

Laughing, Cooper flexed his bicep. "You tell me."

She gave his arm a good squeeze and shrugged. "Meh."

"Oh yeah?" He swept her off the pier and flung her over his shoulder. "How's this for strong?"

She drummed her palms on his back until he let her slide down. Grin as wry as ever, she perched both hands on her hips. "So, you can bench press a whole ninety-two pounds, huh? Impressive."

He yanked on the hose he'd dragged down earlier to use on their boards and doused her in cold water. Maddie squealed, sidestepping him to hightail it up to the grass.

Man, he missed this. Missed the bond they'd shared every day when he lived with them. Would he lose it completely once in Indonesia?

His amusement drained with the water as he let up on the handle. This wasn't the time for doubts. Yet the more he tried to suppress them, the more they suffocated him.

Maddie edged back onto the pier once he set the hose down. Though her eyes hadn't lost their mischief, something deeper shined behind it.

"Freckles, I need to ask you something." Despite his attempt to keep his tone light, the burden on his mind wore through. "You're, um, you're not mad at me for leaving, are you?" He was a grown man able to take on any executive, yet here he was, his voice wavering in front of an eleven-year-old.

A bony shoulder lifted in the air as she shook her head. "You'll come back." No hesitation, she spoke with the kind of confidence he should be channeling right now.

The corner of her mouth slanted. "You know you can't stay away from this face for *too* long." She pointed to a cheesy grin and batted her lashes.

"You're right about that. C'mere." Chuckling, Cooper hooked an arm around her neck. "I'm gonna miss you. You know that, don't you?"

"I'll miss you, too, but North Carolina is your home. It's where your family is. Leaving doesn't change that."

No matter what, she always believed the best in him. Her unconditional love expanded the lump seizing his throat, and he held her a little tighter.

His cell rang from the bench where he'd left it while on the water. "Sorry, Freckles. I need to grab this." He answered his client's call. "How's it going, Barry?"

"All's well, man. I just wanted to say thanks for talking me into sticking things out with my portfolio. I'm back up by twenty-two percent."

"Didn't I tell you it'd rebound?"

"Yeah, yeah. But you know how I get."

Like a lunatic? Yeah, he knew. Cooper laughed to himself. Barry might drive him crazy sometimes, but he was a good guy.

"Are you sure you gotta move to India?"

"It's Indonesia."

"Whatever, man. I'm just saying. It's not going to be the same."

Cooper held the phone with his shoulder and dragged his paddle board up to the grass to wash it off. "The internet works all over the world, Barry. I'll be able to manage your portfolio from anywhere. It'll be fine."

Barry's wife called something in the background at the same time an incoming text chimed in Cooper's ear.

"I'm asking. Just give me a minute, will ya?" Barry said away from the phone. "Listen, Cooper, the Mrs. and I want to have you over for dinner before you go. You know, as a thank-you for putting up with us."

Cooper laid his board down and had to smile. Yet as quickly as it came, it retreated behind the same gravity that'd been weighing on him all day. "Be sure to tell JoAnn I appreciate the offer, but I'm afraid I won't have a chance before I go." The days were running out.

"Next time you're back in town, then."

"Sure thing. We'll be in touch. You two take it easy, all right?" Though he'd tried to keep the conversation upbeat, the words sank in his stomach like a bowling ball. And when hanging up brought a missed text from his realtor into view, the weight only compounded.

I'll be by at six with the prospects. Don't forget this time. If all goes well, we'll be signing contracts in the a.m.

Cooper looked up from his phone just in time to see his brother stepping into his path.

Drew patted Cooper's arm. "Everything all right?"

"Yeah." He pocketed his phone and made another attempt at neutralizing the thoughts turning his head into a pinball machine. "But unfortunately, I have some people coming by to look at the house tonight."

"No worries." Drew called Maddie over and lolled an arm across her back. "My little adventurer has talked me into taking us camping tonight."

"Camping?"

"Just up at Camp Willow Run. We'll be back in the morning, if that's cool."

"Sure." Cooper rubbed out the back of his hair, feeling like he was missing something. "Tomorrow's fine. Have fun."

"You and Quinn too," Maddie said with a little too much lilt in her voice. "And be sure to change," she added right before tugging her dad up to the deck.

Ah, there it was. Nothing like a spontaneous camping trip with an agenda.

Cooper's focus drifted to the dock and into moments he'd accumulated with Quinn over such a short time: seeing her come to life on the WaveRunner, almost tossing her off the pier, kissing her under that lamppost. The boards might be new, but the grooves in the wood already held memories that would stay with him forever.

The brick in his gut steered his gaze to the speedboat that'd been docked all summer. Quinn was right. Though he couldn't fully identify why, he'd been avoiding the boat and its connection to Dad. Maybe even to the move itself.

He crossed whatever barrier had been holding him back, boarded the boat, and ran a hand along the steering wheel. "I'm sorry, Dad."

A flicker of light from the house showed a glimpse of Quinn in the window, lifting Brayden from his crib. She stood there with his son in her arms, and his heart caught up in an image he doubted would ever release him.

Forcing his eyes away and his heart back where it belonged, he withdrew his phone and called his lawyer.

"Jim, hey, just wanted to let you know I spoke with Drew today about the adoption."

"And he's on board?"

Cooper paused, swallowed. "Yep."

"That's great news. I'll draw up the papers in the morning."

The window's gravitational pull lured Cooper back to what he was forfeiting. He rubbed his jaw but couldn't force a response. Everything was set in motion. The fact of the matter was, he'd be on the road in four days as he'd planned.

"Cooper?" Jim prompted.

"Yeah, I'm here," he managed.

"Look, if you're still unsure—"

"I've made up my mind." He pressed his shoulders against the seat and craned his head to the darkening sky. As much as it'd kill him, the only heart he was willing to break was his own.

CHAPTER TWENTY-FOUR

Choice

"You asked him *what?*" Quinn whipped around from the kitchen sink. "Cooper, no."

"Drew's a great father."

The turmoil in his voice withered her own to a whisper. "So are you." What would it take for him to believe that? She turned off the faucet but couldn't stop the ache from pouring through.

Even though she'd rather have Brayden stay in Cooper's family than end up with random strangers, she was supposed to have gotten Cooper to see *he* was the best choice. "I thought you were dead set on leaving Drew out of this."

"Yeah, well, things change when you run out of options." He tossed his ball cap on the counter and braced weary arms against it.

Frustration rose in the center of her chest. She'd stayed silent while his realtor showed the house to that snobby couple earlier. She'd forced her mouth shut when he'd been on the phone with his lawyer, but she couldn't take it anymore.

"*Carpe diem*, right? You've hidden behind that façade so long, you don't even realize when you're not actually living it."

"Excuse me?"

She clenched the dish towel. "What happened to taking a leap? To not confusing fear and love? Was all that talk about faith just a line you were feeding me?"

"What? No." Defense broadened Cooper's shoulders, but she wouldn't cower this time.

"It's easy to leap when you're playing right into what people expect of you, pretending you don't care what happens, that roots only hold you back. But I know better." She backed him up with each forward stride. "I've seen you with Maddie. With Brayden. You can't tell me those ties don't mean something to you, Cooper. I don't buy it."

He stopped, jaw twitching. "Like you're one to talk."

"At least I can admit it," she said softer than she meant to.

"Can you?" This time, he edged her backward. "I don't see you moving home and embracing *your* roots. I don't see you sticking things out with your dad no matter how hard it gets."

She hid her inward wince. "That's not fair."

"C'mon, QT. You're running from the life you really want because of what? Fear of not living up to people's expectations? If you want to talk about letting assumptions rule my life, fine. But at least be willing to look in the mirror."

Despite his eyes softening, a look of fired-up yearning intensified. "How can you not see what you're allowing a scumbag like Brian to rob from you? He's the one who lost by letting you go. If you can't see that, you're—"

"He didn't know." She turned away from the look of pity bound to be on Cooper's face. Clutching the edge of the sink, she lowered her head, her voice faltering. "I couldn't tell him about the hysterectomy. If I had, he would've told me it was okay, that it didn't matter. But I know him, all right?"

"So, you just broke things off and left without even giving him the choice?"

"It was better that way."

He turned her around. "For who?"

"You saw him with Cindy Mae. *That's* the life he wanted."

"That life could've been with you."

"No, it couldn't." She shoved her bangs back with her wet hand. "You don't get it. Adoption wouldn't have been enough for him."

"You don't know that." He inched closer and cupped her shoulders. "You can't keep making people's decisions for them, Quinn. Not for him or your dad." Voice tenderized, Cooper kept earnest eyes on hers as he wiped soapsuds from her hair. "Or for me."

This close to him, she couldn't even make her lungs decide to breathe. She waded through an array of emotions in search of her voice. "I just want to protect the people I care about."

"You sure you're not trying to protect yourself?"

Maybe she was. But with Cooper only a breath away, it didn't matter anyway. She'd lost that battle the moment she walked through his door.

His gazed roamed her face with such urgency, she had to grip his arm. "I don't want you to leave without seeing what I see in you."

Quinn swallowed, her grasp tightening. "That's not fair to ask if you don't do the same."

His chest rose and fell like an echo of hers until he finally brought her close. In the quiet of that still kitchen, she surrendered her fears to an embrace that always knew how to take them away.

Maybe she shouldn't feel this way, but in his arms, she was home. Safe. Right where she wanted to stay.

When she lifted her head from his chest, his eyes seemed to search hers and then pause as if reading the words she hadn't spoken. She traced her fingers along the arms that never hesitated to comfort her. The same ones that cradled Brayden with acceptance and sheltered Maddie with protection. Was it so wrong for her to want to stay wrapped in them a little longer?

Her fingertips grazed the skin above the top of his collar.

He closed his eyes. "Quinn." The husky whisper held a note of warning.

She dropped her gaze to the tiles, her arm to her side.

His hand tightened around her lower back when she started to turn away. The torn look on his face anchored her in place. And for a moment, neither of them moved.

With his hazel eyes still holding her, he inched closer and slowly pulled the pencil from her hair. Soft locks swept down her neck but didn't come close to the gentleness of Cooper's hand running down her jawline to her chin. The top of his thumb brushed the corner of her mouth.

Heart racing, she couldn't breathe. His gaze traced her lips in a kiss as tender as the one that followed. Even more than the first two times, the touch consumed her. The emotion, the connection. It's what she wanted to run to, not from.

A moan escaped his throat when he finally broke away. "You should go."

What?

A look trapped between fear and desire ran so deeply in his eyes, Quinn could almost drown in it. "We should both get to sleep." His gravelly voice strained through breaths as erratic as hers.

Quinn wanted to stay, to fight with him—anything to understand how he could kiss her like that and then push her away. But the war tearing down his face turned her around. He was probably right. What were they doing other than making saying goodbye ache even more than it already would?

She'd barely made it three steps away when Cooper whirled her around by the hand and backed her against the fridge.

"I thought you just said I should go."

"One more minute." His lips sloped to the skin beneath her ear as though trying to stretch every millisecond of that single minute.

She knew as well as he did a minute wasn't long enough. She wanted more. Wanted him. Not for a story or a career break or validating some soapbox she'd been guarding for too long. But because she'd fallen for him.

The emotions woven in that truth ushered through every move, every breath. She leaned him back far enough for him to search her eyes to know what she was asking.

He only hesitated a moment. His hands slid around her waist and lifted her onto the island in the middle of the kitchen. Though the counter was solid granite, it might as well have been a sieve, her body melting through it.

A cry from Brayden's room tunneled from down the hall. Cooper's kiss stalled. When nothing but silence followed, his reluctance gave way, but something had changed. His hands, his mouth, his body—they all moved on instinct, but his thoughts were thick enough to feel. One at a time, they resisted the rest of him until he finally slowed to a stop.

Too many ticks from the clock passed in his pause. He cradled both her cheeks in his hands and kissed her so slowly, she slipped her fingers over his to keep him from letting go. But she knew he would. Knew the moment had ended.

When he leaned back, a sad smile capable of breaking her heart replaced the one that had turned it into a diesel engine dozens of times. Still cupping her cheek, Cooper pressed one last kiss to her forehead and backed away.

Quinn slid off the counter to the floor, praying it would ground her. "I should go check on him."

He nodded without saying anything, and she begged her feet to move. She walked away with her lips caught up in her fingers, holding on to a kiss that had ruined any that would ever follow it.

At the bedroom door, she gripped the knob and waited for her breathing to slow before entering. Moonlight stretched a path across Brayden's shadowy room to his crib. Quinn peered over the rail to a sleeping baby boy who'd forever wrecked her heart as much as his father had.

Whatever had made him cry earlier must've already passed. She pulled the edge of his jungle blanket over his shoulders and gently smoothed her fingertips across his fine hair.

From the window, Quinn caught a glimpse of Cooper disappearing onto the end of the pier right before diving into the lake. After what they'd just shared, she had no idea what he was thinking or what he wanted, but taking a leap obviously wasn't hard for him. Maybe his real fear was taking one with her.

Cooper rifled through his suitcase for the fifth time. He'd packed everything he needed for the road trip, hadn't he? At his bed, he turned in half circles, disjointed thoughts bouncing around his bedroom.

His gaze skidded to a stop over the road atlas lying under his toiletry bag in the corner chair. The route. He hadn't finished mapping it out yet. Tapping his thigh, he shuffled aimlessly around the room once more until he refocused on what he needed.

Jeez, where was his head today? He'd stayed busy all morning and afternoon yet barely made a dent in the last-minute arrangements he still needed to take care of before heading out on Wednesday.

He trekked into his office with the atlas to find a highlighter. At his desk, he ran a thumb over the sticky note on the pen holder and smiled. Of course he couldn't concentrate. Who could after kissing Quinn like he had last night?

The scene flooded in and slumped Cooper into his desk chair. He hadn't meant to let that happen, but her touch, her eyes … He couldn't say no when she reciprocated everything he wanted too. His heart had moved on instinct, and when she let down her barriers, he'd lost all restraint.

Until Brayden cried.

Part of him had wanted to ignore the reminder of consequences, but the part that loved Quinn wouldn't let him. He wouldn't turn what they had into a mistake they'd both leave regretting.

The gravity of what they'd really be leaving behind thrust a blow to his gut.

Cooper dropped the highlighter and soared around the doorframe into the hall. At Quinn's bedroom, another jab trailed the first. This time, a sucker punch. Other than a suitcase on her bed, the place looked like the empty shell of a guest room she'd passed through for a forgettable amount of time.

A hard swallow worked its way down his throat. He swung around to grab his keys.

"Whoa." Drew just barely averted the collision. "You all right?"

Was he? Cooper squeezed his forehead. "Sorry. Fine. Have you seen Quinn?"

"Last I noticed, she was out on the dock."

A sigh of relief unlocked the tension in his shoulders. "Thanks. Would you mind keeping an eye on Brayden for a few?" He pointed behind him, not needing to explain.

Drew simply nodded his understanding. When Ti moseyed into the hall, Drew curled her into his side and dipped his head at Cooper again. "We've got you covered."

He always did. Cooper shouldn't have bucked so long against asking him to adopt Brayden into his family. He'd take care of him.

After jogging from the living room all the way to the edge of the property, Cooper finally slowed at the sight of Quinn standing on the end of the pier.

A dozen dragonflies zipped around the dock. But with her attention transfixed by the lake, she didn't seem to notice. He couldn't blame her for being lost in thought. He hadn't been able to escape his own thoughts much today either. Then again, maybe that was good, because at least now he knew what he needed to tell her before it was too late. If it wasn't already.

In any other circumstance, he would've taken the fact that her bags were already packed as his answer. But he couldn't just walk away. Not this time.

At the opposite edge of the pier, he withdrew his cell and pulled up a Boyz II Men song on a radio app.

Quinn turned at the sound, and Cooper grinned. "Don't worry, QT. Your secret playlists are safe with me."

The slightest quirk of her lips sent his heart racing with hope.

Gesturing to the dragonflies, he made his way across the planks toward her. "Since you already have company, I hope you don't mind if I join you too."

She took in the dragonflies' spastic pattern soaring above her. "Wow, look at all of them. What are they doing?"

"Dancing."

She made a face at him. "Dancing?"

"Mm-hmm. Well, their version of it anyway." He strode close enough to wrap his arm around her waist if she'd let him. "I'm pretty sure they want us to join them."

"Oh really?"

"I mean, it'd be a little rude not to. We are kind of on their turf right now."

She rolled her eyes but couldn't lose her grin.

"Why not?" He edged another step closer. "You've mastered the WaveRunner, conquered a rainstorm in your heels, given yourself permission to make a royal mess in the kitchen. Adding dancing with dragonflies to your list of leaps should be a piece of cake."

He raised a playful shoulder. "I bet if you throw that cowgirl hat of yours on, not even wearing Fruit of the Loom underwear could hold you back."

She shoved him, a laugh tumbling out.

A song came on with classic nineties' beats, and he cranked the volume. "C'mon, I defy you not to dance to this song."

"You're impossible, you know that?"

"I think you mean charming."

She snorted. "More like full of yourself."

"Confident," he challenged.

Her smile was winning the war. But when she still didn't fully cave, Cooper feigned a look of concern at her hair.

"What?" She patted the top of her head.

"It's just an inch worm." He stretched out a hand. "Let me—"

An impressive combo of screaming and flailing began before he even finished. Quinn practically jumped into his arms. "Get it out."

Laughing, he picked a tiny twig out of her hair instead and slid his hands down to the small of her back.

Her eyes tightened, his plan uncovered. "Smooth."

"I thought so." He took her hand in his and sobered. "Dance with me."

She held on to his gaze, and a slow breath gradually relaxed her muscles against his. For what didn't feel long enough, they danced in a moment where the flutter of dragonfly wings replaced every other measure of time.

"You're not going to go dive into the lake like you did last night, are you?" she said against his chest.

The tenor in her voice made him lean back. "I had to cool down somehow."

The skin above her eyes crinkled. "If you didn't want—"

"You?" Was that seriously what she thought? She had no idea. His fingers slid down to hers. "Quinn, look at me. It took everything I had to walk away last night."

"But all the other girls you've been with, why ...?" Her voice trailed, the insinuation cutting to his core.

After painting that persona, what else would he expect her to think?

"First of all, you're not just any other girl, Quinn." Cooper lifted his face to the fading sunlight, closed his eyes, and exhaled. "I've dated casually in the past because it's easier. No emotional connection. No risk of getting hurt. We go out, have a good time, and leave it at that." He groaned at the words leaving his mouth. Even more at how long he'd lived that lifestyle, trying to remain numb and unattached.

When Quinn's chin dropped to her chest, he lifted it to meet her eyes again. "But it's never more than a date. I don't take women home with me. I don't cross lines that shouldn't be crossed. Megan was the only girl I've ever been intimate with, and look how that turned out."

Regret singed the last confession.

Sorrow filled her eyes. "You still view Brayden as a mistake?"

"That's not what I meant, but putting ourselves in that same predicament would've been. I shouldn't have let it get to that point last night."

She blew out a hard breath. "You're right. I let myself get too caught up in the things you make me feel, in the fear of losing you. I wasn't thinking straight."

Hearing her admit she felt things for him spurred an untamable smile. "Well in case you haven't noticed, you kind of make me lose my head when I'm around you too."

Her brow creased.

That probably didn't come out right. Along with everything else leaking out of his mouth so far.

The sunset's rich colors reflected off the water like one of Ti's calming paintings. Breathing in the serenity, Cooper brushed Quinn's bangs back and left his hand behind her ear. "What I'm trying to say is, I'm falling in love with you. And you're right, I've been hiding. I've run when I should've stayed. Lived a façade to avoid pain."

He traced a thumb over her cheek. "But I don't want to anymore. Not with us. I want to do things right." His forehead found hers.

Her fingers curled around his collar, and he brought his lips to hers. Slow and soft, he prayed the kiss would say what words failed to. "This is real. I know you feel it too."

Tears filled her eyes. "Chemistry isn't our problem, Cooper. We've made our choices."

"But are they the right ones?"

He caught a glimpse of hope cutting through her walls. When she lifted a palm to his cheek, his pulse sprinted. He'd broken every rule he had with her. Had handed over his heart, knowing she could pull out of his driveway, taking it with her.

"Cooper, I need you to know—"

"Well, well," a woman from behind them said. "I've underestimated you, Thompson. You certainly go above and beyond when the job requires it."

He turned toward a petite woman with bold streaks of blond interspersed through her short dark hair.

"What are you doing here, Cru—?" Quinn seemed to strain to correct herself. "Christa?"

"You won't return my calls. What did you expect? We have a deadline." The woman fluttered her lashes. "Time is—"

"Money. Yeah, I know. I already sent you what you wanted."

"What I wanted?" A haughty laugh barely escaped the woman's tight lips. "I gave you this chance because I saw potential in you, Thompson. I thought you had a clue how to be a journalist. Instead you feed me this." She flicked a manila envelope in her hands.

Journalist? Cooper looked at Quinn for some hint of explanation.

"Potential? Please." Quinn's jaw flexed. "The only reason you assigned me this piece was so you could watch me fail."

Her heels screeched across the boards. "I gave you this assignment because without it, Corporate wouldn't take a second glance at how well you're doing under my leadership."

Quinn's eyes widened. "You knew about that? About—?"

"Of course I knew." Christa calmed herself, a superior smile curving to the left. "Why do you think I've been letting all those nimrods on staff go? I have less than a month to get this magazine in the kind of shape that's going to make Corporate wish they'd never so much as considered dropping me."

Quinn's brows rooted together. "You wanted me to succeed so it'd make you look good."

"So it'd make *us* look good. Which is why you're going to rework this piece."

Open distaste shaded Quinn's expression. "You wanted a feature. I gave it to you. We're done."

"We're done when I say we're done." Her eyes turned to flames. "Now, you listen to me, sweetheart. I didn't take a risk on you so you could pass off some feel-good story about a guy you were supposed to get the inside scoop on just because he throws a charming look your way."

Cooper's arms nearly went numb at his sides. She couldn't mean … "Quinn?"

Her shoulders caved, confessing everything she didn't have to.

"You haven't told him yet?" Her boss's voice grew thick with agitation. "You were supposed to have him on board by now, Thompson. That was part of the deal."

Deal. The word dug into his side like a rusty screw. He gripped the lamppost as pieces of the last several weeks fused together. The way Quinn had shown up, her questions about Shore Corp, her writing. She played him for some byline?

His muscles convulsed. He had to get out of there.

He strode past the woman's twistedly satisfied expression.

"Cooper, wait." Quinn drew him to a stop by the hand. "I'm sorry. Please, let me ex—"

"I've heard enough."

Tears cloaked her eyes. "I tried to tell you so many times. Tried to make it right by writing a feature on the real you." She breathed in a shaky breath. "It might've started out as an assignment, but things changed."

Cooper yanked his arm away. "You're right. They did."

She knew how he felt about his privacy and staying away from the media. Worse, she knew how he truly felt about her, and she let him go on this whole time like a fool thinking she—

He cut off the thought, furious at how naive he'd been. It didn't matter what he'd thought she felt. He was the one who'd lowered his guard and let himself be played. Anger sparked against betrayal like a flint, the fire too strong, too consuming.

"Cooper, please."

Ignoring the way Quinn's raw voice jabbed the blade deeper, he kept trucking up the yard.

Drew rounded the side of the house. "Is everything—?"

"Not now." Cooper clipped his brother's shoulder on his way by and didn't slow down till he straddled his bike. He should've been riding this the whole time, not driving his SUV, thinking he could play the role of a family man.

Heat waves rippled off the pavement as he jerked in the clutch. She wanted to write a story on the real Cooper Anderson? This was it. He skidded out of the driveway without looking back.

CHAPTER TWENTY-FIVE

Gravity

Back at her parents' house, Quinn stood barefoot on the hardwood floors of her old bedroom. The tie Dad had given her all those years ago slid through her fingers like answers to prayers that had always been out of reach. Two days of silence from Cooper confirmed that obviously hadn't changed.

A muffled version of Ava's ringtone rang from under her pillow where Quinn'd left her cell buried. She let the call go to voice mail to join the unanswered messages from Ti and Livy.

It would be hard enough facing an entire party of people today while pretending to be fine. But at least Ginny's guests didn't know how see-through she felt, unlike Cooper's family. And Ava? The girl would dish out an entire speech on how losing their jobs over this was the beginning of a new adventure. Only problem was they had no place to start.

Quinn wiped under her eyes, refusing to believe it was all for nothing. She would've done a hundred things differently, but writing that final piece on Cooper wasn't one of them. It'd never be printed now, and maybe he'd never read it even if it was. But if Brayden did one day, then it'd be worth it.

A gentle knock at the door quaked into the quiet room. The sight of Dad in one of his plaid short-sleeved button-downs had Quinn dabbing at her eyes all over again. She turned away but doubted it'd gone unnoticed.

"I still remember the look on your face when you opened that birthday box to find a tie." The sound of his chuckle stretched into memories that used to ground her. Maybe still did.

Dad slapped his thigh. "You looked as lost as a ball in high weeds, thinking I'd mixed up yours and Chase's birthdays or something."

"Well!" She couldn't help joining in his laughter, but it didn't take long for it to wane behind a pang of gravity that never fully relented. "It was a sweet gift, Dad." Her fingers skimmed down the blue and silver thatching. "I'm sorry you never got your answer, though."

"Who said I didn't?"

Quinn turned only to find a look of certainty overtaking his gray eyes. Her heart tanked. Was his mind still trapped in the past? She fiddled with the sash on her sundress. "Dad, Brian and I aren't together anymore."

He huffed. "Good riddance too."

Her head flung up. "What?"

"If you didn't break off that engagement, I was gonna have to step in."

"But …" If she blinked enough times, maybe the movement would oil her jaw somehow. "You were so happy when we were together."

"Oh, I tried to pretend to be for your sake." Dad moseyed closer to the center of the room while his words still felt miles away. He studied her the way he always had when interpreting her expressions. "You were happy, sweetheart. What father would want to take that away from you?" He stroked the whiskers on his chin. "But it's hard for us dads, having to watch our little girls learn from their own mistakes."

The room might as well have slanted. "I can't believe … I mean, how'd you know …?

Fatherly intuition smiled from eyes that were as clear and lucid as they ever were. He rested a strong, weathered hand to her shoulder. "You may think that prayer went unanswered, but I just saw this past week that it hasn't."

His insinuation cranked a vise around her heart, crushing what was left inside her. She couldn't take bringing him any more disappointment.

"Cooper and I … it wasn't real."

"Horse manure."

She flinched at his tone. "Dad."

"Well, I'm sorry, honey, but you can't tell me you don't love that boy."

The truth swelled in her throat. "It doesn't matter. He's already gone. It's too late."

A stern eye of discipline met her dejected stare. "Just 'cause things get hard doesn't mean you run away. Not this time."

The consequences of her mistakes echoed throughout a room too small to avoid them. Quinn's legs found the edge of the bed, and she caved onto the mattress. "I'm so sorry for leaving like I did. It was wrong." She lifted watery eyes toward him. "I thought I was doing what was best for everyone. But the truth is, I was scared, selfish."

"Same as the rest of us." A grace-filled smile led him beside her on the bed. "Why do you think we all need prayers?"

Nothing but genuine faith and forgiveness looked back at her. She shook her head. "How do you do it? How do you cling to your faith when God keeps overlooking you?" An avalanche of brokenness tore through the whispered words.

"Overlooks me?" His wrinkled brow scrunched in genuine confusion. "If He showered me with any more love, it'd be coming out my ears."

"How can you say that?" Her shoulders slumped at how much his disease had robbed his mind. A mix of anger and sorrow clogged her voice. "Do you know how many times I prayed for Him to heal you? To heal us both?" Her hand covered her stomach on its own, the hurt still so raw. She willed back the tears exposing the abandonment she should've gotten over by now.

A patient smile passed Dad's eyes as he wiped her cheek. "I know things don't always work out the way we pictured they would, but I reckon that's probably a good thing."

"How can anything good come from sickness and pain? Who does that help?" No one. Couldn't he see that?

"Oh, I think it's helped more people than you think." His gaze found the faded black and white photo of his and Mom's wedding day still pinned on a bulletin board above her desk. "It's helped an old married couple remember that their vows to love each other through anything are as real now as they were the day they promised them. It's helped a nurse find strength to follow a calling most people would've given up on."

Voice soft and vulnerable, he leaned the side of his head against hers. "And just maybe it's helped a headstrong girl learn to surrender her vision of the life she expected for a life she couldn't even imagine."

Just when Quinn was sure her tears had run dry, the streams carving down her cheeks proved her wrong. "Do we have to go through all this pain to get there?"

"In this life? I reckon so." Dad squeezed her to his side. "Finding the blessings in between? Well, now, that's our choice."

She wrapped her arms around him, hanging on to the rare moment of having him fully present the way she wished he could stay. "I love you, Daddy."

"Not as much as I love you—with or without a husband. And with or without some big job promotion."

She leaned back. "How did you—?" Eyeing his smile, she waved it off. "Never mind." She'd given up trying to figure out how her parents always knew everything she thought she'd been hiding from them.

"C'mon, now." He rose and helped her to her feet. "I hear there's an excited birthday girl waiting for the band to start."

"Band?"

As though clairvoyantly summoned, Ginny whirled around the corner into the bedroom. "There you are! I can't believe you actually got Driveshaft to come?"

Okay, she was definitely missing something. "I didn't. I—" But Ginny already had her swinging into the hall and out the back door with only enough time to slip on her shoes.

Sure enough, the band they couldn't afford to pay was busy setting up on a wooden stage alongside the barn. Not for the first time today, her jaw came unhinged.

Chase strolled up beside her with his eyes almost as impressed as Ginny's. "Cooper's an all right guy, isn't he?"

Cooper? Comprehension bottomed out in her stomach and almost set off her tear ducts all over again. He'd paid for them, hadn't he?

"Yeah, he is." The kind of guy who, despite everything, came through for people he cared about, even when they didn't do the same. The kind of guy she never should've let walk away.

Cooper kissed Brayden's head and laid him in his crib. Eyes still closed, Brayden curled into his jungle blanket with his red cheek bearing the mark of having fallen asleep on Cooper's chest.

"I'm sorry I ran out the other night, buddy," he whispered. "I won't leave again without saying goodbye." He brushed a gentle touch through Brayden's soft hair. "Promise." His throat closed, no more words getting through.

Knowing Ti, she would take hundreds of pictures of him to send to Cooper. When he got old enough, they'd likely tell him Cooper was his real dad. Would he understand? Resent him? He swallowed hard and turned. He couldn't think about that now.

With Brayden napping and the girls out grocery shopping, Cooper sank onto the floor against the couch and got back to work on the party favors Quinn had left behind. He glanced at the clock. If he hustled, he could get Ti to bring them over to the party before it ended.

The basket of miniature candies almost laughed at him. So, maybe finishing them in time was wishful thinking, but he had to try. Quinn would be fit to be tied when she realized she'd forgotten them here. Not that he could blame her for rushing out that night when that's exactly what he'd done too.

But after riding for three hours, he'd cooled off enough to come home. Given that she'd completely dropped off the radar, she obviously hadn't done the same. Then again, maybe she had. Her parents' place was more of a home than this place had evidently been to her.

The ache of everything that'd happened stung as sharply now as it had the night her boss had shown up.

He tossed the favor into the basket. What was he even still doing here?

"If you bust out a hot glue gun next," Drew said from the kitchen doorway, "I'm gonna have to take a step of intervention."

Cooper chucked a ball of twine at him. "Can't be any worse than stringing shells on necklaces, hoss."

"Hey, that was all Ti's idea." Drew dropped onto the couch with a mug of green tea and threw the string back at him. "So," he said, the word dangling with insinuation. "You ready to admit you love her yet?"

Cooper pulled a piece of twine in a knot so tight, it almost snapped in half. "Don't start."

"You're the one sitting here playing with tulle. I'm pretty sure you already started it."

He clenched the ball of string. "She lied to me, Drew." Worse than any other persistent journalist, she'd swept in here, getting him to fall for the enemy just so she could exploit him. What didn't Drew get about that?

"And you didn't lie to her?" A pointed look drove Drew to the edge of the cushion. "It's hard to be straight with someone when you're not being honest with yourself."

Just what he needed. A counseling session from his all-knowing brother. He rubbed his temples and tried to tune him out.

"C'mon, Coop. You came back. You're finishing her party favors for her. Get a clue, will ya?"

He jerked up to his feet. "It doesn't matter. I'm leaving tomorrow, remember?"

"No one says you have to."

In a turn, Cooper kicked the basket away from him. "I have plans."

"More like fears."

He swung back around, jaw clinched. "Drop it, Drew."

"Come off it already." Drew pushed up from the couch. "This whole Indonesia idea, the cross-country trip, wanting me to adopt Brayden. Why don't you man up and admit this is about some stupid notion that you've let Dad down?"

Cooper stormed into Drew's face. "I'm warning you. Let it go."

"The way you let it go when I pushed Ti away?" Memories from last summer poured from the gaze he wouldn't release Cooper from.

Chest still heaving, he backed up. "How many times do I have to tell you I'm not you?"

"Obviously as many times as I need to remind you it doesn't matter." Drew turned him around by the arm. "What's your obsession with this, man? Are you that peeved that Dad left the shop for me instead of you?"

Cooper yanked his arm free. "I never wanted that shop."

"Then what's your problem?"

"I don't know, all right?" With his fingers clenched in the back of his hair, he paced until the last night he'd had with Dad kept him from moving forward like it had these last six years. "It wasn't supposed to be like this. He was supposed to be here longer. I didn't get to prove ..."

"Prove what?"

"That I could live up to who he wished I was." Instead, the last thing his dad saw was a self-absorbed dreamer, leaving in anger. The broken confession practically begged for hope that was as absent as Dad was. "I can't fail Brayden too."

"Is that what you think? That you failed Dad?" Slow strides brought Drew toward him. "I was the one disappointed in you the night you left for Hatteras, not him. I thought you were being irresponsible, still acting like a kid who needed to grow up."

Drew ran his tongue along the inside of his cheek. "But you know what Dad thought? He said you'd already grown into the man he believed in. That it was just a matter of you figuring it out yourself."

Cooper's chest tightened as Drew grasped his shoulder.

"Dad wasn't the only one who drowned that night. We did too. In grief, anger. Both turning to whatever we could to cope."

"I'm not coping."

"The heck you aren't. You're so blinded by regret, chasing after what you think Dad wanted for you, that you can't even see that what he really wants is standing right on your doorstep."

Ignoring Cooper's tense jaw, Drew looked at him the way Dad did when trying to break through his thick walls. "If you want to trek across the country—or around the world—to absolve guilt you shouldn't even be carrying, I won't stop you. But you don't have anything to prove to Dad, Coop. You never did."

Drew nodded slowly and then popped Cooper in the arm. "So, do me a favor and take your own advice, huh? Stop trying to be someone you're not. Just 'cause we're different doesn't mean I'm the only one who deserves to start over."

Succumbing to a smile, Cooper faced the ceiling. "Spoken like Dad."

"Yeah, well, I seem to remember you reminding me you have some of him in you too." Drew gave his shoulder another solid squeeze. "That includes being a father. You don't have to be perfect, man. Just present." He returned to the couch and the green tea he'd left on the end table.

"And Coop?" He picked up a manila envelope from the table and approached him again. "Don't be afraid to live up to who Dad saw in you." He handed him the envelope. "Someone already believes you have."

With a final nod, he disappeared into the kitchen, leaving Cooper with a dozen things he wasn't ready to confront.

The envelope weighed in his hand like a fifty-pound dumbbell instead of a few sheets of paper. Unable to open it, he strode out to the deck and dropped it on the patio table next to the folder with the contracts he'd brought out here earlier but couldn't bring himself to sign yet.

A surprisingly cool breeze rolled off the lake with a reminder of how forgiving the weather could be from one day to the next. Unlike himself.

His body folded into the nearest chair. Elbows on his knees, he dropped his head to his hands as moments with Quinn washed in on waves that'd pulled him under from the beginning.

Something furry brushed up against his calf. Trooper. The cat jumped into his lap without an invitation and walked her paws up his chest till her wet nose grazed his chin. Cooper rubbed her head in a futile attempt to coax her down. "Now you decide to show up, huh?"

The cat flexed her front paws back and forth on his thigh while purring against his stomach. He took one look at her sawed-off whiskers and had to laugh, picturing the way she'd won Quinn over. If he were half the man he wanted to be, he would've done the same.

The wrinkled envelope nearly glowed with the confirmation that it was time to man up. With a deep breath, he pulled out the article before he could change his mind.

His eyes hovered over the last sentence. He read it once. Again. Still one more time until the sound of Quinn's voice coalesced with the memory of Dad's.

But of all the things getting to know Cooper Anderson has taught me, none has changed my life more than this: We'll never find where we belong until we're willing to admit we're lost.

The papers fell to the table, his hand back to the cat who'd been able to see the only thing that'd made this place home.

Quinn should've been honest with him from the beginning. But in all fairness, his brother was right. About all of it. If Cooper had been honest with himself, he would've seen how every decision he'd made since finding out about Brayden had been motivated by fear. Not love.

All this time, it hadn't really been about his need to open the boat shop. It was about his need to run away—from the doubts of not being a good enough father and the fear of embracing a family capable of leaving him undone.

But running meant missing out on what Dad had always taught them was worth the risk.

He rose from the chair. Maybe it was too late for that second chance Drew thought was in his cards. Maybe it wasn't. Either way, he'd never know unless he did the very thing he'd asked Quinn to do all along.

Leap.

CHAPTER TWENTY-SIX

Mess

On the stage, Quinn tapped the microphone. "Test. Hello?" Feedback screeched from the amp and quieted the party guests seated at round tables under the canopied tents she'd put up. All eyes fell on her like dozens of miniature spotlights.

She breathed in, smiled at the fireflies in the tall grassy field behind them, and tried again. "Hi, everyone. Thanks for coming out today. Before we move on to dessert, I'd like to say a few words in honor of Ginny and what being a part of this family means."

Quinn fumbled with the piece of paper she'd penciled a jumble of thoughts on while struggling to figure out what to say today. But the tighter she clutched it, the more the flimsy page seemed to dissolve in her hand. A lot of good it'd done to prep ahead of time. Standing here now, she couldn't think straight. Couldn't focus.

Instead of clear words to speak, images of being with Cooper on his dock took center stage in her thoughts—the way he'd affirmed her writing as a gift, the journal he'd given her without a single doubt of what kind of legacy she could leave as an author.

Everything that'd happened these last few weeks closed in with a truth it'd taken her far longer than it should've to realize. While searching for the future she thought would give her merit, she'd abandoned the roots that had given her the kind that mattered most. Yet somehow, Cooper still saw it in her.

She gripped the microphone in the stand.

Soft chatter joined the shifting of chairs and utensils from an antsy crowd waiting for Quinn to remember how to make her voice work.

Her gaze roamed past the tables toward Chase in the back, nodding his assurance. Beside him, Dad had his arm around Mama, both beaming with a love that had never wavered. Not even for their stubborn daughter who'd lost her way home.

Quinn cleared her throat and stuffed the page of ramblings into her back pocket. "Let's be honest. All of our families are a bit dysfunctional." Chuckles erupted across the lawn. "We all make our share of blunders. We leave when we should stay." Her eyes found Ginny's. "We let down the people we love most when it's the last thing we ever meant to do. Because the truth is, life can get pretty messy, things don't go according to plan, and we might even lose sight of who we are."

Chase gave her a pointed look from the back, and she laughed through the slightest film of tears.

"But here's the thing I've learned about family. They welcome us anyway. Not because we have our emotions in check and everything in order, or because we've come back with some impressive rewrite of our life stories." Her eyes ushered a wave of apology to Dad for thinking she needed to prove her worth to him through a job title.

"Instead, family embraces us home exactly as we are. With shaky knees and white-knuckled grips, while learning to trust things are going to be okay even when it feels like they aren't. Because it's right here—in the middle of the mess—where chapters of faith and forgiveness write the kind of stories worth living."

Curbing another onslaught of tears, Quinn raised a glass of sweet tea in the air toward her cousin. "So, today, we celebrate the gift of family and the grace of finding our way home. Happy birthday, Ginny. I couldn't be more grateful to share a small part in your story."

While friends and family members clapped, Ginny ran up to the stage and clobbered Quinn in a hug. "You could never be just a small part."

And there went the chance of repressing those blasted tears.

Once off the stage, with her composure regained, Quinn maneuvered through the tent toward a back table and an untouched plate of cheesecake bites. Embracing her roots included savoring sweet, heavenly comfort food, right?

She popped a bite into her mouth and sank onto a folding chair and into a world of blissful contentment. At least, until two older ladies decided to deem her table their own stage.

After a half hour of being sandwiched between them and their nonstop conversation, contentment evaporated with her fading sugar rush.

Mrs. Goodman patted Quinn's hand. "And what about you, dear? Have you found Mr. Right?"

"Hmm?" Quinn looked up from the brownie crumbs left on her plate, apparently missing the most recent subject change carrying on around her.

"Parties like this remind me of wedding receptions. Don't you just love a good wedding? Seeing the couple so in love." The wiry-haired woman brought a wrinkly hand to her chest as if watching a fairy tale behind her thick glasses.

On the other side of Quinn, Mrs. Carlson dabbed a cloth napkin to her mouth. "Now, June, don't you be forgetting about all the expectancy of the wedding night. Turns couples into a downright ball of nerves. Bless their hearts, they take off like a herd of turtles, don't they?"

"Well, heavens to Betsy, Joan. Who can blame them? All that pressure. Especially with what girls put themselves through these days." Mrs. Goodman set her teacup down and fanned a hand at her friend but then stiffened when her glance swept past Quinn. "Oh, but don't worry about that, dear. They make this thing called cellulite cream." She patted her hip. "Does wonders for the thighs."

"Um ..." Quinn sat up in her seat, scouring for an escape route. Or maybe one of those sparklers she could burn her ears with.

"Now you're just scaring her, June." Mrs. Carlson took Quinn's hand hostage. "Don't you listen to her nonsense. Just concentrate on finding someone you can be yourself with at the end of the day when your hair's in knots and you don't feel like shaving anywhere."

Ignoring Quinn's highly uncomfortable cringe, the woman went on. "You find a boy who'll love you anyway, and you'll find a marriage that'll last long past the wedding night."

"Right." She slid her hand free. "I'm, um, just gonna—"

"There you are." Chase towered above the table. A single arch of his charming smile turned the old women into mush. "I'm terribly sorry, ladies, but I need to borrow my sister for a moment. Urgent matter." Completely straight-faced, he helped her up from the table.

Once out of hearing range, Quinn hugged his side. "You're a lifesaver. You know that?"

"I'll put it on your tab," he teased.

She elbowed him. "How about I won't make fun of you for falling all over yourself in front of Livy tonight, and we'll call it even."

He stopped, arms splayed. "It's called being smooth, thank you very much."

"Sure it is." Quinn peered across the lighted trees toward the stage. "Is that why Livy's flirting with that band member over there?"

Chase followed her line of sight and grimaced. "It's a work in progress."

"Uh-huh. Well, don't work too slowly, or—"

"Quinn." Nurse Murphy jogged up to them. "I was worried I'd miss you."

"Miss me?"

"I assumed you were heading back to Hatteras tonight."

"Oh. Actually, I'm not really sure there's much left for me in Hatteras. Besides…" Quinn looked around with assurance. "I'm where I belong. I'm even thinking of starting my own magazine. Writing about family, maybe include some recipes." Was she absolutely crazy for thinking anyone would read it?

A look of anticipation Quinn didn't understand crossed her face. "Like your old blog?"

"Blog?" Her gaze bounced to her brother and back. "How did you—?"

"I was talking to Cooper about how your posts changed my life when I was in nursing school. He didn't come right out and tell me you were the author. But after we talked again later, I picked up on the hints." She grabbed Quinn's hand. "I can't tell you how relieved I am to finally get to share how much your words impacted me."

"Really?" She couldn't be serious. "They were just silly stories about our family."

"Not to me. Every time I read one, it was exactly what I needed to hear right then."

Yet again, another moment with Cooper rose from inside her with a truth he saw before she ever could. Her words had mattered after all.

"I don't know what to say. Thank you for telling me."

Before she could get another word out, Aunt Loraine sauntered up from behind them. "Look who I found."

A clear view of Brayden's sweet face shook her equilibrium. It had wrecked her to say goodbye to him the night she left Cooper's. The joy of seeing him now sputtered into confusion. "What's he doing here? I mean, where is—?"

"Mama." Brayden stretched his arms out for her, and her world came undone.

Tears brimmed for the umpteenth time. "Did he just say …?" Her voice cracked.

Aunt Loraine handed him over and rested a hand to her arm. "That precious heart of yours makes you the best mama a child could have. No biological restraints can change that."

Brayden nestled his fine hair under her chin, and Quinn held on to one more reminder that her dreams weren't forgotten.

Grappling for stability, she faced Aunt Loraine again. "Where is he?"

"Gone, but he said to give you this." She handed Quinn a road atlas with a bright pink sticky note on the front that read: *Don't think. Just open it.*

"Oh, and this." She held out the pen he'd picked up when they were at Watersview.

Despite the round of laughter the pen elicited, Quinn couldn't shake the nervous anticipation mounting in her chest.

Brayden wrapped both arms around her neck while Chase helped her open the map to an earmarked page flagged by another sticky note.

Cooper had taped a printed-off map to the page that highlighted a route from her parents' house to his. She ran a finger along the second sticky note. *I know it looks short, but the way home rarely is. So, what do you say? Up for a drive? P.S. Don't worry, QT. There are no Motel 6s along the way. I checked.*

Torn between grinning uncontrollably and steadying her heart from racing, she wrestled to take this all in. He hadn't left? He wanted to see her again? But what if—?

"Go." Chase took the map and Brayden. "You don't wanna work too slowly, or ..." His obnoxious grin sloped to the left as he gave her a shove in the right direction.

She turned in time to avoid a collision with Mama, who held out Quinn's purse. Because, of course, somehow the woman's sixth sense knew she needed it. Too choked up for words, Quinn headed for her car.

Inside, an orange sticky note sat on top of a peach Cooper must've put in her cup holder. She lifted the fragrant fruit to her nose while reading his handwriting. *I won't even ask you to bring peach cobbler ... this time.*

He was lucky she didn't have a cobbler to throw in his face. She shook her head, a smile so much harder to tame.

It stayed with her the entire drive to his place and up to the open front door. A little hesitant, Quinn let herself in. "Cooper?"

The call echoed against the high ceiling. Instead of a reply, a tiny meow brought Trooper into view rounding the corner.

As soon as Quinn squatted to the floor, purrs of affection greeted her as if she'd never left. "Hey, you, what are you doing here?" Hoping Cooper was nearby, she played it up. "Did that big bad stockbroker finally give in to your cuteness? I know, he's a big softie, isn't he?"

Trooper weaved in and out of her legs while trilling a shameless plea for more loving.

When no other sound stirred in the house, Quinn gave the cat one last rub and rose. Where was he? The delectable scent of coffee steered her around the bend to find a latte sitting on the entry table with a blue sticky note on it.

In case you weren't convinced, yes, I'd fly to another city just to get a latte ... but only for the right girl.

A twinge of heat pricked her cheeks at the memory of tripping all over herself that day in Brayden's room when she'd talked herself into a hole. Just picturing Cooper leaning against the doorway in his dress clothes with that sideways grin fixed on her sent her pulse soaring. Same as then, she needed a distraction. One sip from her cup of pure bliss led to ten more.

She followed the sound of Trooper's nails skittering across the hardwoods to a train of multi-colored sticky notes lining the floor, each one with an arrow pointing to the back door.

After a reluctant first step, Quinn jogged onto the deck toward one more note on the rail. She tore it off, her heart hammering.

Now that you've downed a solid half of your latte (I know you did), how about you join the guy anxiously waiting for you on the dock?

She peered through the hanging tree branches to a glimpse of Cooper in dark jeans and a loose fitting white dress shirt, facing the lake.

Though racing on the inside, Quinn took slow strides down the stairs and across the lawn. Cooper turned when she stepped onto the dock. A lake-scented breeze blew through his shirt and rustled the soft hairs that had grown a little longer around his ears since she first met him.

All this time, she'd been convinced finding love was like chasing after dandelion seeds blowing across an open field. But the moment his eyes anchored her, she knew searching hadn't been necessary. Because whether she fully understood it or not, love had already found her.

"Cooper, I'm—"

"No, please." He lifted a hand. "Let me go first." He crossed the wooden boards but seemed to stop himself from reaching for her. After lowering his head a moment too long, he brought his hazel eyes to hers again and inhaled.

"Quinn, listen, we both made mistakes. My pride wanted me to believe you were the only one, but that's not fair. I've been lying to myself for a long time." His gaze strayed to the speedboat docked beside them. "The entire self-image I've built has been a front. Something that started out as an act but then turned into an identity I was too caught up in to let go of. Because, honestly? I was scared to find out who I was without it."

Breaking the barrier that had restrained him a moment ago, Cooper reached a hand to the back of her neck. "Until I met you."

She breathed in at a touch even more affectionate than his words.

His fingers caressed the skin beneath her ear. "Now that I know who I can be with you and Brayden, I don't want to pretend to be anyone else anymore."

She slid her hand over his, not trusting her voice.

"I didn't sign the contracts. I'm not going anywhere."

"What? But what about your dad? Your investments?"

"It took a little work, but I managed to find an investor interested in buying me out once the business gets underway. This is what my dad would've wanted—for me to realize none of that is more important than my investment in my son. I belong here with Brayden. And you. If you'll still have me."

He brushed a thumb over her cheek. "You told me to choose love over fear." The soft look on his face melded into an even softer kiss. Too soon, he leaned back and whispered, "I choose us, Quinn."

She couldn't speak, could barely breathe. Was this really happening?

"You've called me out on being a mess more than once since you first showed up at my door." His lips quirked just before the look in his eyes deepened. "Truthfully, I might never stop being one, which is why I'm positive you'll always be the best part of me."

Cooper dipped his head to meet her gaze. "I know we've made some wrong choices." His maddeningly attractive grin hitched to the left. "But what do you say to starting over with the right one? You willing to take one more leap?"

Breathing with more freedom and certainty than she'd ever experienced, Quinn grabbed Cooper's hand, ran to the end of the pier, and jumped into the unknown she no longer feared. Because, with him, she didn't leap alone.

They bobbed to the surface. Cooper swiped his wet hair back, his face a smile of shock. "You're not becoming an adventure junkie, are you?"

As his arms circled her waist, Quinn curled hers around his neck and flaunted his impish grin back at him. "Then who would be your Pepper?"

He tossed his head back, laughing. "I knew you'd come around eventually." Sobering, he brushed off the water droplets coursing down her forehead. "I love you, Quinn Mary Beth. Every stubborn, grammar-correcting, stress-baking part of you."

"I love you too."

"You do, huh?" His dimples sank so far in his cheeks, they probably met on the inside. "Does that mean you're willing to dive into more than just this lake with me?"

She pretended to debate the offer. "As long as you promise it's not our *last* leap together."

Cooper framed her face in his hands. No matter how many times she'd tried to convince herself a look wasn't the same as an actual kiss, his eyes always proved her wrong.

"I promise, QT. It's only the beginning."

Ready

One Year Later

In the back entryway of the church she'd grown up in, Quinn fanned out her delicate veil on both sides while waiting for the ceremony inside to start.

"Relax already, will ya?" Ava waved Quinn's hands away from her dress. "Hello, *I* did your hair and makeup. You couldn't look any more beautiful if you tried."

Smiling in spite of herself, Quinn released a pent-up breath. "Thanks for being here with me, girl. It means a lot."

Ava feigned a shrug. "Well, I do kind of have a magazine to run now that my *business partner's* about to drive across the country on her honeymoon. But with a little tweaking, I managed to fit you in—even on the Fourth of July."

"Considering you're getting to stay at a gorgeous lake house for two weeks, I wouldn't exactly say you got the short end of the stick." She nudged her. "And you better not forget to feed Trooper while we're gone."

Ava rolled her eyes but then leaned a shoulder into Quinn's. "You sure Cooper doesn't want to throw one of his business comrades into the deal? I mean, I did practically set you guys up, after all. Wouldn't hurt to return the favor."

"Set us up?"

Her arms unfolded at Quinn's yeah-right expression. "Oh, c'mon. Who talked you into making a move? *Moi.*"

"More like you had me making a fool of myself half the time."

"Well, it worked, didn't it? Cooper's head over heels for you."

The feeling was more than mutual. Was she really marrying him today? A year had flown by, and yet some days, she would've sworn she was reliving those first weeks of falling in love with him all over again.

"So, listen, I was thinking." Ava fluffed out the petals in her bouquet. "Now that our magazine is running its fifth issue, maybe it's time to splurge a little. You know, buy new desk chairs for the office."

Quinn cracked up. "What is your obsession with desk chairs?"

"Girl, when you sit on a piece of furniture for forty hours a week, you start to bond with the thing, literally." Smiling, she squeezed Quinn's hand. "And at least my randomness sidetracked you for a few minutes, right?" She nodded to the double doors opening into the sanctuary.

Quinn's pulse spiked as music billowed into the corridor. Dad came from one side while Aunt Loraine ushered in from the other and prodded Ginny forward. "You're up first." She motioned Ava to the doors. "You next, dear."

Ava winked at Quinn and whispered, "Just follow my lead."

Right. She chuckled until a clear view of Brayden and her soon-to-be husband at the end of the aisle diminished the entire church to just them.

In a tux tailored to fit him perfectly, Cooper breathed in at the sight of her. His eyes came to life above the blue and silver tie she'd spent years praying over before ever knowing the man who'd wear it.

She swallowed, overwhelmed by an answer to prayer God hadn't given up on even when she had.

Her grasp around Dad's arm tightened as he cupped a hand over hers. "Ready, sweetheart?"

To live the life she couldn't have imagined? "More than ever before."

A WORD FROM THE AUTHOR

If you enjoyed this story, please take a moment to leave a review to help new readers discover Cooper and Quinn's story. Even if it's just one sentence. Reviews are a tremendous help to authors, which in turn allows us to keep writing more stories for you. I can't do it without you!

Ready for Chase and Livy's story? Grab a copy of *Chasing Someday* and escape into another fun southern romance full of heartwarming undertones of grace and hope.

Enjoy all the books in the Home In You Series:
Still Falling: A Prequel
Write Me Home: Book One
Begin Again: Book Two
Just Maybe: Book Three
Chasing Someday: Book Four

Visit www.crystal-walton.com/new-release-mailing-list and be the first to hear about the next release.

ACKNOWLEDGEMENTS

Dave, what would I do without my adventurous husband, encouraging me to take leaps when I'd rather cling to the safe shoreline? Thank you for holding on each time we jump off a new pier in this life together.

Erynn, my characters and I would be lost without you. Thank you for trusting my heart as a writer and knowing how to draw out pieces of the story till they reflect what I carry inside me. I'm so grateful to have you as my editor and friend, even when you distract me with endless memes of a certain blue-eyed hero. ;)

Melanie, girl! Another book down. Another stretch along the journey. I can't tell you how much it's meant to lean on your friendship through the struggle of infertility, the doubts of being an author, and the days when "adulting" barely seems feasible. Thank you for all your input and encouragement while I was pushing through Cooper and Quinn's story throughout my first trimester, when all I wanted to do was binge watch Netflix. ;) Thanks for being such an awesome critique partner and the sweetest of friends.

Charity, Rachel, Vicki, and Kris, thanks so much for sharing your time to read and critique this manuscript. Your fresh perspectives and suggestions continue to help me build stronger stories. I'm so grateful for each of you.

Shaela, your gift at design continues to bless me. Thank you for another lovely cover.

Ruth, your creativity and enthusiasm are always a blast. Thanks for coming up with such a fun name for Quinn's old blog. Hilarious and perfect!

My amazing launch team—Girls!—you keep me going so many times. For real. Your excitement and encouragement are a huge part of what makes plodding through the rough times of being an author so much more bearable. I can't thank you enough for being so excited about Cooper and Quinn's story and sharing in all the pre-release buzz.

My readers on Facebook and my newsletter list, it was so much fun brainstorming ideas with you for this book—from characters' names to grammar pet peeves to funny country sayings. Thanks for adding your fingerprints to this fun story. I hope you've enjoyed seeing some of your input show up on the pages!

To all my fellow grammar lovers, this one was for you. I hope you had as much fun twitching with Quinn as I did while writing it. The struggle is real. ☺

For anyone who's ever walked through the pain of infertility or the loss of a child, you're so near to my heart. I just want you to know I'm standing alongside you in this journey of pressing on toward hope and restoration, day by day.